GHOST
IN THE
COGS

STEAM-POWERED GHOST STORIES

Also from

BROKEN EYE BOOKS

The Hole Behind Midnight, by Clinton J. Boomer
Crooked, by Richard Pett
Scourge of the Realm, by Erik Scott de Bie
By Faerie Light, edited by Scott Gable & C. Dombrowski
Tomorrow's Cthulhu, edited by Scott Gable & C. Dombrowski

COMING SOON
Questions, by Stephen Norton & Clinton J. Boomer
Soapscum Unlimited, by Clinton J. Boomer

www.brokeneyebooks.com
Blowing minds, one book at a time. Broken Eye Books publishes fantasy, horror, science fiction, weird . . . we love it all. And the blurrier the boundaries, the better.

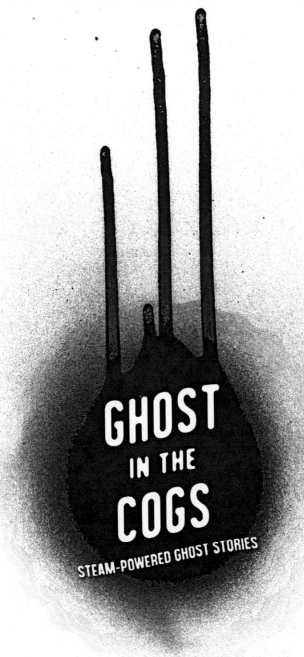

GHOST
IN THE
COGS

STEAM-POWERED GHOST STORIES

Edited by
Scott Gable
C. Dombrowski

GHOST IN THE COGS

Published by
Broken Eye Books
www.brokeneyebooks.com

ISBN-10: 1940372143
ISBN-13: 978-1-940372-14-3

Table of Contents

Introduction

C. Dombrowski
Scott Gable

✿✿✿

That persistent squeaking you hear? Sometimes, it requires more than grease. This time, you're gonna need an exorcist. Or is the proper term ghost hunter? Undead acquisitions expert? Well, you probably get what we're saying.

This world is a special place, a clanking and industrious world where steam hisses and engineers beckon with pipes aglow. It's a world where ingenuity and possibility rattle ahead, hand in hand, at full steam. Delicately contrived clockwork determines the timing. Yet sometimes, there's something more, something whispering amidst the engines. Something other-worldly. These are the tales of the ghosts between the gears, of the clanking spirits, of the possessed and moaning gadgetry.

We hope you won't be *too* scared . . .

"Ships and sails proper for the heavenly air should be fashioned. Then there will also be people, who do not shrink from the vastness of space."

—Johannes Kepler, letter to Galileo Galilei, 1609

Asmodeus Flight

Siobhan Carroll

✿✿✿

The day she turned eleven, Effie's father showed her how to die.

"Even the best aeronaut can be taken down by a spark," he said, his hand tracing the air between the Asmodeus engine and the oil-varnished paper over their heads. Effie swallowed. The ground below the air balloon looked unreal now, falling away into a picture of farmland and houses. But the hot flame that licked and danced before her—that threat seemed real.

Effie's father hesitated, studying the engine's blue glow. Carefully, very carefully, he reached out as if to take the brass globe off its resting place. Effie braced herself but relaxed when she saw her father was not actually going to touch the engine's surface.

"Mr. Sadler, when he was going down, kept his wits about him." Her father mimed pulling at the two rolling hitches that tied the globe to the brass circle. "He undid the fastenings, and . . ." He pressed an invisible globe to his face and mimed blowing his last breath into the smallest of the three valves on the engine.

Effie watched, amazed. She had glimpsed her father making this gesture before, through doorways, when he thought he was alone. She had not realized he was rehearsing his death. If she hadn't been so captivated by his performance, the realization might have chilled her.

"And that's it," her father said, returning his hands to the sides of the globe, framing the flickering blue grate. "That's him in there. Mr. Sadler's ghost. Still flying after all these years."

At a thousand feet, the air around them was clear and cool. The sun glowed red and blue through the paper of the *Dover*, and below them, the world was spreading out like a map in green and gold. But what Effie noticed was the reverence on her father's face as he watched his old friend dance in the air balloon's hot engine.

Four years later when the news of the accident reached them, the memory of that moment made it easier for Effie to compose herself. She walked through the white glare of shock, past her sobbing mother, and approached the gentleman standing awkwardly in the entrance hall.

"Thank you for retrieving it," Effie heard herself say. She watched her hands pluck the globe from the stranger's hands. The engine's surface was cool to the touch, and for a moment, it felt unfamiliar. But peering down through the grate, she saw two blue undulations. The ghosts of Mr. Sadler and her father.

"Thank you," Effie said again. "It's what he would have wanted." And she hugged the globe as though she herself were already falling from the heavens, as though it were her own death and not her father's that she had been called to witness.

✿✿✿

"It's no' for sale."

Effie didn't bother looking up from her knots. The redoubtable Mrs. Brown was as adept at dispatching gentleman buyers as she was in dealing with local tradesmen. Despite her limited height—Effie's assistant measured only four feet three inches to the objective gaze—Mrs. Brown somehow still managed to loom at people. Effie could practically hear her looming now.

"It's no' for sale young man—and don't you go shaking that puss a' me. D'ye think we're country faffle you can swindle with your sing-time songs? Off wi' ye."

"But Mr. Baxter—"

"Mr. Baxter'll be hearing his man's portuning puir wimmin like a common ragart!"

Effie straightened up in time to see the young servant cower away from Mrs. Brown, his face displaying the confusion that typically attended her barrages of (partly invented) dialect. He obviously wasn't sure what he had been accused of but suspected it was deeply improper.

Taking pity, Effie wiped her hands with the stain-rag. "Is that Mr. Stanley Baxter of Endsgate?"

"The same!" The young man's eager-to-please face dissolved in alarm when he realized he might have committed another faux pas. "Er, Madam—"

"You're new to service, I take it? I am to be addressed as Miss Mitchell. And you are?"

"Fielding, Ma-Miss Mitchell. Samuel Fielding."

"Well, Mr. Fielding," Effie said, "Please, tell your master that we are not entertaining offers for the engine, now or in the future."

"Miss Mitchell," Fielding shifted uncomfortably. "Mr. Baxter said you'd say that. He said to say . . ." (The young man closed his eyes, evidently trying to recall the message exactly.) "I cannot imagine my fleet without a high balloon like the *Dover*. Therefore, I am proposing to hire the services of Miss Mitchell, her assistant, the balloon, and the *Dover's* Asmodeus engine, for £2,000."

Mrs. Brown sucked in a sharp breath. Effie tried to keep her face still while her mind raced. Two thousand pounds! The balloon itself was only worth a hundred. The engine, true, was worth more—how much more was unclear these days, given Parliament's ban on West Indies aether and the old aeronautical families' reluctance to part with their engines. But £2,000! With that money, she could secure a land lease for her mother and still have years' worth of income set aside.

"Tell your master I will consider his generous offer." Feeling a flare of pride, Effie added, "Though my answer will probably still be the same." She flushed, wondering if she sounded childish.

Fielding appeared not to notice. "Thank you! Miss. Uh. Mrs." He slid out a rolled piece of paper—evidently a contract—and dropped it on the counter. He managed an awkward bow to her and a hesitating bob in the direction of Mrs. Brown before fleeing down the street.

"What's that about?" Mrs. Brown's dialect was sheathed now that combat was over.

Effie gazed after the servant, her mind racing. "It's the Exhibition," she decided finally. "Mr. Baxter has his aerial display planned for the solstice. To truly outdo Mr. Green, he needs to put a ship close to the Crystal Palace."

Mrs. Brown sniffed. "He wilna do it wi' those lumbrin' creechurs."

"Not the dirigibles," Effie agreed. The new inventions might be cheaper to fly than Asmodeus balloons, but they were clumsy.

"If he hadn'e wrecked his own, he wouldn'e be looking," Mrs. Brown observed.

Effie nodded. Mr. Baxter had lost his *Witch of Atlas* some years ago after launching his balloon in a brewing storm. Since then, he had gained a reputation as a man who had gambled much of his family's money away at card tables but then won it back with some clever investments in the colonies. A dubious sort of man.

"It would be a lot of money for Mother." Effie was suddenly aware that she had been toying with the rag in her hand, smearing her fingers with oil in the process. She re-wiped them, but it was too late: the telltale stains had crept into the cracks of her knuckles. "I'll have to consult with her."

As she turned away, two things flickered at the edge of Effie's perception that, in retrospect, she would wish she'd paid attention to. The first was the blue smudge the contract's seal left on the counter. The second was a figure in the crowd whose posture strongly reminded Effie of Mr. Baxter. But why would Mr. Baxter watch his own servant's delivery? Effie looked back. The man had vanished into the churn of the London street.

✿✿✿

That night, Effie lay awake fretting over Mr. Baxter's offer. Her father's marriage bond guaranteed Effie's mother a small stipend, and Effie's aeronautical demonstrations brought in occasional tides of money. But a reliable source of income would be useful. Unlike the marriage proposals Effie had fielded in recent years, Baxter's offer would also enable her to keep flying. What then was the source of her unease?

Something kept turning at the back of her mind—a smudge of blue as though from a hex seal. Though that was impossible.

Around three in the morning, Effie realized her decision was already made. The Asmodeus engine was her family's legacy. She would not sell it for a million pounds.

Thankful for an excuse to close her eyes, she rolled onto her side.

She was woken by a clamor outside.

Lurching up, Effie saw the orange glow at her window and knew.

Effie plummeted down the stairs in a rush of dark. Figures clustered uselessly in front of the workshop, lit by orange and yellow.

"Fire!" someone hollered, but Effie was already running past them, her bare feet bruising the ground, her nightdress—*improper*, part of her noted—a frustrating drag on the night air. Sparks floated up from the workshop—*Even the best aeronaut can be taken down by one*, she thought—and she struggled with the massive padlock, forcing in her necklace key while some faint voice behind her cried "Miss! Please don't!"

The workshop was a blaze of heat, its walls moving fire. Eyes stinging, Effie dropped to her knees, where the pure air was thickest. She crawled toward the safe. No good saving the *Dover's* paper now. That and the galley she'd stained were gone, but neither of these things were the heart of an Asmodeus balloon.

Something crashed beside her, letting in a gust of air. *I might die here, on the ground of all places*—but Effie set that thought aside. The entire world came down to this: feeling her way to the mercifully cool metal of the safe.

It was empty.

Effie groped inside the space the Asmodeus engine should be. It couldn't not be here.

Suddenly, hard arms yanked her away. She struggled, trying to protest, but her burning lungs lacked air. She was dragged backward through the flaring dark. She was on cold ground, rolling and coughing while ice water drenched her body. Pushing herself up on a numb arm, Effie saw her father's workshop collapse in a shower of sparks.

✪✪✪

"Today," Effie said grimly.

Mrs. Brown glanced sideways. Since the fire, she'd treated her young mistress cautiously, as though Effie was one of her mother's fine Wedgwood cups. "There's no proof Mr. Baxter had owt to do with the fire—"

Effie shook her head, unwilling to replay her frustrating conversations with Scotland Yard. "He offered that contract to cover himself," she muttered. "Nobody will suspect a 'gentleman' of stealing an item he was about to purchase. He knew I'd refuse. The contract seal was hexed. It silenced our alarms—"

"Oh aye," Mrs. Brown agreed, "but coppers want proof if they're to lay hands on a gen'lman." For a moment, Mrs. Brown looked abstracted, perhaps reflecting on some episode from her mysterious past. Then she said, "If you're caught filching, it'll be a hard sing. They won't drop you, miss, but—"

"I'll sell my confession to the newspapers," Effie said, her chin jutting defiance. "It'll be a scandal."

"He'll shirk about for a day or two," Mrs. Brown agreed. "They'll clap you in Bedlam a mite longer."

Effie had visited Bedlam once, and her recollection of that tour—which had, after all, only shown the Lady's Botanical Club the respectable cells—brought her up cold. "You think they'd do that?"

Mrs. Brown gazed at her with flat, hard eyes. "If you weren't respectable, miss," she said, "you'd already be there."

Effie swallowed, taking in Mrs. Brown's meaningful glance at her unusual dress with its flexible stays and higher petticoats. The sideways glances of the shuffling crowd suddenly struck her as menacing. It was one thing to attract such glances as a female aeronaut with a balloon—an outré figure to be sure, but one protected by the aura of British science. But as an oddly dressed woman without a balloon, she suddenly felt her vulnerability keenly.

"Still," Effie said, hearing the stubbornness in her voice and half-hating herself for it. "We're going to find it. Today."

She turned, craning her neck to catch sight of the aerial fleet bobbing behind the Crystal Palace. There was Mr. Green's *Nassau*, the largest Asmodeus balloon ever built, turning in the breeze like a glorious red-and-blue planet. There was an old-fashioned Montgolfier. There were passenger vessels, taking paying customers up in cautious trips to view the top of the palace. And then there were the detestable Mr. Baxter's dirigibles, hovering at a distance from the rest.

Effie and Mrs. Brown dutifully filed in with the shilling crowd. The Great Exhibition had attracted a seething mixture of nationalities—scar-faced Americans, queue-sporting Chinese, green-scaled Inner Earthers—even an odd Frenchman, the latter drawing suspicious glances from John Bull and continental exiles alike. But nominally, at least, the *Pax Francia* treaty still held. The Frenchman wafted through the crowd, an unhappy-looking security agent plodding in his wake.

Under different circumstances, Effie might have joined the crowd in gaping at the Crystal Palace's dazzle of fabrics, its pink diamonds and arching dinosaur bones. As it was, she and Mrs. Brown had one destination in mind: the great aerial docks, futuristically imagined.

The crowd entered the observation platform for the docks. Upturned faces gawped at the shadows of dirigibles and at the statues commemorating aeronautical luminaries: Joseph Priestly, whose quest for pure air had led to the isolation of the aetherial element; the Montgolfier Brothers, who had first demonstrated humanity's capacity for flight; and lastly, Sir Humphry Davy, who had successfully driven Napoleon from England's skies only to expire from his wounds in the Battle of Britain's final hour. A bouquet of flowers lay at Davy's feet. Two guards stood on either side of the display case for the *Veritas's* engine, scanning the crowd. No doubt they were looking for the usual dangers: foreign agitators and religious enthusiasts who mistakenly identified aether "ghosts" with immortal souls.

Forgetting herself, Effie pressed forward with the rest of the crowd for a glimpse of Davy's ghost circling its brass confines.

"Miss," Mrs. Brown whispered. Reluctantly, Effie pulled back. Now that they had actually arrived, she could feel an anxious pit forming in her stomach. She *ahemed* some distracted laborers out of her way. Behind her, she heard a series of surprised wheezes as Mrs. Brown, unconstrained by social niceties, elbowed her way to the front of the platform.

"'Ere you!" Mrs. Brown thundered. "What's this!"

Effie ducked under the guard rope as the crowd behind her exploded into shrieks of alarm. "Grenado!" someone shouted.

"He's workin' for Boney!" Mrs. Brown declared.

As Effie swung herself over the raised platform, she glimpsed a Vril'ya splayed to the floor by one of the guards, its yellow eyes wide with astonishment. Effie found herself hoping the guards would figure out quickly that the "grenado" Mrs. Brown had planted on the Inner Earther was a dummy.

In the shadow of the now-chaotic platform Effie whipped off her skirt, revealing the aeronaut's trousers underneath. She pinned the forged performer's ribbon to her collar, tucked in her pocket, and started forward, trying to look as though she had somewhere to be.

Nobody challenged her as she walked into the aeronauts' workshop. She strode between the benches, trying to glance surreptitiously at each station she passed. In her pocket, the Hobbs pick-lock chafed uncomfortably against her leg. "It'll open all but cold iron, miss," Mrs. Brown had promised. Under different circumstances, Effie would have been taken aback by her servant's familiarity with such devices, but now was not the time to ask questions.

Then she saw the gold-and-purple colors of the *Donna Julia*. Effie slowed to an amble, smiling vaguely at the young men sanding the tackle blocks. They did a double take when they saw her, eyes wide at the sight of a female aeronaut. Effie let her gaze float over the workstation. She saw no safe.

"I'm the new pilot," she said pleasantly. "Mr. Baxter's new engine wants airing. Where am I to get it from?"

It was a gamble, of course. But if Baxter had stolen her engine—*and he did*, Effie thought furiously—it had to be somewhere nearby.

The two men looked both amazed and blank. Then the first one waved his hand at someone behind her. "Oi! Fielding! The miss is looking for a new engine."

Effie turned to see Baxter's mop-haired servant bounding toward them. The air seemed to freeze around her. Fielding's pleasant face changed expressions in slow motion, first taking on a look of surprise and then one of happy recognition.

"Miss Mitchell! What a—I'm glad to see you're back on the field! That is," he said, remembering himself, "Mr. Baxter will be glad. He was terribly disappointed to hear you wouldn't be joining us. What a horrible thing! That fire! Did you lose much of the workshop?"

Effie stared. If Fielding was a liar, he was the best she'd ever encountered.

"The *Dover* won't fly this season, I'm afraid." She smiled, delivering the line she and Mrs. Brown had practiced. "One of my father's friends invited me to assist today. Alongside my chaperone, of course," she added, remembering balloons' dubious reputation as French inventions.

She blushed, and Mr. Fielding blushed. No progress whatsoever occurred until one of the sanders said, "The miss wants a look at the new engine?"

Fielding practically bounced with joy. "He told you about the engine!" Catching himself, he lowered his voice. "It's a remarkable innovation, Miss Mitchell. You have to see it!"

Smiling tensely, Effie followed Fielding out of the workshop and toward the looming dirigibles. They looked like something out of an antediluvian nightmare, huge and iron grey. It was hard not to believe the Nonconformists were right when they said the burning of fossilized aether—the very innovation that had permitted the elimination of the West Indies trade—infected their crafts with the souls of ancient beasts. Effie shivered in the bright sunlight, feeling as though she were indeed coming into the territory of massive predators.

"Mr. Baxter!" Fielding waved his hands toward one of the figures examining the strain on an almost filled dirigible. Baxter—a slender man clad in impractical ruffles—froze. His expression told Effie all she needed to know.

Certainty exploded into rage. She pointed at him. "Thief!" she yelled. "Arsonist!"

This was not part of the plan. Neither, however, was Mr. Baxter's reaction: to lean over the galley and order one of his men to cast off the bowlines.

Effie took off at a run. The bowline had just left its mooring post when Effie caught hold of it. Forgetting any pretense of propriety, she launched herself up the rope, hand over hand.

Below, she saw the shadow of the balloon drift away from the ground and a bewildered Fielding being pulled into the air by the bowline's loop. She hoped the man had the sense to let go before they were too high. Effie, having abandoned all sense herself, hauled up into the galley, almost at the feet of a frightened-looking Baxter.

"You!" she puffed. "Stole! My! Engine!"

Baxter raised his hands as if in protest. "I needed to show it could be done!" He gestured toward the dirigible's glowing engine. Following his gesture, Effie saw, to her horror, a familiar brass globe burning blue within the green flame of an Owen engine. He'd stacked the two devices, a combination of power that ought to be impossible and that would—she saw now—grant this dirigible more maneuverability than it had ever had before.

She realized her mistake a second later when a blow to the side of her head blackened her vision. Effie crashed onto the galley deck. Above her, Baxter wielded a heavy pole. "I didn't mean to kill you," he apologized. "If you only understood! I've seen the future, you see. In the emperor's telescope. Napoleon's got a new alliance. The men from Mars and their mechanical ships. They'll invade from the sky and turn England red."

A well-placed kick cut short the madman's rant. Effie scrambled away, her head throbbing. Somehow, in all her scheming, she had never envisioned the possibility of dying. *If only I can get my engine back*, she thought wildly, *it'll be worth it.*

Her hair was yanked backward. Effie had to clutch a cleat to keep from falling. In the corner of her eye, she saw the dark shape of the pole coming for her and turned away. But before it hit, there was a crash behind her, and the grip on her hair loosened.

Mr. Fielding, having pulled himself on board the airship, was apparently terminating his employment with his fists. "Working for Boney, is it?" He yelled. "You Frenchified villain!"

Effie hauled herself up. It wasn't just her head wound, she realized. The dirigible was listing. With a mind of its own, the monstrous airship was heading straight for the Crystal Palace. The sharp point of a British flagpole sailed into view.

"Brace!" she yelled, her training leaping to the fore. Effie pulled into four-point contact with the galley as the shatter of glass announced the worst. Glancing down, she saw Baxter push the overbalanced Fielding overboard—and was relieved to see the servant tumble onto one of the Palace's iron ribs, just missing a fall through its glass ceiling. The dirigible leapt free.

"No, no, no!" Baxter, his face bleeding, launched himself at the helm. "Why aren't you working?" Buckets of tools skidded down the deck as the dirigible's tilt increased.

Effie, hearing the hiss of air above, knew. Wasn't this the moment she'd practiced since she was eleven years old? Carefully, she reached for a loose line, found its tension, and slid down toward the engines.

All the fight seemed to have gone out of Baxter. He stared up at the dirigible's sagging envelope like a blind man. "It can't be."

Effie landed on the engine's frame. The heat from the fire was excruciating, but she had no time. Even as Baxter turned, she was already snatching the blistering Asmodeus engine from the flames, already raising it—

"No!" Baxter grabbed at her.

And suddenly he was falling, and she was following, the green ground rushing up to meet them both.

The wind was loud around Effie. Screechingly loud. She tried to drag the engine toward her face. *This is how you die*, her father had said.

The engine pulled away from her. It twisted underneath her, crunching into her abdomen, forcing her upward. The wind died.

Below her, a tiny figure—Baxter—hit the ground. Effie turned her face away. Her own fall had slowed to a crawl. The hard fist of the engine pushed her up, the fierce heat of her family's ghosts lowering her gently to Earth.

The engine deposited Effie, burned and bleeding, in the middle of Hyde Park. Energy expended, it settled in the grass beside her. She stared at it as the running people approached.

Something new has been discovered today, she thought dazedly. The Asmodeus ghosts were still conscious. And they could move independently, without flame. Shapes were aligning differently in her head: the famous dexterity of Asmodeus craft, the hideous accidents attending West Indies "slave" balloons, the alien ponderousness of the dirigibles. And somewhere, too, she was remembering what Baxter has said about the Continental Emperor and Mars and an invasion. She wasn't sure how it all fit together yet.

In later years, Effie would say she'd felt the shadow of destiny in that moment. That for a brief second, the Asmodeus engine had shown her the shape of things to come.

But the moment passed. A crowd raced across the green. The determined shape of Mrs. Brown led them, and behind her, a limping Fielding looked confused.

Effie glanced down at the gleaming engine sitting on the grass, its familiar ghosts circling contentedly.

"Thank you," the next aerial admiral said. And she clambered up to greet the future.

When not globetrotting in search of dusty tomes, **Siobhan Carroll** *lives and lurks in Delaware. She is a graduate of Clarion West, the indefatigable OWW, and the twin ivory towers of Indiana University and U.B.C. Her fiction can be found in magazines like* Beneath Ceaseless Skies, Realms of Fantasy, *and* Lightspeed. *Sometimes she writes under the byline "Von Carr." Both versions of herself firmly support the use of the Oxford Comma. For more, visit voncarr-siobhan-carroll.blogspot.com.*

Hiss

Folly Blaine
Randy Henderson

✿✿✿

Mary pushed open the heavy oak door to her uncle's laboratory with stiff, white fingers and led Simon, the housekeeper's boy, inside. Moonlight streamed through tall arched windows that overlooked the rear gardens. Pale flowers shifted in the evening breeze like ghostly dancers.

"There, you've had your look," Mary said.

"We have time. Sir went all the way to the gate." Simon wandered deeper into the room.

Mary followed. He was the newest addition to their family. She would indulge him. "I told you it isn't scary." She shrugged. "Only another room."

Instruments rested neatly on wooden tables and hung on the walls, perfectly spaced between tall cabinets. In addition to the pincers and vises, there were tongs, tiny hammers, handsaws, and thin metal rods. Long tables spanned the length of the walls with curtained areas beneath.

While Simon inspected a row of glass beakers, Mary picked up a scalpel, considered it. She enjoyed how the blade glinted in the moonlight. She touched the tip lightly to her index finger. A prick, and then a spot of brown welled, pooling at the tip. So sharp. So precise.

Mary ran the blade slowly along the pad of her thumb, splitting the skin apart in a neat line. Thick brown sludge oozed from the wound.

She stared, waited. No pain, no fear. Nothing. She felt nothing.

Mary glanced at Simon and pocketed the scalpel.

Approaching the shadows at the back of the room, Simon paused before a large object, easily three times taller than himself. A gray sheet covered the object.

Simon yanked away the sheet. Fabric pooled at the object's base, revealing a large metal sphere covered in curved rectangles of copper and bronze, bolted at each corner. Sets of orderly pipes stacked like an organ fed into the top of the strange device. The sphere rested on squat feet of mortared brick, set right into the laboratory floor.

Was this the "battery" that she'd heard her uncle whisper about with visitors? Simon stepped forward, touching the smooth shell, pinching a bolt between his fingers and twisting. It didn't budge. Wires trailed from the side of the machine to a raised bed next to it where a helmet rested on the long, low cushion.

"What is this?" Simon asked.

"I'm sure it's for his work."

"Everything is for his work, but what's it do?" Simon flicked the helmet.

Male voices from the hallway interrupted them. Mary grabbed Simon's arm and whispered, "Hide." She pushed him toward a curtained area beneath a shelf along the wall. It would give them a clear view of the machine. The two crawled inside, and Mary pulled the curtain shut just as the door opened, and Uncle entered the room, trailed by Mister Davis and several men. Their shoes shuffled across the floor. They moved like they carried something heavy. A kerosene lamp flared to life. Then another.

"Set the body there," her uncle said. He sounded different, more official than she was used to hearing.

Men's legs passed the sliver in the curtain. Mary held her breath.

Body? Simon mouthed.

Mary glared and shook her head.

Together, they peered between the curtains.

Mister Davis picked up the helmet while the other dark-haired men dropped something on the raised bed. It creaked in protest.

"How long will this take?" Mister Davis asked. He stood shorter than the others. "You two, wait outside," he said, and the other men left.

Uncle frowned at the sheet on the ground and kicked it aside. He opened a panel on the sphere. He turned dials, listened, pressed switches. The machine gurgled and then roared to life. Steam trickled and hissed from vents at the side.

"Do you feel it?" Simon whispered, his voice bright. "I feel . . . looser. Stronger."

Now that he said it, Mary realized it was true. She lifted her hands and flexed them. The sluggishness she usually felt, the . . . disconnect between her will and her body had lessened. And her special heart, the one that sang beneath the ragged scar on her chest with a constant *click click click*, pulsed with new vigor.

"You say he died this afternoon?" Uncle said loudly, over the roar of the machine. "Here," he took the helmet from Mister Davis and seated it firmly on the dead man's skull, rocking it into place. "Time's right on the edge, but we may get lucky. Souls tend to cling to the familiar."

"I don't care about his soul," Mister Davis said. "I care about his tongue. We need to know if they've found us out, if our undertaking is at risk."

"If there's not enough soul to bring back the whole man, we risk greater danger than discovery. Let me work."

Mary's head whipped toward Simon, but he'd lost interest and was cupping a glass beaker over his mouth.

The machine quieted to a low hum.

"What are you waiting for?" Mister Davis said. "Ask him."

Uncle pressed a finger to his mouth. "Shhhh." He shifted a lever up on the great machine, and the humming and hissing increased.

The dead man screamed.

Mary felt a surge, a tingling that flowed from her humming heart, matched pulse for pulse by the excited hissing of the machine and the convulsions of the dead man.

"The window!" Mister Davis cried.

Mary looked over in time to see a hooded face ducking between the lilies.

"Damn," Uncle muttered. He hesitated. "Damn, damn, damn." Then he pulled the lever all the way down and rushed from the room. "Gather your men. He mustn't leave the grounds."

Mister Davis followed, calling to his helpers. The room fell silent and still once again, save for the hissing of the machine and the groaning of the dead man. Already, Mary could feel the hum of her heart slowing to its normal soft and steady clicking.

Mary climbed out from under the shelf. Simon held back, clinging to the curtains as though they were his mother's dress.

The dead man's torso lurched upward, his eyelids peeling back to reveal black pits. His mouth wrenched to one side then drooped, tongue lolling out like an overheated dog. The sudden reek of spoiled food washed over Mary. Simon shrieked and backed away.

The dead man's fingers closed around Mary's wrist, and he pulled her toward him. His breath stank of foulness, rot.

Mary jerked away, and her arm ripped from her shoulder with the wet gristly sound of a pork chop being torn in two.

"You-you-you," the dead man stuttered. Something like spit but milky yellow, strung from his lips as he dropped the arm.

Mary reached down and picked up her arm from the floor where it had fallen. The joint had gone soft again. The housekeeper could fix it, but it was such a bother.

She set her arm on the table.

"Please," the man said. Dried blood flecked the corner of his mouth. "So much hurt—"

Mary leaned in closer. "What do you feel?" She licked her lips. "Tell me."

"Needles. In my arms, my legs. Oh God, my eyes. Like someone shoving pins into my eyes."

He struggled to stand and fell back again, his muscles seizing and contorting, head jerking beneath the helmet, his mouth opening and closing like a fish. "It burns," he said.

"Do you really want my help?" Mary said slowly. Her hand moved to the scalpel in her pocket.

"Yes," the dead man pleaded again, air wheezing past his slack lips.

"Truly?"

"I said I do!"

Mary plunged the blade deep into the dead man's chest. He fell against the bed and shuddered. "Thank you." He smiled through a mouthful of black grime. "Thank . . . you."

Mary looked from the man to the machine to Simon who stood peeking with wide, yellowed eyes from between the curtains. She retrieved the scalpel, wiped the blood on the dead man's shirt, and counted to ten. Then Mary grasped the lever and pushed up. The hissing began again. The machine shuddered to life.

The dead man screamed. And then his screams turned to tearless sobs. "Why-why-why—"

"You shouldn't've hurt my arm, sir," Mary said. "It wasn't nice. It wasn't good. Come, Simon," she said and held out her hand. "Uncle will be back soon."

Simon walked to her as though in a daze, and she led him to the door.

"No! No! Please! I'm sorry," the man said. "Let me sleep again."

Uncle returned, breathing heavily. He frowned as Mary and a quivering Simon emerged.

"You shouldn't be here," he said. "What happened to your arm?"

"You know, Uncle," Mary said, leading Simon into the hall, "our little family could really use a butler."

ʮ

Folly Blaine *lives in the Pacific Northwest and is a Clarion West graduate. Her fiction has appeared at* Every Day Fiction, Mad Scientist Journal, *and in the anthologies* Dark Tales of Lost Civilizations *and* Beast Within 4: Gears and Growls. *In addition to writing, she also narrates short stories and audiobooks. (www.follyblaine.com)*

Randy Henderson *is a milkshake connoisseur,* Writers of the Future *grand prize winner, relapsed sarcasm addict, and Clarion West graduate. His "dark and quirky" contemporary fantasy novel,* Finn Fancy Necromancy, *is out now from Tor Books (US) and Titan Books (UK); the sequel,* Bigfootloose and Finn Fancy Free, *will be available in February 2016. (www.randy-henderson.com)*

The Misplaced Body of Fitzhugh Alvey

Jessica Corra

✿✿✿

When Dr. Alvey finally opened his eyes, he was delighted to find himself in his own home. He had no recollection of having gotten there, but one did not question good fortune. The fact that he was indeed questioning it indicated that he was a scientist, and questions were simply his order of business. More importantly, Fitzhugh Alvey had never in his life encountered good fortune when bad fortune would do.

Fitzhugh remembered testing the portment chamber as planned and that it had worked. That at least explained how he had come to be on the floor of his study. He must've returned from his trip. He stood up slowly and attempted to straighten his clothes.

Fitzhugh shrieked. For despite solving one mystery, a bigger one had just presented itself. He could see through his hands. He was entirely transparent, in the manner of one of the spiritualists' ghosts. But he did not remember dying. Surely, if the portment chamber had killed him, his body would be in the chamber and not just his ghost. Only a scientist of Dr. Alvey's caliber would posit a hypothesis upon finding himself probably dead, but science was his first love, and he was only probably dead. Panic was not necessary until he had obtained more facts.

In the next room, he could hear his secretary, Miss Windless, moving about. A glance at the clock indicated tea time, but Fitzhugh was not hungry. He thought to write down that observation, as it seemed to support that he was dead, but he could not hold a pen. He growled his frustration.

"Dr. Alvey? Have you returned?" Miss Windless called.

Fitzhugh froze. His clothing was still mussed, but he couldn't fix it, and that was the lesser concern if Esther should see him now. Clearly, she was aware the machine had worked to some degree. He hid behind his desk as the doorknob rattled and watched. Esther's buttoned boots stepped into the room. "Dr. Alvey?"

Esther knew almost as much about the chamber as he did, being his assistant as much as his secretary. If anyone would be able to help him, it was her. Fitzhugh straightened. "Do not be alarmed, Miss Windless, but there was a mishap with the machine."

Esther's mouth puckered in astonishment, her blue eyes wide. She swayed, and Fitzhugh said, "Please do not faint. I am unable to catch you."

Esther pursed her lips. "Well then. Do tell."

"It would appear that the portment chamber was not able to bring back my body with my soul, and I cannot operate the machine to return for it," he theorized. It was easier to theorize than to reflect personally upon the matter, or he might faint himself. Could ghosts faint? They were pure consciousness according to the most current journals. But then, he *had* awoken on the floor, indicating either that he was not technically a ghost, but something else, or that current science was wrong about ghosts. He would write that down as evidence neither for nor against the theory that he was dead. If he could write.

"Miss Windless, a new journal, if you would," he snapped and began to dictate everything he could remember about his trip and his discovery upon return.

"Yes, sir," she said, and for a time, the only sounds were the scratch of her pen and his quiet tenor.

❁❁❁

Esther Windless was no stranger to the unusual. She had a knack for it, which was how she found herself the assistant to Dr. Fitzhugh Alvey in the first place. Her first cousin Dorothea on her mother's side had become a medium, and a lady scientist was only slightly more bizarre to the Windless family. But these were progressive, modern times, so allowances must be made for such eccentricities as Esther and Dorothea.

In addition to being her cousin, Dot was also her best friend and the person to consult about her employer's matter. Esther had convinced him that research always facilitated action, no matter how badly he wanted to retrieve his body. She had done this less by argument and more by a simple refusal to work the machine.

Esther explained Dr. Alvey's experiment and his hypothesis.

Dot whistled. "So he thinks he's dead somewhere?"

"I believe it is his primary theory, the one that makes the most sense, but I do not think he believes it, no," she said, then paused. "It is perhaps a bit too metaphysical to believe one is dead when one is conscious to ponder it? Descartes's 'cogito ergo sum,' I would say."

"So you do not believe he is dead either?"

"I am withholding my opinion until you tell me what you know of ghosts," Esther said and smiled.

Dot frowned and sat upright. "This calls for tea." She rang the bell.

A discussion followed, the likes of which would have horrified the Windless family into disownment, and it was accompanied by the most delightful lemon cookies.

Dot concluded, "We have accepted the notion of ghosts, insofar as a soul exists. Consciousness is quantifiable in that sense. A soul is potential energy in a body, which becomes a sort of sustained kinetic energy apart. Ghosts. How the energy sustains itself is a fascinating question, but it is enough for now to posit that it can."

"How exciting! You should be a scientist, too," Esther exclaimed.

Dot tutted in an unladylike fashion. "If you will pardon, science could not handle me. I am best left to spiritualism."

"Science could not handle you? What does that say of me, then?" Esther was incensed.

Dot said, "I expect you will force science into line eventually, and you will start by sorting out Dr. Alvey's latest mess. I suggest you try the most recent jump first. I can't imagine the machine would have left his body somewhen else and continued jumping without his notice."

Esther had the distinct impression that Dot did not think much of Fitzhugh Alvey. True, he was a bit unkempt but in a striking way. His black hair stuck up in the back but it framed a handsome face behind horn-rimmed spectacles. He was altogether not unpleasant to work with in any capacity.

Rather than say that , Esther nodded. "I thought so, too. I suppose there's nothing for it. We'll go tonight. That is the other reason I wanted to consult you. In case the machine malfunctions again," Esther swallowed, "you might know what had become of me."

"I would never give you up to your parents, dear one," Dot said, patting Esther's hand. Esther relaxed until Dot added, "I would simply tell them you eloped with the doctor and we would never hear from you again."

Esther choked and said, barely withholding her own laughter, "The truth would be easier on their constitutions than that."

✪✪✪

Fitzhugh was quite enthused to try the portment chamber again.

Miss Windless said, "Really, sir? I would think given your condition . . ." she trailed off, unsure how to politely finish.

He smiled. His assistant had always been a forthright young lady, one of the reasons he had hired her. Laboratories were not the place for dainty specimens of either sex. Miss Windless had presented herself at an opportune time, and he could not resist. That she had saved him from a dilemma involving his latest automaton and a tree had only been part of his consideration.

"Alright then, shall we?" He had spent the hour she had called upon her cousin confined to the study. The internal debate over how he might pass through a wall, given the conservation of energy, had occupied him so thoroughly he had hardly noticed the time.

Miss Windless had explained her cousin's theory of energy states, which was his preferred conclusion as well, but it didn't account for a great many things. His mind reeled at the implications of being a cognizant ghost if, indeed, he were dead. And if he weren't, the implications were greater still and best left to someone in possession of a body for an appropriately overwhelmed response.

He followed Miss Windless into the portment chamber. It was not designed for use by multiple persons, though Fitzhugh would construct a bigger one if it proved successful. A simple chair sat inside a casing of aluminum into which he had built a console containing the wiring and mechanisms necessary to power the machine.

Miss Windless sat in the chair, and Fitzhugh crowded in beside her. He was lanky and had to bend nearly in half to fit. "My sincere apologies, Miss Windless."

"It's alright, Dr. Alvey," she said, but sounded constricted. "I'll shut the door."

Only he was blocking it. Esther could see the door through him but had no way of reaching it as they were positioned. Embarrassment swept over him, and he would have blushed had he the systems to do it. He said, "Maybe I could go back out and come in after you've shut it."

Esther said, "My own sincere apologies, Dr. Alvey," before plunging her hand into his abdomen and sliding shut the door to the chamber. She gasped and withdrew.

Fitzhugh felt nothing, only watched in horror as his assistant clutched her hand. He'd have felt sick, but he was more concerned for the lady, who looked pale in the dim interior, lit only by the burning polyaetherate beneath the desk. "Are you well?"

"You're hot, sir," she said, astonished. "Give me a moment to write it down, but I think this supports our conclusion that you are in some sort of energy state."

"Very good, Esther." he said. He had just called her by her Christian name, and she'd said *our*, but he didn't correct her or apologize for his own gaffe. She had just stuck her hand through his soul. They were a bit past formalities.

Under his careful instruction, Esther started the machine. It sounded much like a storm had unleashed itself inside the chamber. Esther said, "Is it supposed to sound like this?"

"We are fine," Fitzhugh reassured her. The chamber filled with the diffuse, cloying scent of elderberry as the polyaetherate gas burned. "Brace yourself, Esther!"

With a shudder, the portment chamber blinked out of the study. It appeared simultaneously in the alley behind Dr. Alvey's brownstone, ten years previous.

Inside the portment chamber, Esther had fallen off the chair. She was a wisp of a girl, and the sort of bounce the chamber made as it landed would have toppled almost anyone. Dr. Alvey said, "I fell off, too. Excuse me for not helping you up."

"Yes, sir." Esther righted herself on the seat and checked her dress. Nothing was askew enough to be indecent, and Fitzhugh found himself disappointed.

Miss Windless was a model example of a modern lady in terms of intellect and bearing. She said, "Your body should be near here, then?"

"Let's hope."

✿✿✿

Esther was oddly disenchanted. She hadn't felt the time travel. Opening the chamber door to the alley and not the inside of the study was the only indication they'd gone anywhere. Given the noise and shuddering, Esther could believe the machine had fallen out the study window. The past didn't look much different from the present.

"It was only ten years. I didn't want to tax us," Dr. Alvey defended the machine.

Esther smiled. "Alright, let's search the alley. You ought to be here somewhere."

It occurred to Esther that should they find his body and Dr. Alvey couldn't put himself back, she would be required to finagle it into the portment chamber with her. Regardless of its condition. Esther was suddenly quite ill.

"Whatever is the matter?"

She explained. Dr. Alvey's eyes widened, and his shoulders slumped. "I'm so very sorry, Miss Windless. I'm a horrible scientist not to have thought this through."

"That's not true, Dr. Alvey. I didn't think of it either," she said. They walked the length of the alley, trepidation mounting with each step. The only part of Dr. Alvey present was the one which had arrived with her. " I thought for sure your body would be here."

"The machine was slightly closer to the house. Perhaps in the garden?"

Esther didn't know how a soulless body could get itself to the garden without help, but she kept the thought to herself. She could hear the twinge of desperation in her employer's voice. She said, "I shall check."

The gate to the garden was not latched, and she could tell someone had indeed been this way. The dust was disturbed as though something had been dragged through the gate. Esther swallowed. "It looks like something went into the garden. Shall we follow? I don't wish to trespass. I'm afraid I might be seen."

"I can scout ahead," the doctor offered. "Wait here."

Esther did as instructed. Dr. Alvey returned moments later. "I'm sure I went this way."

"Why do you think that, sir?"

"One of my shoes fell off about halfway down the path," he said and grinned.

His face looked boyishly young. Esther didn't have the heart to say that she doubted he'd been walking. Fitzhugh Alvey was a smart man intellectually, but common sense was sometimes lacking. Rather, the man could be naïve. That was how the automaton and the tree had gotten the best of him.

Esther picked up the shoe. She was sure they'd be apprehended as trespassers at any moment. Or she would since Dr. Alvey was half invisible and entirely unarrestable. "Dr. Alvey, from whom did you purchase the house? Are they . . . nice?"

Dr. Alvey sobered. "I suppose that depends on one's perspective. They are my parents."

She had not met them, but if their son was any indication, Sir Alvin Alvey and Lady Alvey were awkward sorts, though no more challenging than her own parents. At least they were not peerage.

"They seem to have taken you into the house," she observed. "Or their butler has."

"I can't be dead, then," Dr. Alvey rejoiced, perhaps prematurely. "Why don't I go in and have a gander?"

"Yes, why don't you?" Esther said, her nerves fraying by the second. "You could simply join your body and sneak out."

"That seems smart," he said. "Thank you for your help, Miss Windless."

"Of course, Dr. Alvey, I am your assistant. It is my job." She bit her lip.

"Yes, but this goes above and beyond duty, I should say," Dr. Alvey said.

Was he going to offer her compensation? Esther didn't want that kind of reward, only recognition.

Thankfully, Fitzhugh Alvey, for his naiveté, knew his secretary well enough. "You have performed most admirably. I couldn't ask for a better assistant."

Esther blushed. That was a bit much. The affection in his voice was rather personal sounding. She looked up at Dr. Alvey through her lashes. He gazed back fondly. She wasn't sure what to make of that. He had always been a kind boss and friendly. She trusted him explicitly, even in such mishaps as this. "We are not home yet. Go on."

"Of course, Esther," he straightened and marched through the back door. Esther rather liked how he said her name.

✿✿✿

Fitzhugh had been obtuse in regards to the current owners of the house. The Alveys were a controversial family, given their progressive leanings, but a wealthy one. Sir Alvin was the first Baronet of Blakeley where he owned a much nicer home than this brownstone, having had the title conferred upon him for scientific advancements.

Sir Alvin had a somewhat paranoid leaning, which his wife, a beautiful, much younger woman, did not discourage. The more time Sir Alvin spent locked in his laboratory, the more time she had to dally. It was Fitzhugh's poor fortune that the Alveys were in residence at the brownstone and not Blakeley when he tried his experiment.

Fitzhugh took a moment to recover from walking through the door. It was like walking through mud, if he were the mud. He suspected his energy flowed around or through the matter of the door, rather than the door parting around him.

He followed voices from the front rooms, careful to stay in shadow. He peeked into the parlor to see his body slumped on a lounge and his parents arguing. Fitzhugh wished he had not waited the hour for Esther's visit to her cousin.

"We have to call someone," Sir Alvin said. "We can't just let him—it—rot here."

Fitzhugh's mother was beside herself. "I am not sure which is worse, that you have another son or that he's dead! We can't call the doctor and say we found him like this!"

Another son? Fitzhugh had two sisters. He crept closer.

"We have a little more time before his condition matters, my dear, so calm yourself and let us approach once more. I have let you rant for near an hour, but the servants will be back soon, and we must have done something. Firstly, I do not have another son. I do not know who this young man is or why he resembles me. I suspect he is a stranger who wished to capitalize upon the fact and ask for money. How he came to be dead in the alley, I cannot say. Biology is not my specialty!"

Fitzhugh was saved from having to create a distraction by a noise in the hallway. The servants had returned, with a struggling Esther between them. As the Alveys' attention turned toward the noise, Fitzhugh dashed through the piano and launched himself into his body, praying he would stick, although he was not a man of faith.

Upon sinking into the body, his soul tethered itself. Fitzhugh had a moment to wonder if this would have happened with any other inanimate body but his own, presuming enough preservation to function, before he felt the exertion of his body restarting and began to cough and ache.

All present turned toward the couch.

"Do beg your pardon," he wheezed. His voice was rusty, his body not certain it should respond to his commands. "Esther, the notebook, if you please."

His mother fainted. The butler carried her to the other lounge and went for the smelling salts. His father muttered to himself, "I'd have vouched he was wholly dead."

Esther shrugged off the cook's arm and crossed the room to hand Fitzhugh the journal, glaring at them all as she went. Fitzhugh jotted down everything that had just transpired and *looked* up to see his father's sputtering face reach breaking point.

"Who the blast are you?"

"Sir Alvey, you have my sincere apology for this predicament. I shall be out of your parlor and on my way at once," he said. He did not trust himself to actually stand yet, but he sounded confident.

His father, for all his awkwardness, could still be an intimidating man. The muttonchops had that effect. "That still does not explain who you are or why you are here or why you were . . . unconscious." Sir Alvin's specialty might not have been biology, but he knew when he touched a dead man, and he did not wish to alarm the wait staff, whom he had dismissed as soon as he had discovered the body of the man in the garden after lunch.

Fitzhugh said, "A distant relation, tenuously. I came seeking employment and your good grace, sir."

Esther cocked her head, but he placed a hand upon her arm, hoping she would remain quiet. He was being familiar, but he had no other idea how to communicate with her in front of everyone. His father's eyes narrowed.

"Do you always bring along a young lady to your inquiries?" Sir Alvin remarked dryly.

"Oh, Esther is, uh, is my wife," he stammered. "And I brought her because, well, you see, I—"

Esther interrupted. "Excuse him, he's embarrassed. My husband has the rare condition called narcolepsy. As a scientist, perhaps you've heard of it? Quite a new diagnosis, but we're relieved to finally know why he has such horrible sleeping spells, and when he did not return directly from his inquiry an hour ago, I thought he might have had trouble, so I came looking."

Everyone stared at her, including Fitzhugh. Narcolepsy had only been named a year or so previously, quite ingenious of her to think of it. To even know of it, really, Fitzhugh thought with admiration.

"I see," Sir Alvin said, though he clearly did not.

"But I can see how disastrously this has gone and shall bother you no more, sir," Fitzhugh said and rose with Esther's help. They walked toward the front door.

It was strange to feel things. Esther's hand leading him toward the door was soft and warm. He wondered if the rest of her felt as nice.

Under her breath, she said, "Dr. Alvey—"

"Fitzhugh, my dear. I did just call you my wife," he whispered back with a wink. She colored lightly. The door to the brownstone shut firmly behind them. They walked around the block toward the portment chamber. Fitzhugh tried not to become apprehensive, having only just regained his body.

"I am afraid there was a mishap with the machine. They did not find me loitering. I was looking for you," she said.

He froze. "What is it?"

"It's gone. It started up while I was waiting and poof!" She threw her hands up to demonstrate.

The color drained from his newly healthy cheeks. "Poof."

She made the hand motion again. "Poof."

Fitzhugh thought he might cry. They would need to petition his parents after all, and how did he possibly exist here as a young boy and as himself? And the technology! It was ten years outmoded from what he was used to. He'd have to compensate somehow. And what of Miss Windless?

They rounded the corner, and there sat the portment chamber. "It came back!"

He turned to Esther.

She did not look astonished. Her eyes twinkled. "It never left, so you needn't fear another malfunction. But I saw the look on your face, *Fitzhugh*, when I said it had gone, and that is precisely how I felt in there with your parents! Your wife! I should say!"

"Oh, Miss Windless, I am sorry," he said. "Shall we go home now?"

"Indeed." And then she said, "Oh, dear, but how will we fit?"

Fitzhugh blushed. "In the interest of science, you might sit on my lap."

"Science," Esther repeated. Her eyebrows rose, and she blushed as madly as he did.

He climbed into the chamber, so she could not see his face. She sat down and closed the door. Fitzhugh was very glad to have his body back to appreciate this. He reached around her to operate the machine and added, "Well, mostly science."

✿✿✿

Dot hit Esther on the shoulder with her fan. She didn't even wait for them to be seated in the parlor before she launched herself verbally at her cousin. "How long have you been back? What happened? Why were you gone so long? Why are you smiling like that? Esther Mallory Windless, you answer me! I had to tell your parents something."

"Yes, and about that little excuse."

Dot sucked in her breath.

Esther waited until her cousin squirmed with the anticipation.

"You were not lying," Esther said and sat back to watch her cousin sputter.

Jessica Corra *is an American writer living in Canada with her Scottish husband. She is a former acquisitions editor for Samhain Publishing, and her work is represented by The Bradford Agency. Jessica believes in wonder, love, and words, and she is a big fan of snowflakes and kittens.*

The Ghost Pearl

Howard Andrew Jones

◇◇◇

A nd the best thing," Applesby said, "is that there's no catch."

Gentleman Jim took the pipe from between his teeth and arched an eyebrow. I'm pretty sure it was more for Applesby than me. He was seated across the table, and I was at Jim's side, usual like, so Jim had to turn to face me, like an actor mugging for the audience.

The three of us sat in one of the little private room's of *Captain Thorne's*, the window behind us. There was a lot of green carpet and a lot of stained bamboo simulating dark wood—real wood being rare in dirigibles on account of the weight—and a little wine. Jim was a hospitable sort when folk came calling.

Applesby fussed with his waist coat. I figured he was exactly what he said, an under butler. He had the look. Soft and well-dressed, but no gentleman. He had huge brown mutton chops and eyes blue and hard as glass.

"I'll leave the clock tower window open." He deposited a brass key on the table with a thunk and picked up the wineglass by the stem, his pinky outthrust. "That's a key I had made of the lord's storeroom. That's all you need. That and the maps." He nodded at the papers face down on the dark table top in front of Jim. They were extremely detailed floor plans of the mansion where the fat man worked. They'd looked pretty thorough—almost as good as I usually drew myself.

Jim barely glanced at the key. He watched Applesby.

Now, it might be you never saw Jim. Six two, he was, without even putting his shoes on. Fair-haired and fit. He could talk like a gentleman, and he looked fine in those dapper clothes. He had a trim blonde mustache and long thin sideburns, and that day, he was dressed in a swell black coat and a white shirt with silver cuff links. They were real silver, too. I was there when he nicked them.

"Applesby," said Jim, "it's a fine plan." Jim could sound all sorts of ways, depending upon who he was talking at. With Applesby, he sounded like an aristocrat, though not one with his nose too lofty. "But there's a problem." Jim tapped the ivory stemmed pipe against his palm. "Jane?"

"We plan our own jobs," I said.

From Applesby's pop-eyed look, I figure he hadn't heard women talk very much.

"But it's a good plan," Applesby objected. "A fine plan." He leaned forward and shoved a whole hand toward Gentleman Jim. "You said so yourself!"

"It's true. But imagine I wandered on to the estate where you worked and planned your day. I've a fair notion of what you do, but I'd probably miss some obvious things, wouldn't I?"

"So you won't do it?"

"I didn't say that." Jim settled the pipe back into his mouth and puffed once. He never smoked the thing long. He used it for effect and because he liked the sweet smell.

"So you *will* do it?" Poor Applesby didn't know whether to look excited or disappointed.

Jim slid the key toward Applesby. "Jane and I will talk it over."

From Applesby's stare, I sensed he just generally disproved of the idea of talking women. He reached tentatively for the key as if he wasn't sure he'd really find it there and pocketed it, his lower lip hanging out like a puzzled bulldog.

"We'll be in touch," Jim said.

"But…" Applesby blustered. "You have to be careful, eh… contacting me. You could give the whole thing up."

"We'll be careful." Jim rose, taking the pipe from his mouth as he leaned forward to shake Applesby's hand.

Still looking bemused, Applesby left. He was a sufficiently well-trained servant that he closed the door after him.

"What do you think of him?" Jim asked.

"I think he's desperate."

"Desperate men make mistakes."

"Right. Probably, he's made some bets he shouldn't have."

"Maybe."

"So his plan's bosh. We can still go after the lord's pearl."

Jim settled back in the chair, twisted it to face me, and puffed his pipe.

"And not cut him in," I added.

"That wouldn't be fair. We wouldn't know about the pearl if it wasn't for him."

"I suppose." If we weren't going with his plan or his key, I wasn't sure we owed Applesby anything, and that pearl almost as big as my fist he'd promised us sounded grand. But Jim had an over-developed sense of fair play. "When do you want to do it?"

"What are you doing tonight?"

✿✿✿

Baneridge is one of those old suburbs stuffed with mansions of moss-caked, gray stones lost behind huge lawns. Even in sunlight, the place looks dreary and downcast, like the moorlands of Calveny, so you can imagine how it looked at two that morning when me and Jim sneaked into the neighborhood to break in through an attic window. Lord Grevon's home felt more like a tomb than a manor.

We hadn't followed Applesby's plan, but we'd made careful note of the times Grevon's various lackeys were supposed to be in various places. Two o'clock is always a good time for burglary. Folks are sleeping their deepest then and are slow to rise.

That floor plan was twenty carat. We could have navigated blind. We nearly did, moving through the dark halls with only one little glow eel lamp between us. By the hazy blue light from its squirming occupant, we maneuvered down to the windowless room on the main floor where I sprung the lock on the room and the vault behind the painting. No key required.

After that, we lowered ourselves out through a first floor window and headed across that lawn. They didn't have any guard dogs, silly fools, although that might not have been as much an oversight as we thought at the time.

You might have expected I was going to tell you all about the heist and how clever we were and like that, but I'm not going to bore you with all the details about how skilled I was or how nimble Jim was despite being a big fellow.

No, this here's a tale about that pearl.

We first knew something was strange as we were making our way out of the Baneridge area. You know how those places are. The black cloaks are out even in the morning, making sure rich folk don't lose any riches. The best way into Baneridge if you're not wanting to be noticed is through the old cemetery. There was an old bush concealing a sizeable crack in the wall, and me and Jim slid through that and into the cemetery. It's a rambling big stretch of ground, and we wound up and down through the hills and past the crypts and the grim-looking angels that long-dead rich folk threw up for their relatives. Some of them lean a little, so if you come upon them sudden-like when you're sneaking around, it seems they're swooping down to get you.

There's owls hooting, too, or sounds you can't place. A scratching in the bushes, say, or a low growl Jim told me was a dog, or the low moan coming from the tomb we passed on the right.

"What's that?" I asked.

Jim looked that way himself and grinned. "Must be a spook."

That's when the thing drifted into our path.

One minute, I was following Jim's gaze, my heart racing a bit on account of the moan. The next thing, a white figure draped in fluttering clothing darted across the path. My blood chilled at the same time my heart slammed into my ribs, and I was surprised enough I didn't notice there weren't no wind for that clothing to be blowing in until *after* I noticed the figure didn't actually seem to be running on the ground.

I'm not generally a screaming sort. Instead, I cursed me a blue streak. "It *is* spooks, you great lummox!" I said.

"Come on!"

We ran, and I'm glad I didn't get too good a look at that white thing. I wish I hadn't gotten a good look at the face with the missing eyes that thrust out at us from behind one cracked gravestone or at the limping child that was partly see-through or at a couple of other things that were even worse.

We were so busy running, neither of us said much until we were up and over the wall on the far side and changing out of our skulking clothes in Madame Taval's cellar.

"It's the world's end!" I said.

Jim's black pants was fine for his outfit, but he chucked his shirt and pulled on a white one and threw on a red overcoat and shoved a black angle cap down over his crown.

I fussed my way into a lady's gown. "The dead's rising up!"

"I don't think the world's ending," Jim said.

"You got an explanation for what just happened?" I asked.

All Jim said was "Let's keep moving."

I grumbled, though he was right. When you're on a job, you stick to the plan and the schedule, and part of the plan was getting out of the neighborhood and well on the way in case we was followed. Madame Taval was sort of a friend, like, so long as we paid her, and wouldn't take kind to spending a few years in the lockup on account of us lingering to gab.

I finished dolling up like a lady, and me and Jim climbed into the hansom cab we'd left with Madame Taval. There weren't no ghosts lurking about, just Madame Taval's crook-toothed son, hooking our horse up by lantern light.

In moments, we were on our way. Our skulking blacks and our filchings was shoved into my bag where they'd give a surprise to anyone expecting to find proper lady's stuff.

With Jim in his cap and coat and me in my proper dress with my bonnet cocked just so and a red veil hanging down, I looked just like a woman out to pay respects to a dying relative, which was our cover story. Proper ladies, of course, didn't lean forward from the passenger bench to talk to their cart drivers.

"Well?" I said.

The horse snorted, and Jim guided us through the cobblestone streets. It was a prosperous neighborhood with streetlights even over the bridge. I thought it was a little strange that a stiltsman should be out so late, but there one was, right along the old brick bridge crossing a Skein tributary. His oil pack was on his back and a long pole in his hand and, naturally, the ten foot stilts strapped to his feet so's he could reach the lanterns that hung way up over the road.

Except this stiltsman turned toward us, and his face was all bloated, like he'd been lying dead at the bottom of the Skein for a week, getting nibbled by fishes and crabs.

The horse whinnied in terror and reared. Jim whipped the poor beast's backside 'til it ran fast enough to win at the downs. What with me and the horse both screaming, we didn't do too good of a job of being discreet, but we got past the dead man on the stilts.

The horse took some coaxing before it slowed.

"Did you see that?" Jim said. "We passed right through his left stilt!"

"Of course we did! It was a ghost!" I was digging through my lady's bag, trying to ignore the fact my hand was shaking. I had a small green case for emergencies. I unsnapped it and pulled out two witch bullets, grey like normal bullets but with silver swirls. I slipped my revolver out of my skirts and was opening the chamber to trade out two of the rounds when the horse whinnied again.

Damned if there wasn't a coal black dog standing in the shadows of a graveyard tree and almost as big as our horse. It weren't normal black. It was more like the shadow of a dog, and it had two blazing eyes like windows onto hellfire.

I never did fire the gun, though, 'cause the cart jumped so bad with Jim driving us so fast.

We lost the dog around the next turn where Jim announced he was taking us to the temple. The plan had been to head straight back to Cliffside and the airship docks, but I figured Sister Toomey might just be able to help. I couldn't think of anyone else who could.

I'd stopped thinking it was the world's end. Near as I could tell, the ghosts weren't wandering down any other streets, and they weren't after the horse. They were after us. And the only reason they could be was that me and Jim had done some filching: the gold and silver necklaces, a fancy watch, and that pearl.

"The pearl's cursed," I said. "Applesby set us up!" I dug through the bag.

"What's your plan, Jane?"

"I say we throw this damned pearl in the Skein!" Hell, I was ready to just toss it into the street.

"You think it'll be that easy?" Jim asked.

I paused, the cloth-wrapped pearl in my fist. "What do you mean?"

"Applesby set us up, alright. I just don't think it's going to be that easy to get rid of."

"Watch me," I said. But I didn't throw it because I trusted Jim.

"Suppose," he said over his shoulder, "you need the pearl to break the curse, and you've thrown it in the ocean?"

I frowned and settled back on the cushioned bench. I supposed it *was* possible. I mean, why set us up if the curse was so easily gotten rid of? And then there was the thought we might simply be able to pawn the thing onto some unsuspecting boob and get our value out of it.

The pearl was worth a small fortune. It would be grand to get its worth, though I had a niggling suspicion that wouldn't be very easy.

The spooks down in central Alston weren't nearly as aggressive or frightening, and we managed not to look at the few we saw drifting along. By then, I was sort of used to the idea we had us a ghost magnet, so long as we could get it over with.

By the time we pulled to a stop at the moon sister temple, it was three bells, which I could hear real well on account of the bell ringing three times up at the top of the temple tower.

Jim parked in the alley, him stopping to hook up a feed bag for the poor old gelding. I was already hammering on the side entrance when Jim jogged up. Something was staggering around amid the old stones in the little moon sister graveyard, but I didn't want to see it clear, so I didn't turn my head.

It took a lot of pounding before Sister Toomey opened up. Usually, she was all sweetness and light, but being wakened at three in the morning puts the brakes on even the best moods. After a few choice words, she said, "You're making enough noise to wake the dead!"

"Funny you saying that," said Gentleman Jim.

"The law after you?"

"Spooks," I said. Right then the thing in the graveyard was scuffling closer.

"Who's that with you?" the moon sister asked.

"Spooks!" I might have sounded a little emphatic.

Sister Toomey sighed dramatically and stepped away. For a split second, I thought her done with us, but three great latches clicked, one after the other, and the door swung wide. She stood in the doorway with a blue candle. Me and Jim scrambled through, and Sister Toomey let out a little gasp when she caught sight of whatever it was. Jim's in the habit of holding doors for folks but not them what's dead, so he slammed it tight, closed the eye slit, and locked up the latches.

"You weren't joking!" Sister Toomey said.

"Spooks," I said, gasping a little.

"What Jane said," said Jim.

Sister Toomey asked us to tell her what in blazes was going on, so after she sent the little acolytes away—they'd come running up to see what the commotion was—we filled her in. Though we left out some of the incriminating details.

Sister Toomey took us to the back of the temple, which she said was especially holy, and lit some candles in the wall niches. Each was inset with pretty mosaics showing the different phases of the moons, all in blue and gold. There was an old wooden door just behind us that something was knocking against when we all sat down on the marble floor.

Toomey studied it in horror. "The crypts," she said.

"Can it get through?" I asked.

"The door's locked." Toomey frowned at the door and ran a hand back through her hair, which was about equal parts gray and black and hung back to her shoulders. She fixed us with a stare that could melt stone. Normally, she was pretty for an older lady, even with one blue eye and one green, but right then, she looked like a fairytale witch.

What with all the commotion, I'd never gotten a real good look at the pearl, and it stole my breath when I got it out. It was perfectly round, like you'd expect of a fine pearl, but it was opalescent and smooth and seemed to glow with some kind of inner light.

Sister Toomey let out a low whistle as she took it but set right to praying over the thing. After, she held it at arm's length and peered at it through the candle flame. Me and Jim watched and pretended that there wasn't some dead thing knocking on the door six feet away. Jim even pulled out his pipe and used one of those candles to light it while the sister wasn't looking.

After a while, Sister Toomey lowered the pearl and spoke in a tired, far-away voice. "This pearl's bad news."

Jim took out the pipe. "Can't say as I'm surprised."

"Can I shoot it with a witch bullet?" I asked.

Sister Toomey shook her head. "No, Jane. That wouldn't help. The pearl must be taken willingly. Until it is, whoever took it will draw the dead to them, every night."

Sister Toomey knew about things like that. Moon Sisters usually do, at least them with the gift, and she had it. We were inclined to trust her, too, on account of all the favors she owed us. Why, if it weren't for the cut Jim gave her, a lot of those little acolytes would be living on the street instead of getting beds and meals and reading lessons and all.

Jim puffed on his pipe. "I was afraid of something like that." He sounded frustratingly nonchalant.

"Why did Applesby pick us?" I asked.

"We've made a lot of enemies," Jim said. "The why's not as important, is it? The trick's figuring a way through."

"We just have to find some bloke to foist the pearl on," I said.

"No one but Lord Grevon and Applesby are getting that pearl," Jim said, and he had that glint in his eye that meant trouble.

"How are you going to get them to take it?" I asked. "They *know* about the curse."

"They deserve it," Jim said.

I reckoned they did. "But Jim, if they know about it, how are we going to get them to take it?"

He smiled real big and put the pipe back in his mouth. "I've got an idea."

✪✪✪

As ideas went, it was fair, though a lot depended on how Jim worded the letter he sent to Applesby's contact and upon Grevon's greed. I was skeptical of Grevon wanting any more money, but Jim said rich men always want more money, no matter how much they have. Like a weed drinker—once you start on the stuff, you keep putting more and more of the little blue puffballs into your beer.

Me and Jim stayed in the moon temple 'til dawn, when the ghosts was gone, then grabbed some sleep in our rooms off Felding street. By three, all of our arrangements were in place, and we were back in the same room at *Captain Thorne's*, though he'd moved his dirigible to a different berth. Thorne flew around a little bit every day over lunch and during the dinner hours so's to give his guests a view.

Me and Jim ate some fish while up in Thorne's, which always struck me as kind of funny, and waited on Applesby, who Jim had told to show up at four. I was looking at the pearl every now and then, seated on the black cloth on the table, and wondering how much it was really worth and who we could trick into taking it if Applesby didn't show. There were plenty of bad folks in the city, after all. In some places, just leaving the thing on the street would just about guarantee *only* a black-hearted man would get it.

I ran this idea and others past Jim, but he was set on getting it back to Applesby and Grevon.

Four came, and then five after, and then five ten. I could tell the time because I was looking at Lord Grevon's gold pocket watch, which is how I know it was exactly five sixteen and forty-five seconds when Thorne's waiter announced there were two gentlemen to see us. Jim didn't show his relief. He just nodded and told the waiter to show them through.

Applesby looked even more nervous than the last time. His little blue eyes kept shifting back and forth. I paid 'specially close attention to his right hand, which was slipped into the pocket of his overcoat.

Much as I noticed Applesby, I paid even more heed to the fellow with him. He was dressed in a black overcoat of finest Moravian silk, complete with a winding dragon pattern. He had a scarlet kerchief of the same stuff—pattern and all—and a little scarlet flower poked into the side of his top hat. Lord Grevon was even harder-eyed and grimmer-lipped than his servant, but he cut a dashing figure, really, and if he hadn't held his face like he'd sucked down a couple of lemons, he might have been a good-looking bloke.

"My man," he said in a reedy voice, "has a revolver upon you. I wish you to know that right away."

Jim laughed genially. "Lord Grevon. Please, join us for a drink."

Grevon sneered. "I have no interest in your fellowship, thief."

Jim completely ignored the hostility. "I admit," Jim said, "it was a fine trick until I figured out how to make it work."

Grevon's cold gray eyes narrowed. "There's no way to make it 'work.'"

"Ah, but you're curious, or you wouldn't have come."

"I came to gloat," Grevon said. "To see you come to your just desserts."

"And why is that, exactly?" Jim asked.

A cold, cold smile frosted those lips. "That little caper those rags printed last month? That steel was intended for *my* factory."

Jim didn't like factories, and you could see it, briefly, in his eyes before he smiled again. "Well, it seems like we got off on the wrong foot, lord. Fate may give us a second chance to work together."

Grevon snorted.

"The trick to the pearl," said Jim, "is to know what to do with the ghosts when they turn up. Jane studied with the moon sisters and saw the how of it after a few hours."

Grevon's eyes snapped over to me. I focused hard against a desire to curtsy.

"Think of it. You know how many secrets the dead know?" Jim lifted the pearl in one big hand and held it up to the light. "It's even more priceless than you thought. Why, with Jane's skills, we can learn all kinds of things that could profit us!"

Jim had more speechifying ready, but Grevon was canny enough to see the potential already. And suspicious, naturally. Although I saw his eyes drift back to the pearl as Jim set it down. "If this is true, why do you need me?"

"You, lord, have access to places we can't get. Oh, we can sneak into Baneridge, but we'd attract attention eventually. But not if we're in the company of a lord. And who knows better which dead are likely to have useful secrets than an aristocrat? We could help each other."

I could tell this sounded a lot more interesting than Grevon had expected. He was trying awful hard not to look at the pearl. His eyes flashed to me. "This is true, girl? You studied with the moon sisters?"

"I've spent a lot of time in the temples," I said, which was true. The secret to lying is to wrap that lie in truth and stuff it full of implications.

Grevon opened his mouth to speak, and I had myself ready with more lies, when the door bursts open.

In come two big gents in black pants, red coats, dark cloaks, and shining gold helms with ebon horse hair crests.

"Black cloaks!" Jim cried.

"Gentleman Jim," the black-haired one on the right said, "you and Jane are under arrest! Get your hands up! One side, sir." With that, he stepped forward, raising a revolver. Applesby went popeyed and Grevon stiffened in alarm.

The black cloaks came past Grevon and Applesby, pointing their weapons.

Jim reached for the inside of his coat, and that's when the black cloak fired. My friend let out a moan and sank backward, dropping like a stone.

I screamed, all girly-like, and put my hands to my mouth, and the black-haired one fired at me.

It was a blank, of course, like Jim had worked out with the Somersby boys, but it was still a shock to see a pistol aimed at you and hear a bang. I jumped back and then remembered to drop. I even groaned because I accidentally hit my head on the chair leg.

While I heard Frank Somersby complaining to his brother that I was a woman—he was really getting into his part—Ed came back that I was a criminal and deserved what I'd gotten. I squeezed the packet in my hand and groaned some more as I rubbed the red stuff all over the belly of my brown dress, as if I was feeling a stomach wound. The Somersbys turned their backs on Grevon and

Applesby and came to investigate us, like they would if they were really black cloaks and we were really criminals. Well, we were criminals, but you know what I mean.

"Jim's dead," Ed said in his deep voice. "What about the girl?"

"She won't live long," Frank answered, though he gave me a wink. I glared at him. I happened to catch Grevon looking my way, so my angry glare slid right into the scene. And speaking of sliding, Grevon's hand swooped up that pearl and popped it into his pocket. He then stepped back and drew himself up like the lord he was. "I'm Lord Grevon of Baneridge."

Ed and Frank both turned.

"I'm sorry, Lord," Ed said, very proper. He holstered his revolver. "We didn't recognize you."

"I quite understand," Grevon said with false cheer. You'd think he'd found an old friend. "You had your eyes upon your quarry, like a keen hunter. I commend you. You're quite sure they're both dead?"

"The poor lass won't last long," Frank said. He sounded a touch too sympathetic to me, but Grevon was too nervous to notice.

"They were attempting to blackmail me," Grevon said, "so I'm afraid I can't muster much sympathy."

"Oho!" said Ed. I guess he didn't know what else to say because he stayed quiet after that.

"We'll send someone around to collect your statement, Lord," Frank said. "Probably tomorrow morning. Now Officer Frunk and I will need to deal with the owners and arrange transport for the bodies and try to make the lass comfortable in her final moments."

"Of course," Grevon said.

I rolled my eyes back, like I was getting woozy and weak.

"Well then," Grevon said. "I shall expect someone in the morning. Come, Applesby."

And like that, they were gone. Me and Jim stayed quiet for a good long while, though, until Ed had closed the door and started laughing. "Frunk? What in blazes was that?"

"Your timing," Jim told them as he pulled himself up, "was perfect."

"I can't believe he took it," I said. Frank handed me a napkin to wipe my "blood" with. He was always a little sweet on me.

"Call back the waiter, boys, and stay for a drink."

Frank and Ed took off their helmets and cloaks and trotted off.

"I don't get how Grevon expected to use the pearl if I was dead?" I asked Jim.

"What's one dead girl to him? If *you* could talk to the dead, he figured someone else could too." Jim pulled out his pipe and lit it.

"You called it," I admitted, dabbing more napkins on my dress.

Jim puffed once on the pipe and chuckled. "I just wish I could be there when he goes to the graveyard some evening and tries it out. He'll be in for a rude awakening."

"No bones about it," I said.

{⟨

Howard Andrew Jones *is the author of an Arabian fantasy series for St. Martin's/Thomas Dunne, starting with* The Desert of Souls, *and three Pathfinder novels, including the recent* Beyond the Pool of Stars. *A former Black Gate editor, he also assembled and edited 8 collections of historical-fiction writer Harold Lamb's work for the University of Nebraska Press. He can be found lurking at www.howardandrewjones. com.*

Frœnka Askja's Silly Old Story

Emily C. Skaftun

000

W ell, I didn't want to taste that anyway," Whale Breath said petulantly, and dissipated into the dark sky. A scant half-kilometer away, the lights from the new electric plant cast an orange sheen on the already-dark afternoon, reflecting between snow and snow-laden sky.

Móðir didn't *need* me to come in. The animals were put away, and she'd probably forgotten dinner entirely, locked away doing whatever it was she did in her workshop these days. I was older than you are now, little ones. But since Magnús had run off with the submarine whaling fleet and faðir died, móðir thought I was alone too much and kept a closer watch over me. I was late.

But I wasn't alone.

I had a number of good and true friends of discarnate nature who lived at the hot spring. They wouldn't tell me their names, so I was forced to dub them with the most unappealing monikers I could manage—in hopes they'd hate them enough to reveal themselves. That was really the only flaw in our relationship.

"She'll be wanting you the instant she's done," Hairy Troll Bottom advised, a stretch to his steamy limbs that reminded me of squinting.

I sighed. "I'm going. See you tomorrow?"

"We'll be here," came a chorus of their wispy, chirpy, drippy voices. Even the ones I couldn't see at the moment chimed in, as usual, in the ritual goodbye. Of course they would be there tomorrow, and the day after that, and the day after that, for longer than I planned to live. They were made of steam. Where else but a hot spring could my steam friends survive an Íslensk winter?

❁❁❁

Móðir had her face pressed to the window like a puppy when I came up the path, steam from my water-heated body curling off me into the dark night. I stepped out of my boots, leaving them in móðir's fancy wind-up drying rack. She held her hands by the bustle at her back, the hump in the silly imported dress she'd had to have. The look on her face was a sort of manic excitement that, since faðir's death, I'd come to fear even more than her cold somber silence.

She waited just long enough for me to hang my coat up over a radiator, mercifully not scolding me for being "late," before whipping the surprise out from behind her. It was . . . something I'd never seen. A collection of bolts and cogs and gears and strips of tin and copper sheet intricately welded into the shapes of limbs and body and massive sheet metal ears, hinged to flop this way and that. It was a type of animal, something I'd seen in drawings in teacher's big reference book. An elephant! One of the whale-large monsters that roamed Africa and other such places. But móðir must have made this one strictly from memory. Its chunky body was a mere wire skeleton cradling blocky copper and wires. Its trunk was long and lumpy, segmented and bendy looking, dropping down between two black marbles sunk into the thing's face to make soulless, lidless eyes.

It was a horror.

Móðir held it out to me, thrusting it toward me as if she wanted me to take the thing from her. I reached out carefully, afraid of sharp metal edges. She'd made me toys before, delicate wind-up birds and sheep and horses, but none of those had looked so menacing, and none of them had made her so obviously proud.

"Well, what do you think?"

The unexpected weight of the thing dropped my outstretched hand as she let go. The tip of its ear snagged in my wool sleeve. "It's heavy," I said, grateful for an honest comment.

Móðir flipped a switch obscenely near the elephant's tail—were elephant tails supposed to be this thick?—and it sprang to life. Its legs moved back and forth and its head shook and its ears tanged like cymbals. I quickly set the thing on the floor, and it scampered off down the hall toward the bedrooms, striking the wall and ricocheting off at an angle.

"What was that?" I asked.

"A gift for you," she said. "A playmate. It runs on battery, so you won't even have to wind it." And she still had the scary enthusiasm in her eyes, so I just mumbled a thanks and asked about dinner.

❁❁❁

In the coming days and weeks more of the animals appeared, all powered by batteries from the new Dreki Anda power station tapping our hot springs. It was indeed convenient not to have to wind the toys, or it would have been if I had wanted to play with them. You understand, I was too old for mechanical monkeys and giraffes and alligators, no matter how intricate their multi-metal scales or how well they clapped pattycake. I turned them on enough to please móðir, then let them run down their batteries until they slowed to a stop.

There were always more batteries, though. Grief-stricken móðir had proven a much more capable negotiator than the battery man assumed, and among other perks for leasing them the land, our farm would always have free power.

I didn't need her "playmates." I preferred the company of the sheep and horses, whose simple, sleepy needs were easily met. I preferred hunting among the rocks and lichen for the Hidden People. I preferred the company of my steam friends. A mechanical shark with thrashing tail and snapping jaws was no substitute, especially one that couldn't even swim. I ruined that one by letting it loose in the spring, where it sank to the bottom like a rock.

The toys frightened me. I was more than familiar with clockwork; móðir had tinkered with it for as long as I could remember. These were . . . different. They were bigger than most of her creations, for one, and . . . angrier. Not cuddly. Not comforting. I'd sliced myself on more than one occasion with a ragged edge of cold metal, and I'd swear some of them were trying to trip me.

But it was more than that. Their behavior wasn't right. I could see most of the gears and pistons that made them work, but even so I couldn't figure out how they made some of their movements, which changed more than made sense. A mechanical elephant should just walk, endlessly, while the switch is on. Instead, sometimes it folded its legs to sit or raised its trunk to the air. Or fixed its bottomless-well eyes on me for so long that I thought it was either out of power or thinking very deeply.

And maybe I wasn't behaving right either because sometimes I'd swear the things had intent, a spooky agency to the way their sightless eyes looked at me. I kept them turned off as much as possible.

One snowy day, in the waning light of a long late-winter afternoon, I made the trek to the hot springs only to find it empty.

Don't get me wrong; it had water in it, steamy hot as usual. Just as I always had, I slipped my toes and legs and body into the reservoir faðir had fashioned from carved stone, but the steam that rose from the surface of the pool held no voices, no shapes, no friendship. It was formless and random, mere gaseous water like móðir always said it was.

My friends were gone.

I didn't tarry long, and I didn't rush back the next day. Water alone couldn't take the chill of winter out of my bones.

❁❁❁

On the third day after my steam friends disappeared, I ran back from the hot spring right past the Do Not Enter signs into móðir's workshop and stopped in my tracks, awed by what her madness had wrought. The place was filled from floor to ceiling with scraps of iron and wood and wires and the assorted parts that made her creations move. As it always was.

But in the center of the space was what had to be her masterpiece: a metal horse, bigger than life-size. It looked ready to rear up and trample us both. It had no mouth and only sockets for eyes, but it somehow looked angry, like Dögun did before she threw her rider. The rest of its body was a bundled mass of metal rods and gears and pistons and gadgetry that resembled muscles and tendons. The creature's massive ribcage held dozens of batteries wired together by a veritable nest of coiled copper.

"Oh," I said, words failing.

"Isn't it marvelous?" móðir said, creeping out from around the animal's flank. If my calculations are correct, it'll do the work of six horses."

"Marvelous," I replied, slinking away.

Back in the house I sat on the floor of my room surrounded by a clanking and ticking chorus of the unnerving toys. They really were the only friends I had now.

"I miss Whale Breath," I said, watching a tin sheep headbutt the wall again and again while a quadruped that móðir claimed was a zebra traced an intricate pattern in a circle around me. Across the room, a raven turned its head so suddenly that I had to look and was met with the stare of its black marble eye. It raised both wings and opened its mouth as if to squawk. Luckily, it had no voicebox. But still, the thing seemed agitated. After a minute or two it lowered its wings in a huff, then raised just one, pointing it toward the zebra that still zigged and zagged seemingly randomly around the room. Even the sheep stopped ramming the wall and looked toward the zebra.

The hairs started rising on the back of my neck. "Are you . . ." I swallowed, "trying to tell me something?"

The raven flapped its wings. The sheep jumped. A number of the other little monsters reacted in some way, each of which felt like a nod. Only the zebra kept doing its thing, tracing strange shapes around me. Were they random? By the time it made a circuit I couldn't remember the beginning of it.

When the zebra came 'round again I picked it up, minding the sharp edges as its legs kept working mindlessly in mid-air. I set it on its side while I wrapped a winter coat around me and stepped into boots, then went outside. The raven and elephant and sheep and a couple of others had followed me, alarmingly, and I held the door open for them as they stumbled into the snow.

There were a fresh few centimeters on the ground, windswept into drifts and bare icy patches but overall still deep enough for footprints. I set the zebra into a clean patch and it took off again, slowly, etching its pattern into the snow. It encircled me, and I took a step back to view the outline as a whole. It had almost come around, and it looked like it had drawn a big-headed shark. Which was impressive but puzzling. And then the zebra took off at a tangent from the shark's head, exploding upward in a spume of trampled snow, and—

"Whale Breath."

❂❂❂

They couldn't talk, but I had my friends back. Sort of. Some of them obviously wanted to play, but others still seemed to want to trip me or cut me with their sharp bits.

I gathered up the friendlies one day, and we all made our slow way back to the hot springs.

The menagerie got all excited when we got there. The raven tried to jump right in, and would have if I hadn't grabbed it. "I'm sorry," I told it. "Water is no good for metalbirds." You see, I had learned from the shark's demise.

The various creatures were all emoting wildly at me. "I know," I said, "it's very exciting." I stripped and slid into the water like a seal.

And instantly regretted it. Hot! Heat! Beyond hot, a feeling like all my skin was exploding, like I was being shocked all over. Pain, unreasonable pain. I flailed my arms, but they were so heavy, those fire-arms, burning even under my fingernails. I opened my mouth to scream, but I slipped under the water and the water shocked down my throat like molten lava. It filled my eyes and nose and ears, and then it was over.

✿✿✿

For a few days, everything was okay. My old friends ringed all around, and though we still couldn't talk, I understood that they'd been trying to warn me about the spring. Oh well. Too late now. Móðir came 'round to the hot spring eventually, and screamed when she saw my body. It looked bad by then, shrunken and hairless and boiled red like a beet. But I didn't mind. I felt I'd come home.

It didn't last. I felt . . . sucked under. I dove into the hot spring and couldn't surface. Down under the rocks through cracks I'd only ever plumbed with my toes, into the earth I went. Things were dark.

And then I woke up to a jumble of scrap metal and wires and gadgets and gizmos and a face before me that made no sense—*Magnús?*—and maybe all of it had been a dream and I was in some kind of mad scientist hospital. There was móðir's face next to Magnús's, and I opened my mouth to ask her what had happened, but my mouth wouldn't open, and I heard her tell Magnús, "Isn't it marvelous? If my calculations are correct—" and I screamed louder than I ever have in my life, but it made no sound.

I had no mouth. I was a mechanical horse.

I couldn't scream, but I could flail my strong limbs, which I did. They moved differently from what I was used to, but panic is panic. I knocked things over, hearing them clatter onto the workshop floor. Móðir and Magnús cursed as they jumped back from me, out of the way, and I wanted to hurt them. But they were my only hope, weren't they? If I was ever going to escape, I'd need them to figure it out. I stopped thrashing.

The sound of Magnús's laughter overwhelmed me, and for a moment I dared to hope that he recognized me in there, somehow looked into the horse's dead eyes and knew his sister's soul, understood what would make a clockwork horse startle. "Yeah," he said to móðir, "this thing will clearly solve all our problems."

❋❋❋

Móðir tried to turn me off, but I wouldn't let her near the switch. I broke out of the workshop and followed Magnús around as much as I could, which wasn't a lot. I could have busted into the house, but it felt wrong. It was still my home, after all. I overheard some things: Magnús's obvious struggle with wanting to help móðir without giving up a promising career as the hvali kafbátur's chief engineer; his intense hatred of the mechanical menagerie (including myself); my own funeral.

He cried. Big brother Magnús. Who would have thought?

Móðir kept making animals, even the toys that she'd said were for me. They seemed to know me, though I couldn't have said who any of them were. At least the new ones were friendly. The ones who'd been hostile before—the elephant and monkey and alligator, and a few others—seemed to be getting worse. They'd peck at Magnús and wind underfoot like naughty kittens and cause basically as much mischief as five-kilo critters can.

My one goal was to make Magnús see me for who I was. I tried to write him a letter in the snow, but I couldn't get my four feet to make anything but a mess at first, and then it didn't snow for what seemed a long time—spring was on the way, finally. I tried nuzzling him, but he reacted with fear. I was, after all, a monstrous metal horse. I couldn't even bring him things: I had no hands, no mouth.

One day I found him sitting in the small family graveyard. The earth over my body was still mounded, hard as winter. "I miss you, sis," he said. "Faðir was one thing, but you too?"

He started as he heard me behind him. I wasn't a graceful creature. "You again!" he shouted. "Get out of here you awful thing. Get!" He picked up a stone and threw it at me, and I just barely ducked away. He picked up another. "I'm not kidding."

And I flashed on a memory, an old memory of winters gone by. We always had the most fun with snowball fights: stagey, almost scripted reenactments of Viking battles with all his friends and me, the pesky sister, tagging along, and I always had the same role. I always died first, hammily, hugely, falling and writhing into mounds of soft snow.

Magnús threw a rock at me, and I let it hit me. It didn't hurt any more than a snowball would have against thick layers of sweater and parka. Which is to say not at all—I was made of metal, after all! But I fell. My four legs didn't want to let me, but I made them. I toppled over, not caring if I'd ever get up; I thrashed my legs in the air and rolled and then, suddenly and intentionally, went still as a corpse. It was the best I could do with no mouth to moan with.

Magnús was silent for a long time. He approached carefully, looking at me. My lidless eyes watched him, but I didn't move a piston. Not until he was right on top of me, and then I twitched once more, scaring him so badly he tripped backward over a rock. Man, did I wish I could laugh.

He came up, eyes wide as saucers. "Askja?" And then I wished I could cry. I nodded and nodded my horsey head, and he hugged me despite my coldness, and maybe, I thought, it would be all right.

✿✿✿

And it was, sort of.

Magnús and móðir worked together to engineer voice boxes out of radio parts, and eventually all we monsters could talk again. Whale breath and the others still wouldn't tell us their real names or their history, only that they missed the hot springs. We tried sending some of them back into the angry, now-boiling cauldron. But while it did soothe them, the effect was never very long-lived. The power plant sucked them right back out of the earth, and then it was anyone's guess where they'd end up. We lost a few that way. I still miss them.

But the real tragedy was faðir.

It took us a long time to figure out why, but some of the toys—the earlier ones—just never came around. When Magnús and móðir gave them voices, they blabbered. They ranted and raved. They became even more murderous.

The only real clue was in snippets of things that felt like memories. The elephant would look at Magnús and say, "Proud of boating. Just like me." And then it would pounce like a cat and leap on its stumpy legs and gore with its pointy metal tusks. But faðir had been a fisherman in his day, and surely he *was* proud of his son's whaling.

The giraffe and the monkey would team up and use tools to trap us, but then they'd look at móðir and say, "just beautiful wedding day."

We think they all were faðir. It seems the spirit can only be fragmented so much before it goes insane.

It makes me wonder, sometimes, what I might have lost.

We returned all the suspect toys to the springs, hoping maybe he'd be back, but if he has been it was only to illuminate lightbulbs, and we never noticed his particular light.

Magnús went back to the whale submarine fleet for a while but returned while still young, married, and raised your parents. He said he was afraid to die out there under the big sea, afraid that no part of his spirit would make it home if he did.

When he died, your parents really, really tried to stop Dreki Anda, to explain why that day's power could not be allowed out through the transmission lines to every house and shop in the town. But the plant's new owners were not "superstitious," they said, and the people needed electricity.

I am sorry that the metal bird will never fly.

You are left with me and my silly old stories, and I know it's not enough. At least móðir's tinkering left me a bit cuddlier than I once was. Yes, it's nice when you scratch my furry ears that way.

Yes, I will take you for a ride if you fetch your frænka Askja a fresh battery.

Where would you like to go?

{{

Emily C. Skaftun *is a graduate of the Clarion West Writers Workshop and holds an MFA in Creative Writing. If she could zap things out of this dimension there'd be a lot less traffic, chewing gum, and rain. Despite the inability (yet!) to vanquish rain, Emily lives in Seattle with her husband the mad scientist and a cat who thinks he's a tiger. She dabbles in roller derby and other absurd opportunities, while writing about fate, flying tigers, and strange fish. Emily is the Editor-in-Chief of the* Norwegian American Weekly. *Visit her on the web at www.eskaftun.com.*

Edge of the Unknown

Elsa S. Henry

❁❁❁

It was a beautiful home. A home with red brick on the outside and a bright blue door. The wisteria and ivy climbing up one side perfectly manicured, and the gate to the front shining with recent polish. To the society of Primrose Hill, it was known as a proper finishing school for young ladies. They delicately marched through the front door each morning. It was said that the owner of the building, Miss Iesult Greensleeves, taught her charges all the most important things. How to make proper social introductions on Hyde Park's Mechanical Promenade. Which forks to use and when. Which gloves are appropriate at what occasion. Whether or not it is acceptable to use steam-powered gadgets to entertain one's guests.

The truth of the matter would certainly curl the neighbors' hair into perfect ringlets.

Miss Greensleeves's Finishing School for Young Witches was no more a place for learning about tea service than it was a place to learn about how to turn one's husband into a newt.

In the parlor, her charges all dressed appropriately in day dresses, each in a different pastel shade. Their bonnets set aside, their hair coiffed in the most recent styles. And each one of them had a wand in their lap and a teacup in their hand. The girls ranged in age from ten, to the eldest, a sixteen-year old witch. Surrounded by prim and frilly flowers, an owlish young lady sat in the corner, her giant spectacles perched upon her nose as she read the latest *Strand* magazine. Unlike the rest, she was dressed in a simple tan gown. The others twittered and gossiped about their promenade in Hyde Park, discussing the latest addition: the steam carousel, which moved faster than any other carousel in the world. She sat apart, reading by herself.

As soon as Miss Greensleeves stepped into the parlor, she counted under her breath to be sure that all her charges were in attendance. She dressed in a deep blue skirt, bustle, and vest and a white high-necked lace blouse. She strode purposefully to the front of the room. With a snap of her fingers, a small tea cart rolled into the room, tiny puffs of steam emanating from the back of it to propel it across the floor.

"Good morning, ladies. I hope that you are all well rested from the weekend. As you know, your final examinations for the year are coming up, as is the Season. Some of you will no longer be with us after that time as we hope you will have been presented at court and will have met a husband." The room burst into a flurry of giggles, except for the owl in the corner. "There will be a few different exams: one in comportment, one in spellcraft, and, of course, one in surreptitious casting. The final piece of your work—" The owl in the corner let out a scream. It was a howl of mourning, keening.

It was accompanied by the *Strand* magazine bursting into flames in her hands.

"He killed him!" She shrieked, waving her hands around.

"Miss Harper, I beg your pardon?" Miss Greensleeves turned her violet eyes upon the owl in the corner. "I'm not sure what the parliamentary vote upon human robotic experimentation could have anything to do with death. No one has been experimented upon yet."

"He's *dead*." She began to cry, her sobs summoning a raincloud above her head, a roll of thunder coming out from it as she gasped. "He got thrown off of a waterfall, and he's dead."

"Miss Penelope Harper, if you could recall your cloud, we can talk about this like reasonable witches. It's not polite to storm inside." Miss Greensleeves was pulling her wand out of her sleeve and casting a spell to quickly waterproof the entire room—if that raincloud began to storm any harder she'd have the mechanics in here for another month fixing the security systems.

Miss Harper sniffed loudly and pulled a handkerchief out from inside the ruffles of her dress, wiping the tears from her cheeks. The raincloud stopped thundering and raining but did not dissipate.

"Miss Greensleeves, I know you're a fan, as well. And we both know . . ." another deep intake of breath before speaking, "We both know that killing the Great Detective by throwing him off of a cliff is entirely unreasonable."

The room went still with only few *nos* and gasps from wide-eyed, disbelieving witches.

Miss Greensleeves spoke very gravely. "Our special guest for the séance portion of your exam is none other than Sir Arthur."

Penelope Harper's eyes were already quite large behind the giant magnification of her spectacles, but it seemed as though they grew three times larger as realization dawned. "You don't mean..."

"I do. You see, Sir Arthur may think he can kill off the character and leave us all to mourn the man who never lived." Miss Greensleeves took a breath and then smiled. All of the young girls shrank back. When Miss Greensleeves smiled, no one wanted to know what she was planning. "But I'm sure with a bit of spiritual mussing about, we might be able to show him why he shouldn't have killed him."

"But does that mean that we have to make it look like it's not real?" Beatrix St. John spoke next, her blue eyes sparkling with curiosity. "You mean we can do whatever we want, as long as it seems as though we've made it all up?"

"I want to scare the shirt off of him, make him think Sherlock Holmes has come back to haunt him and make him pick up a pen again." Miss Harper spoke, reaching her hand up and tossing the cloud into nothingness.

Miss Greensleeves nodded in the direction of Miss Harper and waved a hand. A few books flew off the shelves throughout the parlor, a few more flew down from the upstairs. "These should help you understand the tactics that charlatans use. We can build some props and integrate a few new spells into the security system."

The pastel-enruffled witches flocked to the book stacks: one girl shouted, "I'll write to the Fox Sisters," while another snatched a book entitled *Communicating through the Veil* and another grabbed a book on demonology.

The witches of London were ready to do battle in the parlor on behalf of their favorite detective.

❁❁❁

A few weeks later, a swirl of evening dresses and tambourines bustled through the foyer.

"Ladies!" Miss Greensleeves's Irish accent rang out from the top of the staircase. She was gowned in a soft lavender evening dress, a simple strand of pearls at her throat. The girls were dressed in froths of satin and lace. Even Miss Harper had traded her brown plaid for an emerald green evening gown, a golden locket at her throat. "As you all know, our guests will be here in one hour to participate in the séance. Since there will be non-magical attendees, you know you cannot use a wand for any spellcasting."

"Wands are for show anyhow," piped up Harriet Featherstone.

"Very good," Miss Greensleeves replied. "Now, who is on what piece of the séance?"

Miss Harper stepped forward. "Miss Beatrix and I will be leading the séance." Beatrix held up a clapper in one hand, to show she could knock on the table while holding hands.

"Miss Nessie and I are working on keeping the circle of protection up from inside the classroom upstairs," volunteered Miss Featherstone "We thought it would be best to have additional support in case the security system is still rusty."

Another pair of girls held up a can of phosphorus and the copy of the *Strand*.

"I'm making sure that none of our guests have any spells that would tell them we're working illusions," Miss Jean said. "Oh, and I'll be taking coats, of course. Good hosting and all."

"A reminder to all of you that Mr. Bentley is an inventor under suspicion from the Crown. Do not under any circumstances allow him to escort you home. While he might be a gentleman, his manners about experimenting upon people are utterly atrocious."

The room fell silent, all the young ladies nodding in acknowledgement. No one wanted to become an experiment. Marrying an inventor had its perks of course—being able to talk about all the latest inventions with fluency was certainly a benefit—but the possibility of arriving to an event at the Season with a brand new robotic arm might be seen as amiss.

The time had come. The young ladies all swept to their places. Some sipped at champagne in the parlor, and others lit frankincense and myrrh in the workshop.

Mr. Bentley stepped through the door in his tuxedo and offered little mechanical corgis to each of the ladies in attendance. Miss Harper set hers on the ground and pressed the button for it to start, resulting in high pitched yapping and rusted tail wagging. The security system began to *fweep* in alarm, unaware of the newest mechanical device in the building. With a sheepish smile, Miss Harper turned her new friend off in order to avoid trouble.

All but one of the guests had arrived—the most important guest—and Miss Greensleeves stepped to the door and opened it just as the final knock came.

"Sir Arthur, what a pleasure to have you here for our séance. Some of my young ladies are fans of your work."

He ambled in, allowing the pretty young lady to take his coat and whisk it off to the coat room. Sir Arthur gave Miss Greensleeves a smile and a nod, kind words of thanks for a warm welcome. "Well, I hope they aren't too angry about the most recent issue." He muttered through his mustache, "There've been riots outside of the *Strand*, you know."

Iesult feigned surprise and shock. "Oh, I'm so sorry. It must be terribly frustrating to have an authorial choice so challenged by the public. Well, I hope our little diversion can be of some assistance in cheering you. I know you're quite a fan of the spiritualist movement. My young ladies have been studying it avidly, hoping to learn how to be proper and spiritualist at the same time." She leaned in conspiratorially, "None of that American 'free love' nonsense, though. I promise you that."

The Americans were always a good way to show that you were better and more poised than others. As an Irishwoman, she took points where she could score them

"If you'll come with me into the parlor, we can begin."

Sir Arthur followed as she led him to a seat at the circular table. The twelve participants were ready to take their seats.

"I'd like to introduce Miss Penelope Harper, who will be leading our séance tonight." Miss Greensleeves gestured genteelly to Penelope, who took her seat. Everyone followed suit.

"Good evening, ladies and gentlemen," Miss Harper spoke before pushing her spectacles up on her nose. "This evening, I'm going to ask that we all hold hands. Palms up, if you please."

From another participant, a giggle and a blush as she took the hand of Mr. Bentley. For an inventor potentially hiding out and turning people into part robot, he seemed awfully well dressed.

Penelope sent a speedy glare in the direction of her classmate before fluttering her eyes shut. "Mr. Jeeves, if you could bring down the lights?" The gas lamps automatically lowered. (Not by the power of a butler, though, but rather by the power of a spell bound up in the mechanical security system triggered by the words *Mr. Jeeves*. Witches are tricky like that.)

"Please close your eyes, ladies and gentlemen." She began. As soon as all eyes were closed, the room sank into darkness. Stealthily, young ladies moved into the room, levitating a few objects onto the table and then floating out of the room without a sound. Flicking her eyes over to her fellow witch, Beatrix, Miss Harper squeezed her hand and began. "O spirits, we ask if any of you has a message for us? Can you knock on the table? Knock once if you have a message and twice if you do not."

The table shook with a resounding knock. Only one. From below the table, a small steam powered knocker responded to vocal cues through a nifty bit of spell work.

"Very well, is there any one person to whom this message is directed?" A single knock again. "If you could place a marker in front of the individual the message is for, we will open our eyes in five seconds."

With the participants' eyes still closed, one of the girls helping put on the show lifted a small glowing orb out of nothing and blew it onto the table. It floated in front of Sir Arthur's face, making his moustache cast eerie shadows onto the table.

"You may open your eyes," Penelope intoned. She had to shove a self-satisfied cackle down as Sir Arthur's eyes grew as wide as plates.

"For— " he choked out, "for me?"

"If everyone could please continue to hold hands. Please, do not break the circle." Penelope spoke softly, working her intentions on everyone in the room. The witches present wouldn't be able to let go of each other's hands if they wanted to. "Sir, have you lost anyone dear to you recently?"

"No. No, I haven't." Sir Arthur sounded convinced, as though he was completely unaware of the many hearts he had broken with his prose.

"How curious." She smiled. "Well, we shall just have to find out who it is."

With a rumble, the table shifted and shook, the feeling of an angry spirit filling the room (or in this case, teenaged witchy hormones), and the table and all of the chairs lifted a foot off of the ground.

"Well, this spirit certainly wants our attention," Penelope said calmly while the rest of the séance-goers began to struggle in fear, hanging on to each other's hands for dear life. "Oh spirit, might you tell us who you are?"

On that cue, the walls flashed for a moment, red writing appearing. "You killed me, Arthur Conan Doyle."

Doyle's eyes got even wider, his face marked in pure disbelief.

"This cannot be, this is... Miss Greensleeves, are your students pranking me?"

And then a copy of the *Strand* magazine appeared in the middle of the table before bursting into green flames.

The table began to spin round and round before the whole dining set slammed down to the ground in a huff.

The participants began to scream, still clinging to each other's hands, trailing off when a firm, ticked-off British gentleman's voice spoke throughout the room. "I am the man who never lived and can never die, Arthur Conan Doyle. You will bring me back or face the consequences of damning me to uncertain fictional hell."

With that, Miss Harper allowed the attendees to release hands. While Beatrix was making eyes at Mr. Bentley, choosing to risk matrimony to an illegal robotics inventor over common sense, Miss Harper rose, watching Sir Arthur Conan Doyle grab at the scraps of air that once were the *Strand*. He sputtered and threw his hands in the air.

"Riots! My mother writing to inform me that I have done the wrong thing! The queen is even angry with me, and now . . . my own creation tells me I can't kill him?! Fine. I'll write more. I will. But you're mine, Holmes. I made you, and I can bury you!"

The only response to Doyle's shouting fit was a low chuckle in the same tone as the disembodied voice.

Doyle fled the School for Young Witches, and the girls followed, watching as he and the rest of the guests all scurried away. Some even left their greatcoats behind. The gaggle of girls in evening gowns circled around in the foyer and looked questioningly at their headmistress.

"Did we pass, Miss Greensleeves?" asked Miss Harper, her eyes gleaming with triumph.

"Oh, we'll just have to wait and see if you've successfully terrified the man into writing again."

A few weeks later when the *Strand* announced a return of the Sherlock Holmes stories, a young lady (Miss Harper, to be precise) sitting in the middle of the Hyde Park Mechanical Promenade shrieked from her carriage with glee and shouted across to another, "We did it! We saved Sherlock Holmes!"

Witches will meddle with anything, even publishing.

§§

Elsa S. Henry *is a one-eyed, Scandinavian writer who lives in New Jersey with a husband, two cats, and a hound dog. She writes for tabletop RPGs, Feminist Sonar (a blog about disability), and creepy things that go bump in the night. This is her first published short story.*

The Blood on the Walls

Eddy Webb

❖❖❖

Carnacki's usual card arrived, inviting me to his home on 427 Cheyne Walk to spend the evening having dinner and listening to his latest story. I arrived promptly, exiting the cab so quickly that I nearly forgot to deposit my fare in the brass box bolted to the side. The coins clattered through the pipes, and the automated cab trundled off in a gust of steam. As I entered, I saw that Arkwright, Jessop, and Taylor—his other guests, as well as my friends—were all seated around the table. I joined their amiable talk, and we spent a comfortable fifteen minutes together until our host came out with the food.

"Your last investigation was not so long ago," I said, slicing into the venison.

The table fell silent, aside from the small hiss of steam from Arkwright's mechanical arm. "Indeed," Carnacki said, as he took a bite of his meal.

Quietly, I admonished myself—I had again forgotten Carnacki's dislike of even hinting at his story over dinner. Once we were done and the pipes and shag tobacco came out, he would be as loquacious as any man I have ever met. For the moment, though, I changed the subject, telling Jessop about a new form of typewriter I saw advertised in this morning's paper. As a writer, I am always fascinated in tools that can make my craft easier and more efficient, but I fear sometimes that I alone have such interests.

Once the meal was over, we all adjourned to Carnacki's library. The honor of the big chair always went to our host, but the rest of us quietly fixed our pipes and waited for him to begin his latest ghostly tale.

"To start, and as Dodgson alluded to, this most recent case was quick upon the heels of my previous one. It seems word of my scientific investigations into all kinds of ghosts—real, imagined, and fabricated—has spread far wider than I expected, and there isn't a day that goes by when I don't receive some letter requesting my services. I have actually investigated a few such pleas since we last dined, but none are of much interest or indeed required me to even unpack my electric pentacle and bag of salt. But this latest one is by far one of the most extraordinary things I have ever witnessed in my short career as an investigator."

I leaned back into the comfortable leather chair, closing my eyes and smiling as I puffed on my pipe and listened.

❂❂❂

I received a letter (Carnacki continued) from a man whose name I must not mention, at his own request. Let us call him Mr. Davidson. He is a poor man with noble blood and has recently come into possession of a mansion and a small amount of money with which to maintain it. The mansion, according to his letter, is in disrepair, and it will take a considerable sum to bring it back to its original luster. For a while, he spent all the money he had inherited and more of his own besides in an attempt to bring it up to modern living standards. However, the progress has been minimal. During the reconstruction he has attempted to live in the house with his daughter, but despite his efforts, he is simply unable to retain a staff to maintain it.

Yes, Dodgson, you are correct—he would not be calling upon my services if the issue were not, at some level, believed to be supernatural. His letter to me contains all of the particulars of the situation, which is a rare and treasured quality among potential clients. Here it is, if you wish to read it for yourselves. There are some strange omissions, however, including a lack of a human presence in any of the alleged manifestations—or "hauntings," as Mr. Davidson insists on crudely qualifying them. These omissions led me to consider his case. After we exchanged a few brief messages via my automated telegraph, I agreed to look into his problem.

Within two days, I drove to the house in question to meet Mr. Davidson for a late dinner. He is a large man, and a bit younger than I expected—about as young as Arkwright, I would say, and injured from the Boer War much like she is. He always wears gloves and refused to shake my hand, claiming his war wound never healed properly and made his hands stiff. He seemed eager to dive right into business, so I overruled my usual reticence to discuss such matters over meals. During a simple but filling dinner served by himself and his charming daughter, whom I shall call Melanie, he explained his situation.

"To be frank, Mr. Carnacki, I'm a soldier, not a landowner." He motioned to his daughter, who was pushing her food around her plate. "I am a blunt man used to a hard life, and my wife and my daughter are the only forces in the world that can bring out my softer sentiments. I say this not to try and impress you but to explain that I am not one given to hallucinations or flights of fancy."

"I fully understand and appreciate your assertion," I said.

Looking around for something to put on my bread, I noticed there were no condiments on the table. "I am sorry," my host said, clearly embarrassed to be unprepared. "We haven't had amenities like salt and butter since I gained ownership of the house. I have always meant to stock up, but . . ."

"I completely understand. Think nothing more of it. Please tell me about your wife."

His eyes took on a distant look. "Melanie's mother was lost to me in a zeppelin crash some years ago, but Melanie survived without so much as a scratch or a bruise. The incident itself was horrifying, however, and she never speaks of it, so I haven't a clue how such a miracle came about.

"Since the war left me crippled soon before the accident," he said, motioning with his gloved hands, "I am blessed with a surfeit of free time. I have wanted nothing more than to make a home for my daughter. She is a quiet girl, especially after the accident, and I want to make sure she has a comfortable life and never again experiences such horror. I have a modest pension and a handsome income: my wife invested well while I was away, and I am not wanting for money. I wish simply to rebuild this into a modern and comfortable home for us."

"That is quite understandable," I said. "And I assume that you have run into difficulties in repairing the house due to the spiritual manifestations you mentioned in your letter to me?"

He nodded. "You have seen straight to the heart of the matter, Mr. Carnacki. I wish you to get rid of these spirits, whether by banishing them or proving that it is nothing more than mortal trickery."

I put my napkin to my lips and nodded. "It would please me immensely to do so, Mr. Davidson."

I will not recount the conversation and research I conducted throughout the evening. Rather, I will summarize what I learned. Mr. Davidson knew very little about the history of the house, save that it was in his family for several generations. While he himself had little knowledge of the house—he was raised further out of town and only came to visit once in a while as a small child—he had heard stories that the house had been the site of several unfortunate and fatal accidents as far back as the reign of one of the Kings George. What struck me as odd in his original letter came to the fore again in his recounting of his family history: to wit, no one could seem to remember who had been killed or in what room or by what method.

I moved on to investigating the history of the spiritual incidents themselves. Between the events explained to Mr. Davidson second-hand and my own research of the area's history in the mansion's surprisingly comprehensive library, I learned very little about the past incidents beyond the fact that they continued to be vague and contradictory. The events experienced since Mr. Davidson's arrival, however, uniformly involved blood appearing on the walls. No person or persons were seen, incorporeal or otherwise, but always there was a spray of blood upon the walls that dripped onto the floor as if the very house itself bled. By Jove, if only I had paid more attention to that detail!

Mr. Davidson had explained that the disturbances were reported primarily in the kitchen, so I decided to start my investigation there. I lit a number of candles and set them all over the room, watching their flames for any sign of a flicker or change of color. I looked in every cupboard and turned over every pot, but there was nothing unusual or occult about the fixtures. Sitting in the middle of the kitchen, I carefully opened myself to any kind of psychic or spiritual vibration that might be present. I could find nothing beyond what one would expect in a very old house that has seen tragedy and death. Nothing coalesced into the animate form of a spirit, nor was there any motivating force permeating the room.

Undaunted, I repeated my efforts in the dining room, and then the library, and then the parlor. Each time, I saw nothing, sensed nothing, and found nothing to indicate that any ghost had ever walked through this house.

✪✪✪

At this point, Carnacki trailed off, changing the tobacco in his pipe as he watched our reactions.

"So it was all a hoax?" Taylor asked carefully. He had learned from past mistakes that making assumptions about the direction of Carnacki's story led to chastisement, but he always had difficulty staying quiet during these pauses.

"That is what I thought at first. Since there was such a nebulous gap between the house's history of vague manifestations and the recent, more explicit events, I was developing the theory that someone had been toying with Mr. Davidson."

"Perhaps to force the owner to sell the house to an interested party," I speculated.

"Quite along my own line of thinking, Dodgson." He finished packing his bowl and had it going with a cheery blaze before he continued. "And it was this nascent theory I presented to Mr. Davidson when I proposed the next part of my plan."

✿✿✿

Mr. Davidson didn't quite believe me and asked me to explain it to him again.

"I said I wish to tear into one of the walls that you have renovated," I repeated, carefully.

"Why on earth would you want to do that?"

"If I am right and the renovations predate the arrival of these bloody manifestations, it is possible that someone with an interest in purchasing this mansion had something added to the house. Perhaps, he or she paid one of your contractors to add capsules that exude blood at a certain time or through a trigger mechanism. It could be there is a passage unknown to you that your assailants use to stage these elaborate tricks. Either way, it is only through undoing one of your areas of renovation that I shall be able to narrow down the method of falsifying these ghostly incidents and, from there, possibly learn who created such an elaborate plan." I was sure of my idea, and I knew it came across in my bearing and tone of voice.

The owner adjusted his gloves and nodded. "Very well. If that is what it takes to show that this house is not really haunted, I will allow it. But I would ask that you do as little damage as possible—while I am not a poor man, this house steals money from my pocket faster than a card sharp."

I promised that I would endeavor to do what I could and asked to borrow some of the tools used in the original renovation. He led me to a shed, and from it, I extracted a hefty sledge. I made my way back to the kitchen. As I entered, I found Melanie Davidson standing there, staring at me with a blank look that I am unfortunately familiar with. Reluctant to discard my original theory too quickly, however, I lowered the sledge and stepped forward to speak with her. Mark that, friends! If I should ever again hold a theory more important than the evidence of my own eyes, call me a fool and refuse my invitation to dinner until I learn the error of my ways!

The girl spoke to me in a calm voice. "Please, don't hurt the house," she said. I noted that it was the first she ever spoke to me, and her voice was unusually soft, as if her throat were damaged.

I put a hand on her head. My gesture was one of affection, but in reality, I was assessing her. I barely said more than a word of acquiescence before my hand tingled. She had no odic force—or rather, her natural energies were pulling on mine, drawing my own odic force out of me and into her.

Withdrawing my hand, I turned my attention to my client. "You said your daughter survived the accident that killed your wife?"

Confused, he nodded. "It was a miracle, they said. No idea how she survived."

My old theories were ash in the wind, but new ones quickly formed. "I think your daughter may be significant to this incident. If I may, I would like to perform a ritual to confirm my ideas."

"My Melanie? Involved with this charade? Nonsense, Mr. Carnacki! Pure rubbish!"

"If it is indeed rubbish, Mr. Davidson, there can be no reason to refuse my request."

He was clearly unhappy, but he nodded. "Very well. As long as you don't hurt her."

Allow me to skip ahead in time a bit. You are all familiar with my electric pentacle and the benefits of it detailed in the "Sigsand Manuscript." While both have protected me a number of times from all manner of hostile ghosts, what I proposed was a variation on the original intent. That night, I removed the rug in the center of the parlor and asked Melanie to sit inside of a pentacle drawn in chalk. Her father gave her some blocks to play with as I worked. I carefully aligned the wires as I would normally, but I stood outside the circle as I turned on the steam engine that activated the glowing vacuum tubes.

I cycled the light to blue, the color of safety, and I began to recite the Saaamaaa Ritual. However, instead of the Second Sign of Saaamaaa, which I use for personal protection, I instead invoked the First Sign—that of imprisonment. Within moments of the last line being uttered, I saw that I had been correct: Melanie fell over, as if struck dead by an invisible blow. Mr. Davidson leapt up in surprise and attempted to pierce the pentacle. I was only barely able to hold him back—he used to be a strong man, and some of that bulk remains, but I wrestled him to the ground and kept him from breaking the delicate wires of the pentacle.

"What have you done, you cad?" he snarled as he attempted to escape my grip.

"I have only restored her to her natural state," I said. "She never survived the crash."

This revelation caused him to stop struggling, and I let him go and stood up. "She died along with your wife, Mr. Davidson," I explained.

"That's impossible," he said, staring at his daughter. "I held her in my arms, touched her cheek, carried her from the crash . . ."

"I feel that you, like many others, do not understand the diversity of ghosts. While the romantic notion of translucent figures in white does have some validity, some ghosts can feel as real as you or I. But they are dead, and they cannot stay among the living unless they steal life."

"How . . . ?"

The poor man found it difficult to speak, but I deduced the nature of his question and answered him. "All living things have odic force—a sort of 'electricity of life,' if you will. A person is animated by it, much like a Babbage engine works as steam powers its gears and cogs. In healthy, living creatures, the odic force is strong at birth and renews in diminishing amounts until our death. If our death is premature, that remaining energy can be left behind."

I gestured to the walls of the room. "The odic force from so many lives cut short over centuries has permeated this house, and . . ." My explanation drifted from my lips as I noticed the walls I was gesturing to. They started to drip with blood.

Mr. Davidson pointed at the blood as he crouched on the ground. "How do you explain that?" he said, his voice choked out in a fearful whisper.

"The house has developed a symbiotic relationship with your daughter," I said. "It is recreating what she saw at the crash."

A third voice broke into our conversation. "The walls."

We turned and looked. Melanie was writhing as if in pain, but she spoke in a passionate whisper. I could see the grain of the parlor floor through her body. "The walls," she repeated. "Covered in mama's blood."

"I need to calibrate the electric pentacle to counteract her vibrations!" I said. I realized I was shouting as the dripping sound had become louder, so loud that it drowned out all other noises in the room. "Stay still, Mr. Davidson! Don't touch the pentacle!"

But my words were in vain. Here is a father, stricken in grief and broken by war. His mind survived only because he believed he could provide a better life for his surviving daughter, only to watch her literally disappear before his eyes. He crawled along the floor, his hands so damaged that he didn't even feel the energy flowing through the wires as he tore them up. An uninjured man, or perhaps a saner one, would have dropped the wire in shock. But he pulled them apart as if they were blades of grass before I could reach him. The steam engine burped, pouring out smoke as it ground to a halt.

The ghost of Melanie reached out to her father. She was almost completely faded now—I could barely make her out. Her stolen odic force was almost depleted, and she needed more in order to regain her corporeal form.

I managed to kick Mr. Davidson's hand away at the last moment, denying him his daughter's touch. It sounds so crass to say it in such a way, but that is what I did. I knew that the ghost's embrace would mean his death, so in desperation, I did what I could to prevent it. As his damaged fingers slid away from hers, she screamed, and her face twisted into something dark and abominable. The walls bled more, heavy drops splashing onto the ground in cacophonous thuds. She was drawing the energy of the house into her, one final desperate attempt to regain her stolen life. It was then that I reached into my pocket for my last weapon.

I pulled out a small bag of salt, and I tossed the contents onto her. You all know the purifying nature of salt on ghosts, and the lack of salt in the household—by Jove, if I weren't so blind!—had reminded me that I should carry my own, just in case. I threw a fistful of crystals at the spirit, disrupting her connection to this world. By a stroke of luck, she was too weakened by my ritual, and the odic force of the house was not enough to sustain her. Her screams faded, and Melanie Davidson was no more.

✧✧✧

Carnacki set his pipe down, his story ended, and stood from his chair to wish us a good evening. I shook hands with my companions and saw them to the door until it was only Carnacki and myself left in the foyer. As I shrugged on my coat, I asked one final question that lingered in my mind.

"How did the girl's spirit survive after the crash? Surely, it must have been months until her father moved into the house, and there is no way the ghost could have known she would have a ready supply of life available from the house?"

He smiled and pointed to my gloves as I pulled them on. "It was his hands. A wound is, in many ways, a hole in our collective odic force. That is why our cuts and punctures eventually heal—our life force itself pools there, ready to be taken. But if something draws that excess energy away, the wound festers and stagnates. When a man realizes that his daughter is the only person left in the world for which he has any warm affection, it is natural that he will stay in physical contact with her: hold her hand, touch her hair, and even caress her brow as she goes to sleep."

I nodded, adjusting the gloves. "Which is why his wounds from the war never healed."

"If he were a man less proud, willing to accept the kind of mechanical augmentation that veterans such as our friend Arkwright has as a souvenir of her own campaign, it is possible that his daughter would have died along with his wife. But it was his own touch that kept her tied to this plane and led to all his troubles."

My cab arrived, and we wished each other well as I departed. As the cab rattled its way over cobblestone streets, my mind kept being drawn to the horrible image of watching the walls drip with the blood of someone you love.

{}

Eddy Webb (*with a y, thank you*) *is a freelance writer, designer, producer, and consultant for video games and RPGs. He has worked on over a hundred products, including such properties as Red Dwarf, the WWE, Vampire: The Masquerade, Firefly, and the interactive audio drama Codename Cygnus. His work spans over a decade and across dozens of respected companies, and he's even won a few awards along the way. Today he lives a sitcom life in Atlanta, Georgia with his wife, his roommate, and a sleepy old pug. More information and mad ramblings can be found at eddyfate.com.*

Tipping Point

Nayad Monroe

✿✿✿

Lucinda Blake parted the black lace curtains and peered from the window of her autocarriage as the small caravan of the Winchester Traveling Spirit Menagerie pulled into the fairgrounds. She'd forgotten the town's name, and that troubled her. After one final capture, this would be her new home. Roustabouts and drivers hopped down from the other conveyances, preparing to set up the show. She would have liked to watch them work, but the onslaught of outdoor light brought tears; as the color of her eyes had faded away, even cloudy skies had become intolerably bright. Mr. Gaut had promised that with the return of the vital energies he'd held in reserve, her coloring would darken again. In the meantime, her albino appearance intrigued the customers and lent her a spectral air, he said, so why not make the most of it?

Tremors stirred her hand, so she let the curtain go and felt the relief of the dimness. Despite hardly moving since the start of the day's ride, she felt enervated and listless. Lately, it seemed that her spirit was more loosely tethered to her body than it should be. She could always sense the menagerie stirring nearby, affixing her with hostile attentions. She looked forward to escaping the constant pressure, despite the fact that irreparable guilt would be its replacement. Lucinda wondered where they had found the new girl—what was her name? Emeline?—and what dreadful help Mr. Gaut had offered in exchange for her ability to see spirits. She must be haunted, surely.

Lucinda couldn't be sure that she had done the right thing by taking Mr. Gaut's help herself, but without it, she would still have been a ward of the Ataraxia Institute with no prospects or chance of release, and no one would believe in Lavinia's existence at all.

✿✿✿

Just past three in the afternoon, someone knocked at Lucinda's door. She opened it and blinked down at Mr. Gaut's fifteen-year-old assistant, Oswald.

"I'm to escort you to the apparatus, Miss Blake. They'd like to begin Miss Mabry's training," he said.

"Of course," Lucinda said, taking her shaded spectacles from their cabinet beside the door. She grasped Oswald's extended hand, stepping unsteadily down the small set of stairs to the ground.

The outside air refreshed her somewhat as they walked. "I suspect that I will miss you," Lucinda said. "You've been such a help lately, Oswald."

"Oh, it's nothing, Miss Blake," he said, cheeks flushing.

At the main tent, Oswald walked Lucinda around to the back entrance, to go straight to the apparatus enclosure. He had been with the Winchester Traveling Spirit Menagerie for two years, but she'd never once seen him voluntarily walk through the exhibit, even though no one but Lucinda could see the spirits without Mr. Gaut's patented lenses. Perhaps, it was worse to know they were there without being able to see them, she thought.

"Have you ever looked at the specimens, Oswald? Through the goggles, I mean?"

"Oh, no, Miss Blake. I ain't gonna, I mean. I'm not planning to either. Doesn't affect my job."

He looked so anxious that she didn't press. "Well, thank you for escorting me," she said.

"Sure, it's no trouble," he said, fidgeting. "I'd best get to work . . ."

As he left, Lucinda slipped between the tent's canvas panels. In the shadowy interior, she felt the spirits react to her proximity. They perceived her more strongly in darkness. Pain bloomed in her temples at the sudden surge of spite and malice. Before, she could brush aside their attentions, but the more vital energy she lost, the closer she came to their realm.

As Lucinda approached the room housing the most vital, delicate equipment, she heard voices: Mrs. Winchester and Mr. Gaut.

"Do neither of these girls know how to tell time?" Mrs. Winchester said.

"I expect them any minute, Sarah."

"I suppose Lucinda moves slowly, these days. Are you quite sure of your measurements?"

"Her vital energy is very low. Another capture, and . . ."

"You're certain, Arvin? Have you seen this 'tipping point' occur? If we're to continue capturing these infestations, I require a medium with enough strength to attend to her duties!"

"Now, you know as well as I that Lucinda is the first medium I've worked with, so I haven't been able to make a direct observation . . ."

"Then how do you know she'll die? Terribly awkward if she lives on, even more sickly, while we must explain that there was never a situation for her in this town, don't you think? We must be certain to finish this and contain her spirit, so the new girl can advance the work properly."

"As I've explained, Sarah . . ."

Lucinda missed the explanation as her heart skipped. She found herself rising upward, looking at her own crumpled body on the hard-packed dirt below. Wailing and shrieking rose with her as the spirits clamored at her sudden emergence into the ether. They flailed at their enclosures, trying to cast tendrils after her—Lavinia most of all. Her burning, staring intensity focused only on Lucinda—

And with a snapping noise, she was back in her body on the ground, looking fearfully up toward where she had just been floating. Her lungs drew rapid, shallow breaths above the tightness of her corset as she wondered if they'd heard her fall. She tried to slow her respiration as she eased up to her feet, afraid she might stand too quickly and slip into astral projection again. The voices continued inside, but although she needed to know what they were planning, she also needed to get away and think. Where to go? To her autocarriage? They would only send Oswald again. She scurried along behind the tent, glancing around like a mouse expecting a hawk, so preoccupied that she bumped into someone, stumbled, and fell.

"Oh, my goodness!" The voice was young and feminine, but Lucinda couldn't see much more than a shape and the glare of the sky. "Are you all right?"

Shaking more than usual, Lucinda pushed herself backward and tried to stand, but it was all too much. She sagged and couldn't hold back a quiet sob.

"Now, now," the girl said. Her shape moved forward and settled toward the ground. Lucinda raised a hand to block the light and realized that her shaded spectacles were missing. Her vision adjusted slowly, and a dark-eyed, olive-complexioned face came into focus.

"You must be Miss Blake," the girl said. "Aren't you? I'm Emeline Mabry. I was just on my way to meet you. Did something happen? Are you ill?"

"I can't . . . I can't go back there!" Lucinda said. "Oh, what am I going to do?" Then she was distracted by a motion from behind Miss Mabry, the strange slithering flicker of a ghost. Reflexively, she tuned her inner vision to the spirit's presence. It was a bad one, roiling with sullen, yellow-tinged greens and grays and bursts of black, barely maintaining a human shape at all. She glimpsed moments of cohesion: an angry man's face bleeding profusely from the temple, a mouthful of unnaturally pointed teeth, clenched fists. Lucinda gasped. It had been several months since she'd seen such a one. Extreme fury sometimes twisted them and made them monstrous.

"Oh, you can see him," Miss Mabry said. "That's Uncle Ivor. He tried to impose himself on me on my thirteenth birthday, and when I pushed him away, he hit his head on the mantelpiece. He hasn't let me alone since." Her casual tone startled Lucinda more than the apparition's demeanor.

"Don't worry about me, though. I'm getting rid of the old bastard tonight," Miss Mabry continued, her expression darkening. "Then everyone will be able to see what a monster he is and stop acting like I was the bad girl who tempted him."

"But listen! I can't capture him. I'll die!" Lucinda said. "I heard them. They were talking about it. They're not going to let me go. They're going to let me die and keep me here. We have to get away. They're bad people!"

"You don't understand," Miss Mabry said, her expression going cold. "I need to get rid of Uncle Ivor. You can't leave."

Lucinda understood completely. She remembered the years with Lavinia constantly by her side, the ghost of her stillborn twin, feeding from the ever-more-sickly Lucinda and growing alongside her as a ghostly feral child. Lavinia had been a playmate and an enemy, demanding constant appeasement. She could shriek in Lucinda's ears all night, every night, forever. A beloved, hated sister whose presence was denied by their parents until Lucinda was sent to the asylum for her lies and hysterics. Lucinda knew exactly how desperate a person could be to rid herself of a haunting.

It happened again: Lucinda flew from within her body. The hatred from the captured spirits was there as before, but directly ahead of her was the dead molester, Ivor, twisting his agitated coils through the ether around Miss Mabry, whose aura—visible here—smoldered with palpable deceit and manipulation.

It was the first time Lucinda had faced an uncontained ghost in the ether. She had never managed astral projection purposefully. Her mediumistic ability and Mr. Gaut's clever equipment let her capture spirits and place them in the shielded chambers that kept them from plaguing the living. They became curiosities to study, their vengeful hauntings cut short. Here, though, outside the limits of her physical body, Lucinda lost herself to sudden, ravenous hunger.

She stared at the specter, transfixed with the desire to consume it. Nothing about it frightened her at all. She would have it. Lucinda flew at the ghost, reaching with the entirety of her being and stretching around it like a serpent's hyper-extended jaw, snatching it from the ether in an urgent, unstoppable strike. Crushing down upon it, she absorbed its vital energies in an instant, also pulling along some of Miss Mabry's entwined aura. She immediately knew all that Ivor knew about the nature of his death.

Lucinda snapped back into her body, invigorated, and said to the staggering, pale Miss Mabry, "He never touched you. You killed him for no reason at all. Just to see if you could. And you made it look like self-defense."

"No! No, I . . . he grabbed me! He said such terrible things about what he wanted!"

"Liar," Lucinda said. "I saw it. He's with me now, and I know."

Strength and health coursed through her body, a river in springtime gushing with renewal. The contrast to her shaky weakness of only moments before astonished her, making her realize how close she had come to death, to be so energized by the vital energies of someone already dead. She had drawn a little from Miss Mabry, but still . . .

They almost let me die. They would have let me die! This horrible girl would have helped them!

Ivor stirred within her mind, bolstering her confidence and providing Lucinda with words. "Here's what will happen," she said, stepping close and making full, unblinking eye contact with Emeline Mabry. "You will leave without speaking to anyone else here. You found out that you could kill someone, and you found out what it's like to be haunted. Your haunting is finished now. I advise you not to try it again. If you spend the rest of your life making amends, perhaps, your own afterlife won't be a time of eternal torment. You should consider yourself very lucky to have this chance."

Shocked at herself, she watched Emeline stumble backward a few steps and turn to flee, kicking up dust as she ran. Lucinda tried to take it all in. Within perhaps fifteen minutes, she had gone from trembling exhaustion in her autocarriage to mortal terror to somehow eating a ghost and regaining her strength.

A voice murmured in the back of her mind, *I am not eaten. I am redeemed. And soon, I will be free.* Ivor's presence was milder, softening.

"But it felt like eating you," Lucinda whispered.

You were near death, Ivor replied, fading more. *It will be different with the others. Thank you.* His presence receded.

"The others? Wait!" Lucinda whispered frantically. "Don't go! What do I do now?" There was no answer. The surge of strength she had received did not leave with him, but it settled.

The others. For the first time, Lucinda wondered about the collection of spirits in the menagerie. Ivor had been murdered for no reason and falsely accused. His obsessive rage after death made sense. Emeline had deserved to be haunted. What of the other spirits Lucinda had lured in, one by one, to be captured with Mr. Gaut's inventions, using the "harmonizing frequencies" she didn't understand? Each of them might have been wronged twice—in the manner of their death and in their imprisonment.

And what of Lavinia? Lucinda hadn't killed her. But to an infant spirit, envious of her twin's life and parental love, why would that matter?

This will end now, Lucinda thought. She strode around to the side of the tent and lifted the canvas to duck under, aiming for the back side of the containment pods. The ghosts in the menagerie went wild, throwing tantrums and filling her mind with violent noise.

The pods of brass and copper stood in solid rows, their functionality made into sculptural beauty by artisans hired with the inherited fortune Mrs. Winchester had poured into the venture. Each contained several spirits that visitors viewed by peering through the round windows while wearing goggles they could plug in to ports on each unit. Lucinda reached for the circular handle on the back of Lavinia's pod, turning it to open the access port with amazing ease and marveling again at her sudden strength, but then, she heard voices approaching and dropped to the floor with the access port hanging open above her head.

". . . and then she attacked me, just rushed right at me and scratched my face!" a feminine voice said. Emeline Mabry. Lucinda peered around the edge of the pod as Mr. Gaut entered with Emeline, who was gesturing with Lucinda's dark spectacles in her hand and had scratches on her face that had certainly not been there minutes earlier.

"My dear, how shocking! I wouldn't have thought she had the strength for such a thing . . ." Mr. Gaut said. "But this matter will be finished before dawn, and then, you'll feel much better. I'm sure."

It was too outrageous. Lucinda stood. "Oh, yes. After you've killed me, you'll all feel *so* much better."

Mr. Gaut turned quickly, one hand dropping to his side. "My goodness, Lucinda, you startled me! What's all this about killing? How could you have gotten such an idea? Now, you must apologize to Miss Mabry for this paranoid attack, and perhaps, we can have Oswald run to the druggist for a dose of laudanum. You know how awful your nerves have been lately . . ." His familiar directing tone nearly convinced Lucinda to listen, but he was sweating and fumbling with his coat pocket.

"You're both liars!" she said. A tool cart sat nearby. Lucinda reached for a hammer, planning to bash the gears she'd exposed in Lavinia's containment pod. As she grasped it, Mr. Gaut pulled a strange pistol from his pocket and pointed it at her. There was no sound, but a sensation boxed her ears, and Lucinda's mind flexed with the impact. Her energy level dropped.

"My new set of harmonizing frequencies," Mr. Gaut said. She heard him as if through mud. "They don't affect normal people as such, but it seems that the proper arrangement can work on mediums."

Lucinda, dropping to her knees, saw that Miss Mabry had lost consciousness and collapsed.

"Now why, in your weakened state, would you still be awake," Mr. Gaut said, leaning down to peer into Lucinda's eyes, "while our fresh medium has fainted? I shall have to perform more tests . . ."

But when he got close enough, Lucinda used all her remaining strength to crush his nose with her forehead. It was the one useful skill she had learned from observing other patients in the Ataraxia Institute.

✿✿✿

After binding Mr. Gaut and Miss Mabry with wire from the tool cart, Lucinda gazed at the layers of gears turning inside Lavinia's containment pod—so delicate and precise—and took up the hammer once again. She had to hurry because someone else could come in at any moment. Doubt seized her. What if she couldn't perform astral projection by choice? She would have to. There was no time to practice.

Lucinda raised the hammer, bashing as hard as she could again and again. She felt a sudden stillness when the unit's harmonizing frequencies broke. Then Lavinia emerged at full force, rage concentrated, manifesting claws that tore at Lucinda's skin and clothing. Lucinda, in desperate terror, threw herself from her body and up to face Lavinia in the ether.

For a moment, Lavinia's ghost froze before Lucinda's unexpected appearance in that realm. She appeared as a collage of jumbled faces, potential selves incompletely formed and collected like a swarm of wasps, buzzing and vibrating in place. Lucinda tried to speak—to say wait, please, let me apologize—but she had no voice, and Lavinia launched herself forward to attack again. Lucinda could only defend herself by consuming her.

She fell back into her body, plagued by the layers of conflict and anger absorbed from Lavinia. In contrast to Ivor's adult appreciation of Lucinda's help, Lavinia tore through her mind, zigzagging madly, uncomprehending. Lucinda struggled to organize the experience as she took in the surge of vital energies that came with her sister's ghost. Incoherent stabs of feeling came and went. Lucinda sat with her arms wrapped around her knees, rocking and squeezing her eyes tightly shut, trying to regain control.

The storm began to recede. She sought a connection with Lavinia, something like the communication from Ivor. This time, there were no words. Lucinda absorbed emotions from her sister: confusion, weariness, relief, acceptance. She tried to project back regret and caring as Lavinia faded. It was the only thing she could do for Lavinia in their final moments together.

There were thirty-six more spirits in the menagerie, all of them wild and unknown. Lucinda wasn't weak anymore, and she wouldn't be a victim.

She would set them all free, and no one could stop her.

{{

Nayad Monroe *wrote her first story, a* Fantasy Island-*inspired mermaid tale with a twist ending, at the age of eight. She likes to think her work has improved since then. Her short fiction has been published in several anthologies, including* Steampunk World *and* Sidekicks!, *both edited by Sarah Hans, and* The Crimson Pact: Volume Two, *edited by Paul Genesse. Nayad is also the editor of two mixed-genre anthologies:* What Fates Impose *and* Not Our Kind. *Her author page on Goodreads.com has all the info: www.goodreads.com/author/show/3250170.Nayad_A_ Monroe. But if you just want to see her get silly, follow @Nayad on Twitter.*

T-Hex

Jonah Buck

$\diamond \diamond \diamond$

"*Carthago delenda est*," the phantom said as it meandered through the aerodrome hangar.

"Carthage must be destroyed." Charlotte LaFitte mentally translated the Latin. Benefits of a classical education.

Clad in Roman armor, the apparition swirled toward the audience, its body little more than mist. With each step, the spirit left gooey footprints. After a few seconds, the grey-green ectoplasm evaporated.

The audience watched in rapt attention. Ladies with oversized hats placed velvet-gloved hands over their mouths. Gentlemen in severely tailored suits tugged at their mustaches in macabre fascination.

Moving like someone who had just cut himself free from a trolley accident, dazed but uninjured, the apparition approached the hundred-odd onlookers. Charlotte looked for all the signs, but she didn't see any lights, strings, or hidden vents that could create the effect. The audience began to clap.

"*Carthago delenda—*"

Prescott Blasko pulled a lever on the huge machine behind him, and the spirit collapsed into a pool of diaphanous vapor. The pale aether dissipated as the lights came back on inside the hangar.

Charlotte blinked. She sat near the back of the crowd, directly under a painting of Abraham Lincoln's seventeenth inauguration. As always, Lincoln was turned in three-quarters profile to hide most of the steel plate clamped over his forehead from the failed assassination attempt in 1865. The artist had tastefully minimized the tubes and wires that poked out of the president's skull, pumping tinctures into his bloodstream day and night. In another bout of artistic liberty, the painter depicted the light that constantly poured out of the president's pupils as a muted, benign-looking blue instead of the more realistic seasick green.

Even Lincoln seemed to be watching the demonstration of Blasko's reverse transmigrator.

Blasko opened a hatch on his machine, and chilled air billowed out. Blasko waved the ghost smog away and plucked out the Roman-era amulet inside. The owner was now in his wife's arms, having fainted dead away.

Charlotte was impressed. She was in the process of writing her second book debunking frauds and charlatans who used séances to fleece the lonely or the gullible.

Some fraudsters simply claimed to have psychic powers, regular old fashioned mediums. But an increasing number used the fruits of the new mechanical age to trick the public.

Blasko's "reverse transmigrator" stood almost twenty feet tall, the size of a small house, with dual boilers on either side. It reminded Charlotte of a gigantic laundry press, the big industrial kind that occasional sucked in hapless workers and spat them out as bloody gobbets. A small aperture, roughly the size of a bread box, served as the machine's mouth.

If it was hokum, it was very impressive hokum. Two big Pinkerton guards stood to either side of the machine, tri-barrel carbines slung over their shoulders.

"As I said in my introduction," Blasko addressed the crowd, "this isn't a séance. This is a scientific exploration."

Blasko didn't seem particularly comfortable speaking in public. He talked in a rush, and he tended to gesticulate wildly with his hands. Taking a deep breath, he continued.

"Death is like a one-way mirror. No matter how you squirm or squint, all you can see is your own reflection, your own insecurities or vanities peering back. You can't see who... or what... might be watching from the other side."

Blasko gestured to his invention. "This machine pierces that veil. By placing an item in the tray, it can sense spiritual tethers between this world and the next. Anything with a strong personal connection will do."

Blasko and his machine caught Charlotte's attention a few months ago, and she'd accumulated a small pile of newspaper clippings detailing his itinerary and routine. Charlotte knew he came to Detroit hoping to raise funds to perfect the device. Most investors had laughed him off. He had been forced to give his demonstration in a rented dirigible hangar rather than a posh convention center, but this was still a substantial crowd.

Detroit was a logical place to hold the demonstration. The city manufactured everything from the Edsel five-speed automatic brains that kept President Lincoln alive to the "Armored Teakettle" steam tanks that patrolled the Richmond and Charleston Military Pacification Zones. Mining interests, the automaton industry, the Fortean League, and high-end gangsters all rubbed shoulders here. No city in the Union was more likely to contain a richer, more lustful fool to finance Blasko.

Yet he impressed Charlotte. She'd spent the last five years investigating the paranormal as a professional skeptic, and she'd never seen anything like Blasko's device and the effects it produced.

"Who else would like a demonstration?" Blasko surveyed the crowd. "As you have seen, the machine can operate even on older artifacts, but anything with sufficient personal value to the deceased will do."

The crowd murmured.

"I have something." Charlotte stood up. She hadn't known she was going to say anything until it was out of her mouth, but now, the entire crowd stared at her. Her face suddenly felt hot with embarrassment at her own eagerness, but this was a unique opportunity.

"Ah, Charlotte LaFitte. I thought that was you."

Charlotte could feel her face turning redder. She'd hoped to watch the entire show undetected. Now, she was at the center of this circus. *May the flaming bridges behind me light my way forward.*

"This may surprise you, but I'm a fan of your work," Blasko said. "I'll be the first to admit that the paranormal field has more than its share of swindlers. Good riddance to them. I'm here to prove my device does what it promises. Proving it to your satisfaction would be a feather in my cap. Would you be willing to sign my copy of your book after the demonstration?"

Charlotte found her voice again. "Alright, you've caught me," she laughed. "I'd be happy to sign your copy. First, I have a proposition for you. My credibility is on the line too, now that I've opened my big mouth."

She reached into her bag and removed a small wooden jewelry box. Something rattled inside it.

Blasko smoothed his slicked hair into place. Even oiled like a locomotive's brakes, a cowlick stood up on the back of his head. Charlotte had to admit, she found Prescott Blasko charming. Most stage mediums were all huff and bluster.

Blasko fidgeted nervously with his bifocals when he wasn't speaking. He reminded Charlotte of a graduate student in mechanized medicine defending a thesis, nervous to the point of stuttering.

"I have an object inside this box," she said, holding it up. "Only I know what it is. If your machine can work its magic on the item inside, you'll convince me."

"Hmm," Blasko rubbed his chin. "I hope you won't think ill of me if this doesn't work. The thickness of the box may be problematic. My machine is only a prototype. It would probably just read the box, not the object inside."

Charlotte considered. It would certainly give Blasko an easy out if the reverse transmigrator just so happened to malfunction reading her item, but his explanation wasn't unreasonable. Nothing ventured, nothing gained.

"Alright, would it help if I wrapped it in a handkerchief instead?"

"Oh, yes. That would reduce the interference considerably."

She secreted the object out of its container and quickly wrapped a hanky around it. She stuck the box back inside her pocket.

The box and its contents were a gift from her father when she was a little girl. He'd given it to her a few weeks before he died. She kept them with her at all times. If Blasko's machine could manifest her father...

Despite its original purpose, the box didn't contain any jewelry. It contained a tooth. A single five-inch long, ossified tooth from a long extinct carnosaur.

Her father had been a paleontologist. He'd been on an expedition near the Charleston Military Pacification Zone when he was kidnapped by one of the rebel militia groups that the Union occupation had never succeeded in stamping out. The LaFittes were a wealthy family from old California ranching money. They'd paid the ransom. The rebels killed her father anyway.

The tooth had been his most prized possession since he'd found it as a young man. It was a sort of talisman, part scientific curio, part lucky charm. Maybe he should have kept it with him.

Charlotte's mother had always been a frail woman, prone to nervous fits. Her father's death pushed her over the edge, leaving her vulnerable to the likes of Stephen Astor.

Astor was a tall, striking, bald man with enormous personal charisma and a broken moral compass. In all likelihood, Astor would have made a killing as a used auto-buggy salesman or any other job that required professional schmoozing, but he was too lazy for real work and had a fiendish morphine habit to support.

As Charlotte eventually discovered, Astor had only a single useful talent. He could crack his toes.

Of course, he didn't market that as his skill. He said he could contact the dead. Astor would charm his intended target, get them talking, and then begin his act.

Using the information his mark had just told him, he could fabricate a fairly convincing story. He would sit at a table with his target, asking questions of the spirits and receiving loud knocks in response. One knock for yes, two knocks for no.

By keeping his hands in plain sight the entire time, it was a solid act. The noises came from seemingly nowhere and answered a few basic questions before going back to playing poker with Saint Peter or whatever the spirits did when they weren't talking to Astor.

In reality, each knock was just Astor's toes crackling on the floor. He'd latch onto someone like a tick, bleed them dry, and then move on.

Charlotte's mother fell for his gig. Astor had quickly moved in with them at their California hacienda, performing nightly séances.

Astor was manipulative, wheedling, and far too free with her mother's money. He introduced her mother to morphine. To enhance her psychic abilities, he claimed. Really, it kept her compliant to all his demands, and there were many demands.

It wasn't hard to figure out Astor was a sham. The "spirits" answered questions incorrectly sometimes, even basic personal information. Charlotte was a teenager before she figured out the toe-cracking trick, but her mother was too far under Astor's spell by then.

Their once-beautiful house fell into disrepair. Vast chunks of land were sold off, along with most of the herds. All of it went toward financing Astor's elaborate, bacchanalian séances, which could involve whole crates of cognac.

She spent most of her days locked in her room, listening to the constant chaos outside. Often, she had her nose in a paleontology book, thinking about the magnificent prehistoric beasts that once roamed the earth. The tooth was constantly at her side.

More than anything, she wished her father was still around, that he would return like Odysseus after a long journey and strike Astor down.

One night, she was in her room when she caught a whiff of smoke. Looking out the window, she saw Astor and his cronies standing in the yard, wine bottles in hand, illuminated by the growing flames.

Charlotte saw flames building in the stairwell, so she bailed through the window. The only thing she had time to save was her box. The entire house became a raging inferno.

On the ground, she couldn't find her mother anywhere. Astor had simply left her in a morphine stupor inside when the flames began crawling up the walls. Five grown men were required to keep her from charging back into the house. Astor was duly arrested on a variety of charges amounting to aggravated scalawaggery and spent a few years in jail.

She'd taken the insurance money, sold off the remaining scraps of land, and finished her schooling. Now, she had a successful book exposing predatory supernatural scammers and was working on another.

Despite everything, Charlotte wasn't motivated by hatred. Certainly, she took a certain pleasure in unmasking con artists, ensuring they wouldn't repeat Astor's legacy.

But a part of her wanted to believe. Her mother had taken a great deal of comfort in Astor's false skills. If Charlotte found the real deal, maybe it would vindicate some of her mother's choices.

So far, she'd found nothing to prove her mother right. The people she'd exposed ranged from harmless attention seekers to a supposedly prophetic robot to schizophrenic cult leaders. None of them could deliver on their promises.

Blasko intrigued her, though. She'd never seen anything half as spectacular.

As Blasko took the handkerchief from her, their fingers touched for a second. Placing the cloth in the slot, he closed and dogged the hatch. A green light blinked, indicating the chamber was hermetically sealed.

Blasko flashed a nervous smile. "Well, here goes nothing," he said to the audience. All watched in anticipation.

Yanking a lever, Blasko activated the machine. The reverse transmigrator hummed, the sound growing louder. The lights dimmed and wavered.

Something was wrong. The hair on the back of Charlotte's neck stood at attention as arcs of current lanced between the boilers. Blasko took a step back from his creation as it began to rattle and shake.

"This isn't right," he shouted to one of the guards. The machine's hum built into a howl. "We're drawing too much power. Vent the steam!"

A haze began to form in front of the machine. Crackles of electricity rippled through the mist. There was a lot of vapor, far more than the machine had produced to manifest the Roman soldier. Charlotte backed away from the stage as the cloud towered higher and higher.

The Pinkerton guard placed his hand on a valve. A spark as bright as the sun shot between the metal surface and his fingertips. He screamed, his body going spastic. His lips peeled back, and his jaw clenched so tight Charlotte could see his teeth fracture. A split second later, his hair ignited, and the skin started to bubble off his bones. Shouts of horror rippled through the audience.

A roar answered the screams. At first Charlotte thought it was the machine straining, perhaps breaking down.

She looked up. The billowing mist had a distinctive shape, twenty feet tall and forty feet long. Huge, clawed feet made from gauzy fog stood on the stage.

At one end of the mist, a tail swished back and forth. At the other end, a pair of glowing eyes, like cracked red marbles, stared down at the audience.

The beast's teeth were longer than Charlotte's fingers. Ectoplasmic drool dangled from the curved fangs.

People sometimes reported sensing smells with hauntings, perhaps a hint of rose perfume in the bedroom of a murdered woman. A horrible charnel house odor assaulted Charlotte's nostrils now: the smell of blood and rotting meat and virulent musk, the smell of a predator.

That tooth had been precious to her father, his most cherished possession. But something else had a personal connection with it, a very personal connection that she hadn't considered.

A triumphant roar filled the aerodrome. The reverse transmigrator had just peeled back the distant eons and summoned forth something primordial and savage. Sixty-five million years' worth of primal, unfulfilled hunger stood amongst them.

Blasko darted toward a thick cord running out of the machine. The dinosaur reached down and clamped its scrap shearer jaws down over his torso. Picking Blasko's writhing form off the ground, the monster shook its head back and forth like a dog killing a snake.

Bones snapped and cracked in a rapid-fire salvo. The dinosaur tossed its head back, and the shape, no longer recognizable as Prescott Blasko, tumbled down its throat. Charlotte could see the kicking, twitching form slide down the prehistoric monster's gullet and then just… fade away.

At another time, Charlotte might have wondered what became of something swallowed by a ghost. Did it digest your soul?

The crowd fled toward the exits, knocking over chairs. Blasko's remaining guard emptied his carbine at the prehistoric phantom. The bullets passed straight through, leaving vapor trails in their wake. Compared to the size of the monster, the weapon was little more than a pop-gun. Even against a flesh and bone dinosaur, the carbine wouldn't have done much good.

Turning, the dinosaur lifted a massive foot and brought it down on the man with a crunch. The Pinkerton squirted against the wall.

The monster turned its attention on the writhing, panicked smorgasbord of the fleeing crowd. Behind it, the reverse transmigrator rattled and spewed blasts of blue lightning like something out of Dr. Frankenstein's lab.

Almost directly under the behemoth, Charlotte was out of the monster's immediate sight. A huge foot swept out and stepped off the stage, barely missing her. She was transfixed and horrified at the same time, too shocked to move.

Oh, God. This is your fault, all your fault. You gave Blasko the tooth. You should have known. You should have seen this, a shrill little voice screamed in her head, paralyzing her.

Charlotte shoved the voice out of her thoughts. She needed to do something.

She was the closest person to the reverse transmigrator. If she shut it down, the carnosaur would disappear just like the Roman soldier, right? She had to try.

Clambering up onto the stage, she scanned the array of switches, valves, and lights. A maze of cords and pipes crisscrossed the floor.

Charlotte didn't want to touch any of it. Bolts of electricity shot between the two boiler towers. The corpse of the electrocuted Pinkerton guard was still stuck to the valve on the opposite side of the machine, little more than sizzling meat.

She had to find some way to deactivate the machine without touching it. She looked around for something, anything. The first Pinkerton's revolver carbine lay on the stage, a few feet from his twitching corpse.

An idea came to Charlotte. A terrible idea but the only one she had. She snatched up the carbine, feeling its deadly weight in her hands. Shooting the apparition was pointless. She'd seen that.

But the reverse transmigrator's boilers were operating under such high pressure, a single hole would destabilize the entire machine and probably cause a full-scale blowout.

The resulting explosion would send a boiling wave of shrapnel and steam cascading outward. Without more distance, she'd be roasted like a suckling pig.

Behind her, the crowd struggled to fit through the exits.

The dinosaur waded toward them, moving leisurely. There was no way so much prey could escape in time. It would be a bloodbath if the monstrous specter tore into the crowd.

"Hey, hey!" She waved her arms and shouted, trying to draw the creature's attention away, to at least distract it for a few seconds.

There was no way it could hear her over the cries of terror from the mob. Cursing, Charlotte lifted the carbine and fired a shot into the ceiling. The noise cracked through the confined space.

Lifting its head, the mammoth beast turned. Two glowing eyes gazed at her from across the room, across time, across death. She felt something deep inside herself go loose.

Taking the loud noise as the call of a challenger, the predator took a step toward Charlotte, its feet booming on the ground.

Oh, balls.

She wanted to distract the creature, not attract it. Charlotte took off running, her heart thundering in her chest like a timpani drum.

A roar like the crack of the apocalypse, only louder, sounded behind her. She needed to get away from the reverse transmigrator right now. Scampering off the stage, Charlotte pounded toward the hangar wall.

Behind her, footsteps grew closer and closer and closer. The ground shook with each new impact. The entire world felt like it was shuddering apart.

With luck, she'd be out of the blast radius if she made it to the wall, one hundred feet away. The footsteps grew closer. Fifty feet away. She could hear the floor breaking with each crushing impact. Ten feet away. Hot, fetid breath tickled the back of her neck.

Charlotte spun and raised the carbine to her shoulder at the same time. The dinosaur was on top of her, its gaping mouth filling her vision. Shimmering teeth confronted her.

But she could see through the phantom beast to the sparking outline of Blasko's machine. She pulled the trigger once, twice, three times, barely aiming.

Dragon tongues of steam shot out of holes in the boilers. The huge mouth flickered for an instant, and the entire world flashed a brilliant white as the boilers ruptured. Flanged metal and a hellstorm of pressurized steam blew outward like an artillery burst.

Charlotte was lifted off the ground and thrown backward. Whether she was caught at the outer edge of the blast envelope or ensnared on the monster's fangs, she had no idea. She felt no pain, only white heat.

Slowly, the blinding light faded. Charlotte blinked, trying to force the cobwebs from her vision. There was no roaring, no horrible pounding footsteps. In fact, she didn't hear anything at all.

She'd… she'd done it! The monster was dead, really and truly dead. Destroying the machine forced it to dematerialize. Relief flooded through her.

As her vision cleared, she saw something. It was a group of people, all sitting and watching her. They were oddly dressed, wearing fashions she didn't recognize.

Women in pillbox hats sat, hands over their mouths. Men tugged at their ties in macabre fascination. What in the world? Where was she? Oh, God. No.

Charlotte turned around. A huge machine hunched behind her, quad-core boilers humming. It was a sleek, updated version on the reverse transmigrator, standing up on a stage at some posh venue.

An otherworldly glow issued from the clear, breadbox-sized hatch at the front of the machine. Charlotte stepped closer and peered through the glass panel, already knowing what she would see and dreading it.

Her jewelry box sat in the center of the tray, wrapped in unearthly light. She looked down at the mist of her hands and arms. The crowd started to clap.

{}

Jonah Buck *has always had an interest in pale, semi-human creatures that flit across the sunless landscape to terrorize the living, so he's now studying to become an attorney in Oregon. His interests include professional stage magic, paleontology, exotic poultry, history, and cheesy monster movies. He would like to give special thanks for this story to Lila Walsh.*

The Monster

Erika Holt

❁❁❁

They said it could not be done: flight over long distances.

All previous dirigibles had proven too fragile, inefficient, or uncontrollable for the needs of modern day adventurers. And as for gliders propelled by internal combustion engines, the foremost proponents of which were brothers who, despite bearing the surname Wright would—I had thought—no doubt be proven wrong? Preposterous. While the whole world put faith in the newfangled technology of gasoline and gunpowder, I had believed British steam power and mechanical ingenuity were the ways of the future.

There I was, at the end of a journey of some 4,200 miles over land and sea, the first man to enjoy a bird's-eye view of those majestic vistas, when a capricious and sudden gust of wind brought my journey to a premature end. "Crash" was an overly dramatic word, though my craft sustained some minor damage. An "expertly executed emergency landing necessitated by exigent and untoward circumstances" would be a more accurate description.

It seemed I had become caught up in events of an astonishing and cataclysmic magnitude. Just hours or days before my landing, the whole side of a mountain had come crashing down. The valley in which I found myself was filled with boulders of considerable size with still-green treetops poking out. Now, most fellows engaged in winged pursuits whose craft had become lodged between the sharp edges of two massive hunks of limestone might be inclined to panic. Not I! My design was far too clever to have me worrying over such trivialities.

You see, inspired by the great Herbert George Wells's masterpiece, *War of the Worlds*, I had thought, why not add legs to my craft? A tripod would be just the thing!

My hydrogen envelope was compromised, so I hastened to eject it before it collapsed entirely and engulfed my gondola. I attempted the valve to divert steam from the flight engine to the locomotion engine, but it wouldn't budge. Hanging my waistcoat neatly on the back of my captain's chair, I redoubled my efforts. Finally, the thing gave, and the locomotion engine roared to life. I was heartened when unfurling the legs proved easier, and I worked the three levers to bring the ship up to standing. What a sight it must've been! My ship, rising from the rubble like an alien being! Were anyone around to see. Even using my binocular telescopes, I spied only destruction. Here a wooden beam, there a bit of twisted metal. A scrap of blue fabric fluttering in the breeze. The crumpled roof of a house. Prickles ran down my spine. It appeared this valley had been inhabited at the time of the slide. Bodies probably lay beneath the very rocks over which I passed.

At the abrupt end to the rubble, railroad tracks and a town emerged—or that part of the town that had escaped destruction. I veered south, parking my craft behind the cover of a boulder. My exit hatch was dented and slightly out of square, but after a few good kicks, it opened, deploying the staircase, which came to rest at an awkward angle. I donned my waistcoat and polished my shoes. Just before squeezing out, I tucked my prized, handcrafted mechanical revolver into my waistband.

The journey, though short, was difficult, requiring me to climb and balance on rough terrain for which I found my shoes ill-suited. Breathing labored, I paused to lean against a boulder, forgetting about my revolver until it poked uncomfortably into my back.

"Bugger me!" a voice growled.

I don't know what I found more shocking—that I was not alone in the rubble or that a woman had just used such vulgar language. Perhaps she was trapped, and great pain had caused such an uncivilized utterance. I whirled this way and that, fearing to see viscera splattered on the rock, but found no sign of the poor woman. I called out but received no answer. Perhaps that unfortunate exclamation had been her last.

By the time I arrived in town, I feared I looked a mess but needn't have worried. The place was deserted, pristine but empty buildings and yawning windows a bit eerie in the heavy quiet. Nailed to a door, a scrap of torn paper fluttered. It read:

May 1, 1903: By order of the right honourable Premier Frederick W. A. G. Haultain, Frank town shall be immediately evacuated under threat of another slide and extreme risk to life and limb. Looters will be—

The rest had been lost to the wind. In my pocket journal, I made note of my location for posterity's sake. Quaint details would make for a better story upon my return.

Rounding a corner, I saw two men in the distance, scarlet Norfolk jackets strikingly similar to those worn by the British army and marking them as men of authority. Excellent. I shouted a greeting and waved, feeling it prudent not to take armed men unawares.

"You there!" the taller of the two said in a stern tone. "The town is under an evacuation order. You're going to have to come with us."

Their shiny boots crunched on the gravel as they approached, faces serious but side-arms still holstered.

I was about to protest, to inform them of my identity and remarkable achievements, but to my great surprise, I lost all control of myself. I found my hand reaching for my revolver. Pulling it out and pointing it at the officers.

"No way I'm goin' back to the pokey with the likes of you two boatlickers!"

It was the woman's voice again, and it was coming from my mouth! I did not want to say these things and yet found my lips forming the ugly words. The police stood with raised hands wearing expressions of disgust.

I shared these emotions wholeheartedly. "No no!" I tried to say, but nothing came out. Instead I continued to brandish my revolver as I backed away and then ran off.

Only when I reached the rubble did I regain control of my faculties.

I grabbed the sides of my face, tugged my hair, and gave myself a good slap with my free hand. What had come over me? I stared in disbelief at the revolver clutched in white-knuckled fingers. Was this woman some sort of witch?

"Where are you?" I shouted. "How dare you force me into such despicable acts!"

I tried to drop the revolver but was unable. I shook my arm like a child trying to get a spider off, but my fingers would not unwrap from the grip. I tried jamming the thing into the back of my waistband and . . . it stayed.

I flexed my fingers. Having finally unhanded the thing, I didn't reach for it again but instead tore off my coat and threw myself against rocks hoping to dislodge it. But even after I scraped areas of skin raw and bloody, the weapon stayed put. Panting, I stopped. The hard metal pressed against the base of my spine.

Back in my ship, I stared at my wild-eyed self in the mirror for a few minutes before turning around to examine the revolver. Its burnished wooden grip riveted to an elaborate brass firing mechanism. The slim, dual barrel disappearing beneath the woollen fabric of my trousers.

"Leave me be, you hag! You devil!" I shouted into the air, and this time, I received an answer.

"Aw, stop your moaning, you lily-livered ball sac. Half the mountain came down on me, and you don't hear me whining."

So. It was worse than I feared. Or, at least, as bad. If her words could be believed, I was—or rather my revolver was—possessed by the spirit of a slide victim. An uncouth one at that.

For a while, I gave over to wailing and made renewed attempts to rid myself of the thing, which resulted only in further injury to my body. Finally, I slumped to the floor. "If you let me go, I swear I will leave this place and never return."

"Trust me, pal, if it were that easy, I'da been outta here at the first whiff of your ass crack when you jammed me down your pants."

Heat rose in my cheeks. "How am I to be rid of you then?"

"Damned if I know."

I took to my feet again and paced about. Despite being a man of learning, a man of reason, or perhaps because of these things, I was at my wit's end. I did not believe in ghosts. Or had not until confronted with this incontrovertible evidence. Exorcisms and séances were well outside my realm of experience. But even I had not been able to live free from the influence of ghost stories, a frequent feature in weekly serials and a popular discussion topic at parties. It was said that spirits often lingered from injustice. I stopped pacing.

"Has someone wronged you?"

"Oh, honey," she cackled, "you'd be here all day if I were to tell you how many cockchafers have screwed me over."

"Ahem. Well. Do you have a name?"

"Alice Rose. But everybody just calls me Liss."

An unexpectedly feminine name for such a crude woman.

"And what may I have the pleasure of calling you, hon?"

"Reginald Darwin Corwallis. The third," I added. In truth, I was the first, the only, but fancy titles carried impressive weight. The spirit gave no indication of being impressed.

"All right, er, *Liss*. Beyond these . . . men . . . who have wronged you, do you think there might be some bigger injustice at play here? Like—"

"How the mining company wouldn't give me work, you mean?"

"Well, I can't imagine mere lack of employment would result in this. You don't think . . . could the mining operation be somehow implicated in this disaster?"

Liss made a noncommittal grunting sound. For a while we kept to ourselves in silence.

Feeling all-overish and unsure of when or if this spirit would control me again, I moved gingerly to brew myself a cup of Earl Grey from the tea dispensary. The finely calibrated piece of machinery must've been jostled on landing, however, for the water was merely lukewarm, the tea weak. But the routine calmed me. My hands nearly stopped shaking.

"You know, the more I think on it, you might be onto something. 'Bout the company. Always had a suspicious feeling, and not just because they were too stupid to know a woman could swing a pickaxe just as good as any man!"

"When the camp boys came up outta that hole at the end of the day," she continued, "they always had a crazy-assed look. Like they were scared of somethin'. But none of 'em would ever say a peep 'bout why. Probably cuz they woulda lost their jobs. Maybe there was something funny going on. Maybe we should check it out, especially since you say solving this mystery might help me go free. And speaking of free, the coppers won't never expect to find us there. Good a hidin' spot as any, least for a few days."

My cup and saucer began to rattle. I set them down. "I didn't say . . . you're not suggesting . . . it would be far too dangerous! The town has been evacuated due to the extreme risk of another slide! Anyway, the entrance must've collapsed." A wave of relief swept over me. We wouldn't be able to get in.

"Won't know unless we look."

I spluttered a moment. "Th-that is just foolishness! I won't go."

"Well, I ain't movin' unless you're movin', so yeah you will."

"No!" I threw myself to the floor and threaded my arms and legs around the pipework, holding on with all my might.

Something of a tug-of-war ensued, my body the unfortunate battleground. The spirit sought to unwind my limbs as I sought to hold on, successfully for a time. But a man of mortal flesh and blood cannot hope to compete with the supernatural strength of a fiend. As my muscles fatigued, my non-dominant hand, my left, wrenched free and inched around to draw the pistol. I found myself staring down the barrel of my own gun.

"Get up."

And with that, any pretence of resistance evaporated. What could I do? I was but a slave to this foul spirit's whims, plucked from the domain of science and thrust into that of fantasy. Danger notwithstanding, we would venture into the heart of things, the mine, the mountain, to uncover the secrets hidden there, if any.

To my captain's chair I shuffled, engaging levers with less than due care to bring my craft precariously to standing. I pushed to full speed, moving as a true alien might, guided by Liss to the mine entrance.

Or where the mine entrance should've been. As I'd hoped, it was entirely blocked.

"Well, that brings an end to it," I said. "Let us remove ourselves from this terrible place and contemplate a rational solution to our . . . shared problem."

"Doesn't make sense," she said. "I can't feel 'em down there."

"Whatever are you on about? Feel who?"

"As we've been going, I can sort of . . . *feel* them. The dead folks. It's like passin' through a pocket of winter wind. But here, in the mine? Nothing. I think somehow they got out."

"Nonsense! You can see for yourself that's impossible. They're probably just buried too deep, the poor souls."

Then another, terrible thought struck me. What if the reason Liss couldn't feel the miners was that they lived on? Trapped beneath tons of rock, unable to escape? I'm ashamed now to say that I didn't raise this possibility aloud, didn't suggest we mount a rescue effort or even go for help. But it didn't matter. Liss was so sure of herself, she insisted we look for an alternate exit. And she was right. After only a few minutes, we discovered a shaft bored through a thin seam of coal that reached the surface. They'd dug their way out.

I made no effort to hide my craft, fully hoping the police would find it and save me from this ludicrous situation. I stuffed supplies in a pack, filled two waterskins—one with water, one with tea—and topped up my lantern with oil. And then into the crevice I peered, a warm gust of air riffling my moustache as though the mountain breathed.

I plunged into the abyss, keenly aware of the weight of rock around me and that I was utterly alone, save for a possessed revolver. At the bottom, I lit my lantern and experienced a heady rush of relief when no explosion ensued. The air was close and humid, and though it was cool, perspiration misted my forehead. A malodorous scent crept up my nostrils, like rotting vegetation or perhaps flesh. My stomach clenched, but the spirit had been certain there were no bodies.

I don't know why, but I whispered, "Liss?"

"Yeah?"

"Sssshhh!"

"Well you called me," she said just as loudly.

I resolved not to do so again.

There was evidence of ordinary mining operations: reinforced shafts, carts, broken pick axes, the detritus of unclean men. Save for a few blocked passageways, the mine's interior was in remarkably good condition.

I spotted a nearly hidden shaft—or tunnel, rather, given the craggy, unhewn edges. The miners had erected a barrier across the entrance, mostly dislodged during the slide. Only a single board remained, reading "Danger! Keep out!" The hastily scrawled, vivid red lettering was startling.

After a swig of tea and at Liss's insistence, I ventured onward into the tunnel, which was quite roomy, allowing me to forget just how far underground I must be. Strangely, the temperature seemed to be rising. I was sweating in earnest now.

A noise ahead brought me to a stop. Shuffling footsteps, tentative, halting. My heart rate quickened, and for a moment, all I could hear was blood pounding in my ears. And then the steps came again, and I was gripped by fear. But if I was to discover this mountain's secrets and rid myself of this pestilent spirit, I had to go on.

I switched the lantern to my left hand and drew the revolver. Liss hooted at the touch, the sound echoing off the walls. The footsteps ahead stopped. Perhaps, it was a miner, trapped all these days underground.

Inching around the corner, I probably would've fired, but Liss was quicker, intervened to stay my trigger finger. For it was neither demon nor ghoul but a horse, still hitched to a cart and outfitted in heavy leather gear. Blinders gave its face a strange shape in the flickering light—the probable cause of my momentary panic.

It craned its neck around to try to see us, and an eye rolled in fear, but it didn't flee. It just stood and snorted, nostrils flared wide.

"Aw, poor pit pony," said Liss. "We gotta help him. Easy, big guy."

I felt my feet began to move and snapped, "No need! I'm perfectly able!"

The thing shied as I approached but didn't fight as I undid buckles. "Good boy," I said, patting him on the shoulder. Really, I should've put a bullet in the poor creature's brain as there was no way of getting him out. But I had a feeling Liss would object, and that was a battle for later. The horse pushed past us and hurried back toward the mine proper.

Moisture slicked the tunnel walls, and the stench was so powerful I gagged. I shuffled along and caught myself just short of tumbling over a precipice. The path plunged downward, and the walls parted into a yawning cavern. With one hand on the clammy wall, I extended my lantern out over the void, my arm shaking only a little.

For a moment, I saw nothing but darkness. Heard nothing but the sound of a hundred or a thousand drips, dripping. Felt as though my lungs would compress under the heavy weight of air. But then a fetid gust blasted me, and I was confronted with a supernatural horror the likes of which even Herbert George at his peak could not have conjured up.

A heavy wrinkled lid in what I'd taken for rock opened to reveal an eye. A giant eye. Inhuman. Bluish, milky white in color. Blind, probably, but I had no doubt this beast was aware of my presence. It uncurled an impossibly long neck to bridge the gap between us in a moment. I cried out and stumbled back, falling. My lantern tumbled from my hand but remained lit, revealing slitted nostrils. Its mottled grey skin was leathery and armored in overlapping scales. Strands of slimy moss hung off like tattered clothing. Two smaller heads reared up on either side of the central head, swaying on spindly stalks like snakes readying to strike.

"Holy shit," whispered Liss. "*Turtle* Mountain! I never thought—"

The beast opened a beaked maw in a silent scream, and the small heads lunged. I threw a hand over my face and closed my eyes, sure the end was nigh.

But Liss had other ideas.

"Stand up!"

Not waiting for me to comply, she forced me up on jelly legs, revolver in hand.

"Back off! I don't want to hurt you!" she yelled with my mouth.

What? Now that I was armed and upright, I wanted nothing more than to kill this creature.

The creature tipped its main head, slightly, as though pondering. Seizing the opportunity, I concentrated hard on pulling the trigger. Perhaps Liss was distracted by the beast, for I succeeded. The monster shrieked as a bullet pierced one of the smaller heads. The stalk went limp, and the head dangled uselessly.

"Goddammit, Reggie!"

Now, the large head came for us. Liss didn't hesitate, letting loose three more bullets.

"Run!" she yelled, but I was already running. I had lost my lantern, but there was only one way forward in the darkness. Liss fired again over my shoulder. The creature's head pursued, the massive bulk of its long neck shaking dust and rock loose, which rained down on my head. I heard a final shot and a click. Empty. I ran right into the board containing the warning and was winded on impact. I crawled out of the tunnel mouth and collapsed on the floor, scrambling away from the opening, desperately hoping it was too narrow for the creature to follow.

I lay there wheezing until my breath returned and a chill overtook my sweat-soaked body. Everything was quiet. I lit a match to get my bearings.

It flared to life, and I saw the monster lying just inside the tunnel entrance, one milky eye now a dark, dripping mess, bullet holes peppering its face. As the flame dwindled, I stared at it, and it seemed to stare back at me. It looked not so monstrous now but old and feeble. Tired. Defeated.

The light died.

❂❂❂

Some thirty years later, that image and the memories of my terrible journey through darkness back to the surface still haunt me. That and Liss, who continues to inhabit my revolver, solved mystery notwithstanding. The officers of the Royal Canadian Mounted Police did find my craft as I'd hoped, but unfortunately, this resulted not in my emancipation but in my incarceration for a period of some ten years. The whereabouts of my ship remains a mystery, my pleas to the Canadian government for its safe return falling on deaf ears.

I never married, and following a few more adventures consisting mostly of setting up shop as a widget-maker and finding affordable lodgings in Vancouver (passage back to Britain on my meagre earnings being out of the question), Liss and I settled into a companionable relationship, though I believe she's never forgiven me for taking that first shot.

I breathed not a word of our discovery but became a bit obsessed with the town of Frank and its Turtle Mountain. The going theory for the collapse was that an anticline formation of shale and sandstone overlaid with limestone had been weakened by an unusual freeze-thaw cycle, expanding fissures. However, the indigenous peoples of the area—the Kutenai and Crowfoot—called Turtle Mountain the "mountain that moves" and would never camp at its base. Perhaps they knew the truth. If only the townsfolk and mining company had been as wise. Near a hundred residents had lost their lives that day, as well as a camp of transients numbered up to fifty, Liss included.

When the mine entrance was excavated, the miners discovered the horse we'd encountered—Charlie—still living. Intent on spoiling the poor animal after his horrible ordeal, the miners fed him a rich meal of oats and brandy, which unfortunately proved to be his end. Bittersweet to be sure, but I'm glad he saw daylight one last time.

Though mining quickly resumed, the mine closed permanently in 1917. The mountain has scarcely moved since the slide, and I'll admit to having mixed feelings. While I wouldn't wish another disaster upon the good people of Frank, who stubbornly persist, some small part of me hopes that the creature in the mountain still lives, that we—that I—didn't kill it.

For, as perhaps only an old man can know, there are too few wonders left in this world. Gasoline, gunpowder, and airplanes have overtaken steam technology, and facilitated violence and destruction of unprecedented magnitude. If this is the face of modern progress, I want nothing of it. I will stick to crafting mechanical toys that bring smiles to children's faces.

And, if I had destroyed the one wonder I'd been extraordinarily lucky enough to encounter, well, I will never forgive myself either and can only conclude that it is I who am the monster.

{$

Erika Holt *is a lawyer by day and a writer/editor by night. Her stories have appeared in numerous anthologies, including* What Fates Impose *and* Not Our Kind, *and she is an assistant editor of* Nightmare Magazine *under bestselling and multiple award-nominated Editor-in-Chief John Joseph Adams. The rockslide recounted in her story "The Monster" is a real event which you can find out more about by visiting the Frank Slide Interpretive Centre in south-western Alberta or by just driving the Crowsnest Highway, which carves a path through the 90 million tons of limestone that still fill the valley. You can find Erika on Twitter (@ erikaholt), her website (erikaholt.com), or blogging with the Inkpunks.*

The Book of Futures

Wendy Nikel

⚙⚙⚙

On a seaside cliff on the far edge of town, a single gas lamp sent Dr. Lucia Crosswire's thin shadow cowering into the tangled pines. Her heels crunched steadily along the winding cobblestones, and a well-fed rat darted across the path, screeching at the disturbance to its nocturnal traipsing.

Nighttime strolls along the outskirts of Clifton weren't generally advisable for an unaccompanied lady, but Lucia wasn't concerned. With her pistol securely in its strap upon her leather tool belt and her newly invented electroshock weapon at her other hip, she was confident that she'd come out ahead in any altercation. Besides, the townsfolk of Clifton were highly superstitious when it came to the reclusive monks of Mont Saint-Vogel. Rarely did young ne'er-do-wells trespass on the monastery's hallowed ground and certainly never after dusk.

Even the forest itself seemed to cower from the expansive hilltop monastery, its pines bending outward from the stone pillars and walls. Far above the arched entrance, an angel held a balance, its trays askew. *Thou art weighed in the balances and art found wanting.*

Lucia pulled her cloak tightly to herself, her tools and instruments clanking in the many pockets.

A red cord hung beside the massive door. When Lucia tugged it, the iron cogs surrounding the doorframe shifted and clicked into place, a discordant clatter in the night's placid silence. After a still moment, a mournful bell tolled somewhere deep within the stone walls.

The door opened. A figure blocked the way, clad in a hooded gown of rough brown cloth that obscured his features and form. Its only adornment was a dull medallion, engraved with the image of a bird. *Be ye wise as serpents and harmless as doves.*

Preferring to err on the side of wisdom, Lucia rested her fingertips on the tiny clockwork mechanisms of her electroshock weapon. "Are you Brother Primicerius?"

"I am." The figure stepped backward, fading into the monastery's inky recesses. "Please, come in so that we may more discreetly address the events of late."

Lucia narrowed her eyes and gripped her device more tightly but didn't back away. She'd come this far based solely on a strangely whispered message emanating from a wind-up bird delivered to her investigative offices in the town far below. "Trouble. Please come. 10 o'clock tonight," it'd repeated each time its key was wound. The only other clue to its origin had been the return address on its packaging, indicating that the sender was a Brother Primicerius at the Mont Saint-Vogel monastery.

Lucia stepped inside. The door closed with a dissonant clank.

"Forgive me the request of your presence at such an hour." The voice in the dark seemed to come from everywhere, nowhere, somewhere within Lucia's own head. A spark flared, a match lit, and the shadowy hood of Brother Primicerius hovered before her as if disembodied by the night. "The brothers of this sacred place have sworn a vow of seclusion from the outside world. Therefore, I felt it best to wait until the hours of rest for this meeting, so your presence here would not be a distraction. This way."

He turned, momentarily blocking the candle's light and plunging Lucia into cold darkness. Her heart thudded in her chest like the measured strokes of a pendulum, but she followed, matching him step for step. Around a corner, at the end of another long, silent corridor, a gentle light glowed from beneath a closed door.

"You must swear to me," Brother Primicerius said, "that never, though you suffer a thousand years of torture, will you reveal the contents of this room."

Though the people of Clifton often whispered and gossiped about the mysterious goings-on upon the hill, Lucia had never heard of anyone being tortured for this information, so she replied confidently, "I swear I will not reveal the secrets of your order."

Brother Primicerius nodded grimly. "My brother is the vicar in the village below. He's assured me that he's confided in you in the past and that you are worthy of this great trust."

"Yes, he called upon me last spring to investigate some thefts at the cathedral. Has there been a burglary here?" Even as she said it, she knew it was unlikely, for who would climb all the way up this hill to steal from those who'd taken a vow of poverty?

The door had no handle, but Brother Primicerius pressed a series of springs on one side as deftly as an organist playing a chord, and after a moment of shifting and clicking within, the door slid to one side, revealing the chamber.

"A library?" Lucia gazed in awe at the rows after rows of books. Their spines stacked upon one another until they reached the top of the domed ceiling where an elaborate wrought-iron chandelier hung, dark and unmoving. This was the great secret of the monks of Mont Saint-Vogel? Books?

"These are not ordinary books," Brother Primicerius said as if reading her mind. He walked among the tomes, touching one and then another with awed reverence. "These books contain prophecies from the beginning of time, from every man who walked the earth and claimed to have some deeper insight into the future. It is our sacred duty to weigh each line, study each prediction, and determine which prophets were true, which visions are yet to come."

A library of prophecies . . . Lucia looked with new appreciation on the rows of shelves. "But what do you want of me?"

On a table in the center of the room stood a bronze case with intricate carvings on the lid. Brother Primicerius unlocked it. The case unfolded like the blooming of a mechanical flower, revealing a heavy black tome. In blood-red letters upon the cover was the title: *Liber Futures*.

"The *Book of Futures*," Lucia translated.

"In the holy book of Acts, we are told that Paul drove a demon out of a female slave whose owner had been earning a great deal of money through her fortune-telling. This book is whispered to contain all her predictions of the future."

"Wars and rumors of wars . . ." Lucia recited.

"That and so much more." He snapped shut the bronze case, enclosing the book once more. "It arrived at the monastery a fortnight ago. It is also my belief that this particular relic brought with it some sinister force."

"Sinister force?" Lucia's keen eyes darted about the room where each flicker of the candle and turn of her head made it seem as though shapes were moving among the bookshelves. Her voice came out louder than she intended, its tone barely concealing her skepticism. "Demons, you mean?"

"Perhaps the very one which the apostle drove from the slave girl."

"I don't know what you've heard of my investigations," Lucia said, taking a step toward the door, "but my expertise is in human crimes with human wrongdoers. The spirit world is entirely unknown to me."

The monk's hood bobbed in acknowledgement. "That is precisely why I summoned you. For our expertise is in the spirit world, yet none of our attempts—no prayers or chants or exorcisms—have had the slightest effect. My brothers have asked that I put aside my own convictions and consider the possibility, however small, that these crimes have a more . . . natural cause."

"And what are these crimes?" Lucia asked with some relief at her new understanding of the situation. How strange it must be to live like these monks in a society where demons are the first accused and human culprits only considered when no other explanation can be found.

"Each night," he said, "as the brothers take their rest, this library is locked. Its door, you may have gleaned, is unique. The combination is known solely to me, and I consider it my sacred duty to alter the code each Sabbath. Were any man to apply the wrong combination of levers, the mechanisms within would release a poison to kill him in an instant.

"As you can see, there are no other entrances to this chamber, yet every morning, the brothers discover that their books have been misplaced, picked up and set elsewhere. Also, each night, one book—one each night—is missing entirely, and the one from the previous day is returned, as though it had been there all along.

"To a demon this would be but a mischievous prank." He paused, deep in thought. "But if the culprit is, indeed, of flesh and blood, his motives may be far more devious. With the words these pages contain, you can see why we guard them so carefully, why their disappearance causes us such distress. If someone else were to be taking these pages and using them for their own purposes—"

"Yes, I see what you mean." Lucia wandered about the library, noting the orderliness of each table, the meticulous nature by which these monks arranged their books. She touched the cover of one, careful not to move it from its current position. "The books in this library—would they have monetary value? Perhaps to collectors?"

"Oh, yes. Even the books whose prophecies have been deemed false would still be deemed priceless for their rarity. Except, of course, the books on the history of Mont Saint-Vogel itself, there, on the northern wall."

Lucia studied the shelf indicated, reaching up to straighten an ancient leather-bound book that stuck out further than the rest: *An Accounting of the Property Deeds, Construction, and Dedication of the Most Blessed Monastery of Mont Saint-Vogel*, the thick spine declared.

"Were any of these record books stolen?" she asked.

"No, of course not. They're just tedious accounts of feast day celebrations. Ordinations, deaths, and burials. Money given to the poor or spent to procure the other books. They'd be of no value to man or demon. I've compiled a list of the books taken."

He held out a scrap of parchment upon which had been written a list in elaborate calligraphy of a dozen books, ranging in subject from the biblical prophet Samuel to a girl in an impoverished island country whose visions dated back only three years from the current day.

Lucia pocketed the list and circled about the room, peering into each darkened nook and tugging gently upon each shelf. She stopped suddenly. "Have you had any visitors to the monastery recently?"

"No."

"And when you received the *Book of Futures*, was it brought here, or did one of your monks fetch it from elsewhere?"

"It came from the Ottoman Empire, relayed via airship to the New Breckinridge port."

"Highly guarded?"

"On the contrary, sent as inconspicuously as possible. The bishop of New Breckinridge paid a boy three coins to deliver it, claiming it to be a particularly thick prayer book."

Lucia pulled a magnifying glass from a pocket in her cloak and snapped it open. She inspected the lock mechanisms of the door, which bore no sign of forced entry.

"Did anyone else in the town know of its arrival?"

"No, not a living soul."

"And what lies beyond the walls of this room?"

"The chapel and the dining hall, both locked."

"And below?" Lucia stomped her heeled boot on a tile, which held firm.

"The catacombs, I'd assume. Please, Dr. Crosswire, based on what you've seen, you must agree that this is an impossible crime. There could be no temporal explanation."

Lucia looked about the room. "It certainly is strange, but before I say for certain, I'd like to test one theory, and for that, I will need you to trust me with the combination to that door."

❁❁❁

Five minutes later, Dr. Lucia Crosswire bid the monk a polite adieu and set off back down the winding path toward town.

Twenty minutes later, she emerged silently from the shadows of the pines and crept to the monastery's eastern side where the hooded monk had unlatched a window before saying his evening prayers and laying his head upon his small, unpadded cot.

The corridors were black and cold as a crypt, but Lucia found her way to the library by the light of her small, hand-cranked lantern. At the door, she carefully studied the set of springs and pressed the ones which Brother Primicerius had indicated. The door slid open with a wisp of cool air.

The library was illuminated by the golden glow of a single candle. Lucia tucked her lantern away and kept to the shadows, stepping carefully. When she reached the farthest corner where the entire length and width and breadth of the room could be seen without moving her head, she sat and settled in for a long night.

The candlelight reflected on the *Book of Futures's* bronze case, warping and twisting the golden light into shapes both strange and hypnotic. It was unsettling, the way that it drew her eye, and she could see why the monks of this place were superstitious regarding it.

Lucia pulled a pair of spectacles from her cloak and placed them on the bridge of her nose. She flipped through a series of overlapping lenses. One revealed the temperature of the white-hot flame, gradually cooling to the purple edges of the room. Another showed gray and white, only displaying any shade of color when she glanced down at her own hand. In yet another, the air took on the appearance of blue waves, which rippled like a rock thrown in a pond at the slightest hint of sound.

Over and over, the cogs clicked as she cycled through the lenses. Each time, her gaze was drawn to the center of the room, where the bronze box sat still and unchanging, like a creature lying in wait.

If only there was one with the ability to show spirits—a lens that could tell her if there were mischievous imps hovering above the pages of the holy men's books or seeping out of the book's bronze box. If only she could forget Brother Primicerius's words about demons and vengeful spirits and ghosts.

Click.

Lucia held her breath, listening. She slid the auditory lens into place just as the noise came again.

Click.

The waves spread from the center of the room where the *Book of Futures* sat upon its wooden table. The table itself shook ever so slightly, and for a single heart-stopping moment, Lucia thought that Brother Primicerius had been right, that there was something sinister contained within that holy relic.

The next moment, it all became clear. A smile spread across Lucia's face.

✿✿✿

"You'll be pleased to hear, Brother Primicerius, that I have solved your mystery. I discovered what has been happening to your books."

Lucia stood in the doorway of the library. The monk had come to retrieve her before the morning bells roused the others from their cots and to their daily meditations and work. The monk clasped his hands in what Lucia could only assume was a gesture of excitement, for as before, his face remained entirely hidden.

"You have? Please, tell me! What was it? Was it the spirit within the book? The one driven out by the apostle so long ago?"

"On the contrary," Lucia said, stepping to one side. "It was none but a small boy."

The child standing before them looked to be but twelve or thirteen with a slight frame, ragged clothing, and large, curious eyes that even now barely rested for a moment and darted about the library.

"A boy? Why, this was the same boy who delivered the book to the monastery!"

"Indeed. It seems that upon receiving the book, you and your fellow monks were so caught up in your acquisition that you didn't even notice the young intruder following upon your heels to the library. Once in here, he hid among the copious shadows, watching as you went about your work, enthralled by all he saw. When all of the monks retired for the evening, he found himself alone in the library."

"Good heavens! Has he been here this whole time? And what of his family? They must be worried sick!"

Lucia turned to the boy. "Go on. Tell him what you told me, Pierre."

The boy dropped his chin to his chest, as though suddenly recalling that he ought to feel remorse for his intrusion. "I've got no family, sir, nor a home. This library is the most amazing place I've seen in my life, and it was my curiosity kept me here. Was my curiosity made me take that book, sir, not evil spirits."

"Tell him which one you took first," Lucia prodded.

"It was a book about the history of this place. I tucked it in my shirt and kept it with me as I snuck out that night. I wanted to know what the monks were doing, that's all. I intended to drop it on the front stoop the next day, but then I found the map."

"Map? What map?"

Pierre proffered up the book, open to a sketch of the entire layout of the monastery.

"Good heavens," Brother Primicerius said. "I'd no idea that was in there."

"And look," Pierre said, "there's a hidden route to the library, up from the catacombs. Soon as I found that, well, I couldn't help myself, sir."

"You entered through the catacombs?" The monk quivered in his robe.

"I only wanted to see more of what you did here. The lock on the mausoleums was rusted, and from there, I used the map to find my way. I returned everything I borrowed, I swear. Please, you won't kill me, will you?"

"Kill you?" From deep within his cavernous hood came a thick sound like the grinding of gears. It took Lucia a moment to realize that the monk was laughing. "Of course, I won't kill you. In fact, seeing as you find our work so fascinating, I would love nothing more if you would join us, become one of our order and help us in our sacred task."

"Truly? I could?" The boy's head jerked upward, a hopeful smile brightening his dirty face.

"Truly. Why, I'd wager you already know more of our secrets than most the ordained brethren do!"

⚙⚙⚙

Dr. Lucia Crosswire strolled down the hill from the Mont Saint-Vogel monastery, grateful to be out in the open as the sun lightened the morning sky. Somewhere in the stone structure behind her, the morning bell gonged, calling the monks from their cots. Soon, Brother Primicerius would reveal that they had another among their number. Would he tell them all how it had come about, or would that be yet another secret?

An airship passed overhead, its horn bellowing like a behemoth, and Lucia wondered if any of the books within the library of Mont Saint-Vogel had foretold those mechanical marvels. In all the time spent within the mysterious room, it had never occurred to her once to search her own futures within the pages. Only now did the curiosity tingle the back of her neck, making her wonder what she'd have found.

But just as swiftly as the airship disappeared from view, obscured by the forest's pines, the desire vanished within her, overpowered by her good sense. The future, she decided, was one mystery best left unknown.

{§

When **Wendy Nikel** *isn't traveling in time, exploring magical islands, or investigating mysterious phenomena, she enjoys a quiet life near Utah's Wasatch Mountains with her husband and sons. She has a degree in elementary education, a fondness for road trips, and a terrible habit of forgetting where she's left her cup of tea. Her short fiction has been published by* AE, Daily Science Fiction, *and others, and she is a member of the* SFWA. *For more info, visit wendynikel.com.*

Death Wish

Parker Goodreau

✿✿✿

My employer had crafted the paragon of a charmed life. Though not of the highest or wealthiest birth, Ajith Shankar had weathered better than most when the British airships arrived, their whirring motors spreading fine clouds of ash across the ocean. While others backed failed rebellions or became puppets of the Company, Ajith thrived: a new magnate happy to don a suit and press any white-gloved hand.

Any who offered him the business end of a bayonet in place of a handshake experienced more than their share misfortune in India. Only half the people who wanted to kill Ajith ever tried. The other half, I took care of.

The secret to his success lived in a small wooden box by his bedside where he would rest his hand through the night. But even so close, it did no good against his wife's sudden illness.

Her room fell quiet when we entered. Attendants backed away from their fidgeting over her funeral dress. Muted lamplight gleamed on her jewelry and damp, waxy skin. Ajith knelt by the bedside, one sweaty hand picking at the tasseled edge of a cushion. "Dismissed," he said. The servants shuffled out together, closing ranks against the tide of sorrow that swept the room.

"Erom," he said, "you as well."

I blinked. "I am always with you, Raj Ajith."

He turned, forehead creased, and took the little jinni box from his pocket.

"With my life I trust you, but I have never owned your mind. And you may not like what I am about to do."

I bit my tongue and held my ground. I could not say whether I stayed for his sake or for the jinni's.

He placed the box by his wife's hand. His fingers fumbled as he wound the key, but at last, the clockwork chimed its familiar tune. In a voice that crumbled the second it hit open air, Ajith sang. The language ached with age, its roots deeper and weightier than Hindi or Sanskrit. It made the clumsy pidgin of the British seem weak and squalling as a newborn. I could not know sorrow or anxiety while the song lasted. The melody dwarfed the whole world.

The room filled with prickling, cloying mist, and we coughed until our eyes watered. Ajith sobbed as if his dams had burst beyond repairing. When the mist cleared, the jinni knelt beside him, fawn-brown hands stretched toward Ajith's crumpled face. "Oh, Shankar Sahib." Sighs shifted its black veil. "You know already what I must say."

"No." He yanked the hands away, keeping a white-knuckled grip on its wrists. He stared at the delicate fingers, wet from smoothing away his tears. "You will bring Maina back."

The jinni bent over their hands, white-hot eyes disappearing in the shadows of its headdress. "I cannot."

"Refuse," he said, "and I will order you back into that box, and I will destroy it."

Blind with shock, I leapt halfway across the room, arm outstretched for the precious box. Both their heads whipped toward me. I paid no heed to the glare of my master. The jinni was looking at me. Slowly, it closed its eyes and shook its head. I dropped my arm. Ajith's gaze stayed on me even as I backed away to my post.

The jinni gathered itself and spoke. "Master of my fate, I would do this for you if I could. If you were to find yourself so tied to the will of another, you could not capture the sun for him, no matter how he scourged or threatened."

Ajith thundered to his feet, dragging the jinni after him. "How dare you speak to me so?"

"With the utmost respect," the jinni answered in a measured voice. "I tell you only the truth. I can no more reclaim the dead than I can create life."

"What good are you?" He tossed the jinni aside as if it were no more than the mist that clung to its shroud. Of course, the jinn are not so easily hurt. Even so,

I slipped away from the door and knelt where it had fallen. Its cheeks ran with streams of molten silver. Ajith scoffed and stormed away from the bedside.

"I can't." It grabbed my arms, its fingers burning through the fabric. "I truly can't."

"I know, Laksha."

Laksha drew back and curled its hands before the veil as if in prayer. Its eyes drifted over my shoulder, and I turned.

Ajith's staccato pacing petered out near a niche in the wall. He reached into the shadows and yanked free the cage inside. The cage clattered; the inhabitant jerked awake. The little yellow bird belched steam as it warmed up. Ajith had commissioned the mechanical marvel when his wife proved to be allergic to the real thing. Europeans liked to think themselves the foremost experts in automata, but others had carried on the methods of the Golden Age inventors. The delicacy of the synthetic-feathered body, the seamless and silent gears, were owed to the artist-engineers under Ajith's patronage. The bird was far more complex than the towel-baring automated servants triggered by running water in the lavatory or the greened copper figureheads on English airships who folded their hands in prayer when the wind was against them.

The machine cocked its head at Ajith and began to sing. Ajith stared, knuckles jumping as he pumped his fists.

His head swiveled toward us, eyes gleaming in his deeply shadowed face. Laksha gripped my hand. He stumbled toward us, catching himself on the corner of Maina's bed. His gaze skimmed over her body, and a tremble shook the last of his composure away. He looked less healthy than the corpse. "I know what you can do," he rasped.

Laksha recoiled, scrambling behind me as I stood. Ajith had been Laksha's master, body and soul, longer than I had known them, but I had never feared what he might do with that power. Never before.

He laughed, and my hand went to my gun belt. "Away with you, Erom! I have business to conduct with my slave."

"I will let no harm come to Laksha."

"Who's going to harm it, man?" Ajith said, voice hitching with gasped chuckles. "I've simply figured it out, like always. The hard thing about wishes is knowing how to get what you want. Precision, surety . . ." He staggered forward and caught himself against me. His cologne smelled dank, sodden with tears. "Loopholes," he whispered, gripping me by the collar. "You swore an oath, remember. And much as you pretend otherwise, you are not invincible. If you reach for your gun again, I promise you will not leave this place with your hands."

Laksha gripped my hand. "I will hear my master's wish." Trembling fingers clutched my arm, the heat crawling across my skin. "It is my duty."

"The jinni sees sense at last," Ajith crowed. He dropped onto the bed's edge as if he had put his wife's body from his mind. "It is a simple thing, really. I would not deprive my men of the opportunity to do the real work. All I need from you, for now, is a plan."

❖❖❖

Ajith's household became a tortured place. Mechanics and artisans worked hour after hour, faces empty and sweat-stained, until they fell asleep haphazardly draped on their worktables or squirreled away in dark corners. Doctors were called in for macabre consultations. The craftsmen were forced to observe her autopsy, scribbling notes and sketches with shaky hands.

Servants whispered that the palace was becoming unclean, their mistress dishonored by the delayed cremation. They became nervous of Ajith's past creations: creeping between the lions at the main gate as the mechanical jaws roared, jumping when metal monkeys chattered from the garden trees. The automated servants in the baths soon ran out of soap and towels since none of their flesh-and-blood counterparts would restock them.

Perhaps the worst thing was Ajith's cheer. Though his body grew haggard, he strutted and grinned, acting more the bridegroom than the widower. His laughter filled the house, oblivious to our haunted exhaustion.

At last, it was ready. They settled it in Maina's sitting room and bedecked it with her finest clothes and jewelry. Girls crept in under Ajith's beaming watch to paint the wooden face. It did look a great deal like Maina. The joints and eyelids were softened by leather overlays. The wig of human hair was arranged just as she would have had it. Still, the machine was limited. Even the talented minds behind Maina's songbird had balked at the idea of fully lifelike machinations for a human automaton. The mechanical breast moved with a facsimile of breathing, and the eyes blinked—stiffly and too predictably—but its only real trick was offering a wood-plated hand to be kissed.

The house enjoyed a moment of respite. The work was done, the unsettling tribute made. Now surely they would be given instructions for the cremation and things would proceed as normal. But Ajith gave no instructions. At first, perhaps, it was too horrible for him, but by the time he stood caressing the automaton's delicate hand, I think he had forgotten his desecrated, rotting wife. While he fawned over his creation and ordered "her" room made fresh for it, I slipped away to organize a hasty funeral. Only with my false assurance of Ajith's blessing would the servants light the fire. Relieved as they were to have her out of the house, they all feared their master's new temperament.

I returned to find Ajith enclosed with the machine in his wife's rooms, the box clutched in his hands. He startled when I shut the door. "Ah, there you are. What happened to being with me always?" he joked, but his smile was faulty.

"What are you doing, Raj Ajith?" I left my usual post, coming nearer than I cared to the automaton. In the dim light, it might have been my late mistress, though eerily still and smelling faintly of metal lubricant.

He knelt by the chair and placed the music box on the machine's lap. "The last step." He placed a hand over the box, covering the white roses carved across its top. The music I expected never came. Instead, he sang to the silence. The old words, twisted into a new song. Mist seeped sickly thin through the seal of the closed box and filled the room until I could not see my master, only hear him coughing. When the mist settled, gathering in the drapery of the automaton's clothes, I wiped my stinging eyes and blinked. The machine blinked back.

"A moment, my dear," Ajith said. He brought out a veil, the half-sheer, embroidered style favored by Maina, and laid it over the automaton's hands. The jointed fingers curled, slow and arthritically stiff. Its arms lifted with painstaking grace, a choreographed dance. It settled the veil across its face to cover the painted mouth. Its arms drifted back to its lap. Ajith beamed and patted its folded hands. "There now, say hello to Erom."

The automaton shifted, like a breath drawn in and sighed out. It looked at me, head tilted on its flexible brass spine. "Greetings, favored guard of my husband."

"Laksha," I breathed.

Ajith grimaced and waved me off. "The jinni sleeps in its box as always. If you cannot be polite to my wife, return to your post."

"You are using the jinni most cruelly," I said, knowing it would do no good. "It is its own . . . person. Laksha can never be your wife, no matter how you command it to act."

He grasped the automaton's hands. "Do not force me to dismiss you, Erom," he said. "Maina will need protection now. It would be a shame to lose you."

It was true. In the past, Ajith had revealed Laksha's existence only to those he trusted most. Now, trapped in this grotesque machine, Laksha would be vulnerable, even if Ajith only made it keep up the act in private. People would be curious about the automaton, and as a mechanical achievement, it had to be immeasurably valuable. If it were stolen, or God forbid, damaged . . .

"I will stay," I said through gritted teeth. "But only for . . . Maina's sake."

Ajith sighed. There was a twinge of regret in his frown, perhaps, but he shook it off.

I stood at my post, blocking my ears as he wooed his machine. Laksha's voice, thinned and accented to mimic the deceased, made my skin prickle. It spoke as little as it could and moved only when Ajith obviously expected it. We stole glances at each other, its glass eyes expressionless. The longer I stood, with the doorjamb branding an aching crease down my spine, the more the room regressed to the surrealism of that morning when Maina was found dead. Had I disposed of the body, or did it still lie behind the drawn bed curtains? Was Maina dead, or Laksha? Did a machine truly live if you stuck a spirit inside it? Was a spirit truly alive when forced to possess a dead thing?

At last, satisfied with himself, Ajith kissed his creation goodnight. He gave no indication of when or if I would be relieved of my post. We waited until his footsteps disappeared down the outside corridor and both collapsed. I sagged against the door; Laksha draped over the arm of the chair. Its shoulders heaved, but when it lifted the wooden face, its eyes were tearless. After a long, painful moment, Laksha said, "I never thought I would miss the box."

"I wish there was something I could do for you," I said.

Laksha hummed, a lungless sigh. "This is far from the first time I have longed for you to be my master."

"I didn't know." I drifted away from the door, reluctant to get close despite myself. I had the queerest feeling that the automaton would smell of rotting flesh. "I thought you were . . . content."

"I would not have said so before. Even now, I feel most disloyal. I would never want to hurt Ajith Sahib. Nor you. And I can see it does hurt you. I should have held my tongue."

"Blast it!" I slammed my fist against my thigh, the only thing I could be sure of not damaging. "I should have never sworn that oath!"

"I am most glad you did," Laksha said. It lowered its face, pressing steepled fingers against its veil where the motionless mouth was hidden. "I am most glad you are here still. But if it presses your honor too much, please do not suffer on my account."

"It is not my suffering that concerns me."

Laksha's head turned, looking at the bed where a corpse had lain not long ago. "I wonder if he expects me to pretend to sleep. Have you thought about how much Maina Sahib would hate this?"

"How so?" I asked. There were so many distasteful things about the situation. I could not guess which would bother the late woman most.

"Do you not recall the quarrel she waged with Ajith Sahib when the British came? When he would not use me to support the resistance?"

"Oh yes," I said. "He was more bothered about spies catching wind of her talk. But it seems to have been a wise move on his part."

"Wise, perhaps," Laksha said, "but it makes this seem all the more foolish. After his effort to avoid dangerous wishes, she would be furious to see him do a thing like this. To preserve her memory in the most perverse way imaginable."

"I care little for a dead woman's fury at present."

There was a hiss like steam let free. We turned our heads toward the darkness of the wall niche. Free of its dented cage, the automated bird hopped forward, light glinting off the copper beak. With a crack of breaking glass and a splash of spilled oil, the lamps went out, and the room fell to shadow.

"Erom!" Laksha's wooden hands pawed at me in the dark. I gripped its arm and pulled it to its feet. Flames sputtered in the broken lamps, casting shapeless swatches of gold across the floor. The bird chirped down at our feet. It was a ball of fire, its feathers burnt to black wicks. The bird threw itself into the folds of Laksha's skirts. Flames licked up, devouring embroidery and sinking into the fabric. The jinni screamed, the huge and hollow keen of a creature facing a fate never meant for it.

I yanked my knife free and slashed at the fabric, dragging smoldering sections away from Laksha and stamping them out. The bird, featherless now but still chirruping sweetly, launched at the automaton. Laksha stumbled back, caught a foot on a rug, and tumbled, meeting the floor with a crack. The bird dove after, clawing and biting, tearing the veil and scoring the fresh paint from the wood. I grabbed the flapping machine, searing my fingers on the metal, and threw it out into the hall, bolting the door after it.

Laksha scrambled up. The automaton was half-naked, jagged-edged scraps fluttering around it. "Your hand—"

"Later," I said. "I have to get you out of here. I don't know who . . . how that bird . . . it must have been tampered with, cursed—"

"Possessed." Laksha staggered back and leaned against a bedpost. The voice behind that unmoving mouth filled the room with ancient prayers. All I wanted was to sit at its feet and listen, but I took a deep breath, choking on the smell of burnt faux feathers, and turned away. First, I searched the chest at the bed's foot for a cloak. Laksha stood spellbound as I draped the cloth over its hunched shoulders. The prayers went on while I led Laksha to the door, holding it behind me as I nudged my way through.

No sign of the bird. I grabbed Laksha's hand and ran.

"What are we doing?" Laksha asked in gaps between prayers.

"Ajith." I tugged it down the next hall, yanking it to keep upright against our speed. "We need to get you out of that—"

Something huge and golden bounded around the corner, the wide maw yawning toward us. I jerked back, skidding and slamming into the wall. A metal lion from the gates stalked toward us, gears clanking in limbs that were never designed for this.

"You will not find my husband," the lion said, Maina's voice ringing hollow in the metal chest. "He dishonored the dead, and now, he has joined them." The giant head lowered, turning the lion's open mouth into a wicked grin. "Be a good wife and throw yourself on the pyre."

I knocked Laksha to the ground as the lion sprang. The metal tail lashed my arm. Blood seeped down my sleeve. The lion skidded, claws squealing on the tile. Grunting, I got to my knees and scrambled for the nearest door, Laksha tucked against me. The lion came loping after us. We slammed the door, catching Laksha's cloak underneath. The lion pounded at the wood; claws snagged in the cloak, yanking Laksha down. The automaton struggled to get off its knees, wooden fingers trembling at the clasp that would have freed it. I yanked the cloak off. The fabric disappeared with a vicious rending noise.

We collapsed against the door, our shoulders pushing back against the battering of the metal lion. Laksha sobbed, tearless, face still. "Shankar Sahib, dead! Inna lillahi wa inna ilayhi raji'un." It turned to me, glass eyes half-closed. "Leave me, my Erom, if you love me at all. You have no oath to keep anymore. We cannot hope to escape a spirit, not while bound in matter."

"Then we unbind you," I said. "If we get you out of that monstrosity, maybe Maina will—"

"How could we?" Laksha asked, voice soft and unsteady. "Ajith was the only one with that power. If he is dead, the mastership passes to . . ." It faltered, glanced at the door, and clasped its hands to its chest. "Perhaps . . ."

"What?"

Laksha stood and absently brushed off the remains of the torn, ashy dress. "Get up and hide yourself."

I pulled myself up, braced against the door as the lion continued the assault. "Please, do not let her kill you."

"I hope very much to avoid that," it said. "Go, and do not reveal yourself. If I die, at least I am a slave no longer." Laksha laid a hand on my cheek, and for a moment, I felt neither wood nor leather but its own flesh, searing with smokeless fire. I drank in the heat as long as I could, then stepped away.

Concealed behind a pillar, I watched the jinni throw open the door. The lion crouched at the threshold, face and shoulder dented and claws trailing curls of shaved wood. The metal haunches swayed, ready to strike.

"Mistress of my fate!" Laksha cried and fell upon the threshold. The lion hesitated. "In honor and memory of the departed Ajith Shankar, I present myself to you, prepared to fulfill the desires of your heart as I am able."

The lion bolted upright, teeth bared. "What is this?"

"You are the heir," Laksha said. "While you are here to command me, I am yours. What is it you wish?"

"That abomination melted to nothingness!" Maina's words were nearly lost in her echoing shriek. My ears popped as if I'd gone up in an airship.

"I will gladly comply," Laksha said. "But before I do this, be sure you have no other wishes. To destroy the machine, I must either die or be freed of it."

The lion's tail swished, grating across the floor. "Free yourself, then. I want nothing else but to see my Ajith again."

Laksha rose on creaking knees, eyes closed and hands open to heaven. "I will guide you to him, so you may be together in your next life. Say these words after me, and we shall both be free."

Ancient language roiled through the room. As Maina repeated the words, her replica began to glow, a singeing light that made me hide my face. The air smelled of clean fire. A fingerprint of heat pressed against my cheek. *Find me. But not too soon.*

When the song ended, the metal lion lay stiffly on its side. Where the automaton had been, there was nothing but a smudge of silver ash.

I left India that night.

ʃ{

Parker Goodreau *is a writer and artist from New England. Since they were eight years old, they've been pleading for scary stories. Back then they got an ad-libbed rendition of "The Cask of Amontillado," which may explain a few things. Now, after being raised on vampires, hauntings, and 3 AM horror movies with more screaming than dialogue, they're writing their own stories. It was the next best thing, after they learned they couldn't make a living as the next Poe Toaster. They are most comfortable writing about teenagers, monsters, and teenagers who are monsters. Their free time is split between a busy schedule of goofing off on the internet and creating a weekly webcomic about superpowers and lying.*

City of Spirits

Christopher Paul Carey

ΦΦΦ

I drift in the City of Spirits, borne on currents of soul-stuff and dreams. Below, soft moonlight glints on canals ringed like the waterways of lost Atlantis. In their center, a maelstrom of phantasms swirls around a massive turret. I, too, am drawn toward the tower, eddying among vaporous wisps that have yet to move on from the domain of the living.

A susurrus of anguish builds the deeper I sink into the vortex. Had I lips to part, I might cry aloud, but the abode of my consciousness is as aetherous as the undertow of souls. Instead, as my masters in the order have taught me, I align my awareness with the celestial macrocosm. The radiant warmth of the Most Holy Sun Absolute permeates my essence, and I return gently to my body.

Beside my bed, an orgone wheel whirs in the darkness, its spokes gently fanning my face with cool spring air and a pleasant hint of ozone. Has the mechanism drawn the deleterious elements from the atmosphere and somehow increased my sensitivity to the netherworld? I am unsure. I have felt unsettled since arriving yesterday evening in this *utopie des fantômes*. But then, my training puts me in deeper sympathy with the living; should it be so strange I am more attuned to life's opposite?

I swing out of bed and switch off the wheel. A moonbeam glances upon the wall clock, whose hands trudge pitilessly toward daybreak but a short hour away. I tie up the tangles of my dark hair and tread barefoot across the uneven floorboards on my way to the water closet but pause before the room's tall window. A half mile from my hotel, across a bull's-eye of canals, rises the dark turret from my dream body's nocturnal excursion.

A thrill quavers through me, and for a moment, I forget my morning breathing exercises. I begin to chide myself but stop. It is not every day one has arranged for a visit to the Odic Forge.

❁ ❁ ❁

Mr. Boisgilbert himself greets me as I step off the platform at the docks and set foot at last on Nininger's innermost island. Gondoliers cry out behind me as heavy traffic plies the canal. Above, schools of fish-shaped aerolifts swim lazily through the cerulean sky.

"Miss . . . Meteora!" The short, podgy man lifts his high hat, his smile crooked with uncertainty in whether to call me by my given name or my surname. I shine back at him to banish the awkward moment, accustomed to the unease my sole appellation thrusts upon new acquaintances. Blast the monks who took me in as a babe and christened me thus. One day, I shall dream up my own patronymic.

Boisgilbert clasps my hand warmly as I rest my parasol on my shoulder. "It must be a long and tiring voyage from Athos."

I sigh with not-so-feigned fatigue, discerning no crease of suspicion on the man's round face that he knows of my true homeland in the Himalayas. "A worse trip for the looming war, what with the Protectorate's thugs all about."

The man nods, but I cannot fail to notice his furtive glance at the young man untying the boat that has brought me here, as if he thinks the gondolier may be a spy eager to report us to his superiors. Nininger, though a neutral city-state, lies surrounded on all sides by the Industrial Union of America, a close ally to the Protectorate. I am relieved at the outcome of my little test. Boisgilbert exhibits no sympathy toward the saber-rattling Gilded nations.

"Put your mind at rest, Miss Meteora," he says. "No war will ever besiege Nininger. We're a peaceful folk here. We wouldn't think of tearing down anyone else's dreams, so who would think to tear down ours?"

I smile politely, though my trained ear hears the lie within the inner octaves of his voice. "Why indeed? *C'est le meilleur des mondes possibles.*"

The man brightens and motions me to accompany him. We walk across the wooden boards to the edge of the docks and pass up a high rise of steps to a pedestrian-filled embankment circling the tower. Here, a young man with amazing blue eyes flags down Boisgilbert and takes him aside. It is clear the two have pressing business.

While they speak, I catch Boisgilbert's eye and motion to a bench some distance along the embankment. My guide, listening intently to the young man, smiles and nods me on.

I walk along the smooth white tiles, noticing the distant looks in the eyes of the passersby. In recent years, Nininger has become something of a lodestone for the psychically inclined. Those who stroll the court are doubtless mediums in the service of Boisgilbert, charged with maintaining the Odic Forge.

I sit down on the marble bench, placing my handbag with its precious contents beside me. Clasping my hands in the manner of the Third Requisite Exercise, I draw my attention inside my body, moving it along the microcosmic orbit to cultivate my relationship with my inner unity. I will need to be as focused as possible for my encounter with the forge. In the stark daylight, my astral aura should go unnoticed by the mediums about me, their crude psychic abilities being of such a low order they cannot possibly penetrate my spiritual refinements.

A shadow falls over me, and I open my eyes. A rugged-faced man in a dark denim suit looms above, his mouth gaping. My eyes fall to his rough, callused hands and then rise to take in the bulges of hardened biceps straining against the arms of his jacket. Instead of looking on with the blank stare of a medium, he rakes me with an almost lustful gaze.

My pulse races as the Third Requisite fails me. I have been rash to practice my exercise in public. The shadow has allowed the man to discern my astral body's lavender glow.

"I don't mean to interrupt, ma'am, but I don't recognize that style." The man's voice twangs with the rural accent of the Industrial Union. He extends a gloved hand. "I apologize, miss. The name's Meinhof. Captain—retired—of the Industrial Army."

"The secrets of the spirits are not to be discussed, Mr. Meinhof," I say firmly, hoping to dissuade the man from further conversation.

He continues undeterred. "Most folks here go in for a séance or use the speaking dial to communicate with the spirits, ma'am." The man's thick, joined eyebrows rise. "And here you is, chattin' it up in the broad daylight by your lonesome. You one of them Odic channelers? I seen you strollin' with the big man himself over yonder." His arm moves strangely as he motions to Mr. Boisgilbert across the court, a hiss of ozone-scented steam escaping from a shoulder vent in his suit. I suddenly realize the man's arm is mechanical, like the thousands of prostheses I saw being mass-produced in the factories during my stay in Altruria while journeying from the Himalayas—a grim promise of the coming war.

"Oh, this?" he says, lowering the arm. "Don't let it scare you none, ma'am. A souvenir from my days in Lomellini's army. The plutocrat as took it from me, he ain't among the living no more." He raises his gaze to the tower behind me, a gruff laugh escaping him. "Fact, for all I know, he's cursed to swim 'round that forge for all eternity."

I gather my bag and rise from the bench, a shiver running through me at the memory of this morning's dream sojourn.

"Now before you go, ma'am, mightn't I make an offer?" I begin to protest, but he speaks over me. "Now hear me out. Whatever Boisgilbert is paying you, I'm on good terms with someone out east in the union who can double it."

"You think me a mere channeler for hire?" I cry in protest, my indignation not entirely false. With my hands, I mimic a meaningless arcane gesture at the man. "Now be gone before I call forth the spirits of the forge and strip your mind bare of its wits!"

The man backs away, fear dwarfing his indignation. He makes a warding sign and stalks off just as Mr. Boisgilbert appears beside me.

Boisgilbert swears and then begs apologies. "I'm not sure how that I.A. goon got on the island, but I'll make sure he's escorted off immediately." He signals to his companion, the young man with the icy blue eyes. The pale fellow rubs his hands together, then holds out his palm—fingers pointing in the direction of the departing man—and blows on it. Instantly, the man who accosted me stops in his tracks, his shoulders slouching as if all will has left him.

"Headhunters!" Boisgilbert curses under his breath. "Industrial Union goons buzzing about like gnats, wanting to buy off my mediums—to use them as living weapons in their infernal war, of all things! Bah! They know nothing of what we do here!"

The outburst cannot be feigned. Perhaps, I can approach Boisgilbert directly after all, gain his cooperation to complete my mission. But I know instantly the folly of this hope. He thinks too highly of his petty role as showman to this circus of the dead, peddling tickets to rich and famous for one last glimpse at their departed loved ones. I cannot risk that he will hurl me from his city like he is about to do to the Industrial Army agent.

"Ah, well, Clarkson will take care of this one."

Mr. Boisgilbert takes my arm and guides me across the plaza to the entrance of the immense wall that encircles the great turret. The entire layout of the city—concentric rings of buildings and canals surrounding its most precious treasure—reminds me of my monastery, where only the initiated may gaze upon the esoteric wonders of the inner circles. But there the similarity ends; in Ionia, no mere material wealth can buy access to my order's secrets.

I sneak a look back at the court and shudder. The man named Clarkson stands directly before Mr. Meinhof. Ropey swathes of ectoplasmic matter spin from Meinhof's raised palm and engulf the Industrial Army agent's head.

"Come," Boisgilbert says, steering me toward the tower's gate. "Let Mr. Clarkson deal with that unpleasantness."

I turn away from the unnerving scene, though I am still shaken as we arrive at the gate. I close my parasol and leave it with an old cloaked woman muttering quietly to herself in tongues. As we pass through the great frowning arch into the turret, coldness shivers through me.

"An unfortunate side effect of the forge," Boisgilbert explains, noticing my discomfort. "My spiritualists say there's nothing to be done about it—the Odic fires burn cold."

No foyer greets us inside the tower. Rather, the rough granite walls of the confining corridor curve to the left. I have the impression that we gradually spiral toward the building's heart. The air smells like damp stone.

A luminous mist lights the way, perhaps generated by the forge itself, which is said to provide the electricity for the entire city-state. The farther we proceed, the chill only grips tighter.

An odd feeling sweeps over me, like a childhood memory has suddenly washed up on the shores of my mind. Have I been here before? No—I spent my youth on another continent, cloistered in the halls of my Ionian monastery. Rationality fails to dispel the familiarity.

My calves strain as we climb ever upward. The curve of the corridor is now regular, indicating that we no longer move toward the turret's center but rather corkscrew around it. The cold now reaches deeper than flesh, cutting through my astral form like an otherworldly breeze and rattling the ungainly structure of my only recently cultivated mental body. The power beyond the wall is more potent than any energy I have encountered, be it psychic or spiritual. For the first time, I doubt my masters and the mission on which they have sent me. Can the frail mechanism of copper and brass and wood I have brought from Ionia handle the Odic current of the forge?

But my masters have assured me it can—that the orgone siphon is not a spatial or material construct but, rather, a structural one, like the higher bodies I have spent my entire life organizing within my being. To the uninitiated, the word "energy" conjures up images of electrons swirling around atoms like hyperactive satellites. We of the order know differently. The world is only relationships and nothing else. Matter and energy are but illusions, facile metaphors for the unevolved spirit.

At last, the corridor levels out and ends at an immense lead door. Boisgilbert produces an oversized, many-tongued key but hesitates before placing it in the lock. He turns to me.

"Are you sure this is what you want, Miss Meteora? The price for visiting the forge is steep, and I am fully prepared to refund your payment if you change your mind now. But once we open the door, I must revoke my offer."

"You have my money, Mr. Boisgilbert," I say, smiling sweetly to show him I mean no offense.

"Yes, well, but . . ." He throws up his hands in exasperation. "Surely, we can communicate with your parents through an ordinary séance. My mediums are the best in the world. They will allow you to speak with your loved ones just as clearly as I speak with you now."

"But it's simply not enough that I speak with them, Mr. Boisgilbert. I must see them with my own eyes—not some sickening simulacra spun from ectoplasm but, rather, the true forms of their spirits." Now my tone becomes sharp. "You have assured me this is possible with the Odic forge. Have you misled me, sir?"

Boisgilbert sputters. "Of course not!" Then the man's composure returns, and a grin splits his rotund face. "I just wish you to know what you're getting into. The true Odic forms of the departed are in no way filtered as they are in a typical séance. The experience can be . . . overwhelming."

"I have read the literature you provided and gone through the proper interview process. Do you deem me unprepared now, after I have gone to the expense of traveling halfway around the world?"

The man nods, grinning as if he has at last judged my character worthy. He jangles the key into the lock and swings wide the doors. Brilliant white light pulses over us from somewhere ahead and below. He motions for me to proceed, and I enter the vast chamber.

I stand on the railed edge of a Brobdingnagian rotunda. The turret's curving, rough granite wall throbs with snowy light, reflecting from a cavernous well in the chamber's center. Twelve alcoves spaced equidistantly around the wall each cloister a single cloaked medium—the engines of the Odic forge. I peer over the rail into a sea of swirling phantasms, like those I witnessed last night in my dream excursion. A deep, sonorous sound reverberates as if a titanic heart beats somewhere below in the depths of the well.

"The navel of the world," I breathe, for so it is revered by many, even my Ionian masters.

"And now, Miss Meteora, if you will."

I follow Mr. Boisgilbert around the rotunda's rim and onto a platform of stone and steel that tongues out over the abyss of souls. Upon a little circle jutting from the end are two small benches of purple-veined white marble. We sit, facing one another while a chaos of phantasms eddies below to the thrum of the giant hidden heart.

The portly man removes a timepiece from his suit's breast pocket and dangles it before me from its golden chain. The watch begins to swing, assuming the rhythm of that vast heart in the depths as my eyes follow the motion. The literature Boisgilbert sent explained the process well enough. I am to be coaxed into a mesmeric state, so I might draw the spirits of my dead parents into the Forge from the other world. My loved ones will then appear before me in their true, unfiltered essences.

Or they would, should I care about such foolish entanglements of flesh and emotion. But I do not, for my own essence has been forged in its own crucible of the spirit. Should I die, I know my higher bodies will carry me beyond this world of attachments and desires. No, I am here for a purpose nobler than mere selfish whim.

I am here to save the world.

I concentrate my essence on a point just above and between Boisgilbert's eyes. It only takes a moment, so prepared am I for this instant. The timepiece's swing steadily decreases as the aetherous blood of my astral body flows from my heart chakra into my companion, saturating his consciousness. Already Boisgilbert succumbs, the mesmerist himself mesmerized.

Is it my imagination, or do the whisperings of the phantasms grow more agitated and the light of the forge harsher, brighter, colder?

I remove from my handbag the collapsed orgone siphon and carry it past Boisgilbert's bench, where I set it up on the lip of the platform. I unfold the mechanism's brass joints, positioning the copper oval to leer down into the soul well.

So far, the mediums are oblivious in their alcoves. So concentrated on maintaining the forge, they have not noticed the deviation I have caused in the ritual. Still, I must move fast.

I flip the switch at the base of the siphon, and the fan whirs to full speed.

At first, the merest wisp of luminosity slips up from the well into the copper loop of the apparatus, disappearing as an adjacent reality swallows it. Another wisp—more radiant, more substantial—siphons into the eye, followed by a small glowing cloud and a continuous spray of mist. The apparatus purrs contentedly as if nurtured by its meal of soul-stuff.

I gasp as a greenish, glowing figure appears over the stone platform's rim: a form cast in the image of an old woman, tentacles of aetherous hair writhing from beneath a semitransparent shawl. The phantasm waves its hands in panic as the droning blades draw it toward the oval. Its face elongates inhumanly, maw stretched in a rictus of terror. Then its entire form lengthens and thins as the astral current pulls it into the oval ring where it disappears from our world as if it had never been.

I have imagined this moment a hundred—no, a thousand—times, but a tremor rattles through me at seeing the reality. My stomach turns, and my teeth clench, visceral reactions betraying my lifetime of training. I turn my thoughts from the specter I have hurled from our plane of existence to the image of those destined to die in the coming war should I falter in executing my masters' plan. Why should I feel guilt and doubt now? Only despair and anguish laces the lingering souls of the dead. Draining their corrupted energies from this plane and restoring the balance of positive and negative forces is the only chance for peace on this world.

Calling upon all my will, I return some semblance of calm to my body, though my spirit yet quakes beneath the burden of the awesome task.

Another phantasm appears over the lip of stone, borne on the astral current. Then, it too is siphoned into the mechanism's copper eye, banished to a parallel plane. A third succumbs, a fourth, and then, before I can exhale, a dozen more funnel through the oval.

I step back as a ghastly cloud—green-yellow shot through with veins of crimson—forms around the siphon in response to the furious tow of spirits. As I back up, my right knee gives out to a violent blow from behind. My hands flail as they try to stop my fall, but all sense leaves me.

I return to awareness in a haze. The back of my head pounds, and I cannot breathe. I reach for my neck where I find strange thick hands about my throat. A foggy visage hovers over me: Boisgilbert's flushed and sweating face. I dig my fingers beneath his hands, trying to pry my way out of his death grip, but I am too weak. I scrape my nails into the backs of his hands. "The war," I manage to gasp. "To stop the war."

Boisgilbert bellows in response as he lifts me up several inches and slams my head down against my stony pillow.

"It won't work, won't work!" The cry comes from somewhere behind my prostrate body. "Don't you understand what we do here? The purpose of the forge?"

I try to rise, but something has changed inside me. Though my coherence—the unity of my higher bodies—remains, it is as if the thread connecting them to my body lies on the verge of breaking. My awareness floats somewhere above flesh and blood and bone. I am not dead, yet neither am I fully alive.

I hear a muffled curse, and then look down on Boisgilbert from my astral vantage as he drags my physical form back from the encroaching cloud. My spirit follows sluggishly behind my body, like a balloon pulled along on a slackened string.

"We're bringing the spirits together, helping them move on," I hear Boisgilbert mutter in heated anger. "We are the ones holding back the war! To expel these lost souls is only to doom them to eternal torment, to hasten that which you seek to prevent!"

Wordlessly, my spirit moans with the truth of the man's words. My masters'—no, solely my own—hubris has led me astray.

With all that is left of my unity, I will my body to rise, pulling up by ethereal strings as if dancing a marionette puppet. Below, my body staggers to collapse beside the apparatus. The effort of moving my physical form has strained the connection to my higher bodies to the breaking point. In my last mortal act, I thrust out my hand and hurl the apparatus over the platform's edge and into the mouth of the Odic forge.

A sharp snap resounds through all that I am. I break free of my corporeal shell, pulled along by the astral current that follows in the wake of the plummeting apparatus.

The well of screaming souls consumes me.

❖❖❖

I drift in the City of Spirits, borne aloft on currents of soul-stuff and dreams. Soft moonlight gleams through my shimmering, translucent form, reflecting up from canals ringing a massive turret toward which I am inexplicably drawn.

Through force of will, I pull myself from the maelstrom of phantasms swirling about me. Gently, I drift back over the city and sink down into my body, eager to awake and begin my day—for this morning I intend to hire a gondola to carry me to the tower.

As I switch off the fan that has lulled me into my aetherous sleep, a strange thought rises above all others, unbidden and unexplained.

Perhaps this time things will be different.

{{

Christopher Paul Carey *coauthored the novel* The Song of Kwasin *with Hugo Award-winning author Philip José Farmer and has continued Farmer's Khokarsa series with* Exiles of Kho *and* Hadon, King of Opar. *His short fiction may be found in anthologies such as* The Many Tortures of Anthony Cardno, Tales of the Shadowmen, The Worlds of Philip José Farmer, Tales of the Wold Newton Universe, *and* The Avenger: The Justice, Inc. Files. *He is a senior editor at Paizo on the award-winning Pathfinder Roleplaying Game and has edited numerous collections, anthologies, and novels. He holds a master's degree in Writing Popular Fiction from Seton Hill University. Chris and his wife Laura live in Western Washington. Find him online at www.cpcarey.com.*

Team 17

T. Mike McCurley

✿✿✿

The emptiness of London waits below us in silence as we slowly descend. The gears above us turn, and the massive chain drives make rhythmic clanking as our truck is slowly lowered. The air is cool and clammy, and wisps of morning fog roll back across the crew with whom I've been allowed to ride.

There's a general silence in the vehicle. I can see Ryan, the red-haired catcher, crossing himself and murmuring prayers. A canvas pack full of collection plates sits at his feet in the truckbed. Lars and Kat, the twin Swedes, sit with their foreheads pressed to one another as if sharing some secret conversation that none of the rest of us need be privy to. Their cannons are clamped in quick-release brackets beside them. Extra belts of ammunition shed a wan green luminescence that lights them from below. Even the ammunition for their weapons is made from rarefied aether. Beside me on the bench, Anna Purevoy is deep in a meditative state, preparing for what is to come. Miranda, the unit's second catcher, is studying maps in the passenger seat of the cab next to Hans Bruder, the angry-looking driver who is hunched over the steering wheel. He's the team's sniffer—the psychic in charge of locating the spirits. The last of the Collectors is Seamus Slade, the team medic, who leans against the tailgate of the truck, oblivious to the long fall should that gate open. He's got what I've been told is his usual devil-may-care grin and a hand-rolled cigarette that he sparked as soon as we were free of the drop bay.

"Landfall in twenty," Hans announces. He ignites the truck's boiler, so it's hot when we touch down. I look up and see the *USS Grantville* overhead, her searchlights knifing through the fog to illuminate the empty streets below. There is one other crew in a truck swinging from chains like ours. Team 9 will go south while we move north. Other crews will be deployed farther into the city.

Wordlessly, Lars and Kat stand and grab their cannon. Each of the enormous gunners takes a side of the truck, aiming down and sweeping their weapons back and forth. They have their goggles down and locked.

The echo of a single shot comes from the Team 9 crew. Their overwatch has fired on a target below us, and I hear an exasperated grunt from Lars.

"That git from nine just cost Lars a bottle of gin," Slade explains, flicking the butt of his smoke over the side. It tumbles slowly toward the ground, a glowing dot that dares you not to watch it all the way down. I take the bait and stare.

"If they actually saw anything," Anna says. She is looking at me as if she has never seen me. Before today that was true.

"In five!" Hans calls back. He pulls on the brim of his hat, tugging the black leather down tighter across his brow.

Miranda tucks the map into her vest and drops her goggles into place. I look around as they all go through their last-second rituals. Ryan puts his medallions under his shirt and flips the pack up onto his shoulders before turning to give me a V-for-victory sign. Anna is chanting under her breath, and I can feel my hair stand up as aetheric energy builds around her. In the back of the truck, Slade hops up into a squatting position, slipping another of his cigarettes—unlit this time—into his mouth.

The wheels touch the ground, and a moment later we hear the undercarriage bars hit the pavement. Before the sound has fully registered, Hans has dropped the truck into gear, and the tires chirp as we accelerate away from the drop spot.

Buildings rush by as we chug through the street. Hans knows how to coax all the power from the boiler, and he doesn't hold to a straight route. With the exception of Anna, who does not need them with her ability, we're all wearing the goggles now. Luminifirous aether trapped in the lenses paints the streets a pale green.

It seems sad to see all the empty buildings. Streetlights stand like soldiers awaiting orders, their lamps dark and silent. There is no hiss of gas, no blaze of blue-white light. Nothing illuminates the roadways but our headlamps and the overhead glare from the *Grantville*.

"When it comes, it comes without warning, news boy, so look sharp," Slade says. He's smiling, so I can't really think that was too harsh.

"The spirits here are all angry," Anna says. When she looks at me, her eyes glow blue with channeled energy. "If they get half a chance they'll eat you before you can scream. If one of them touches you, you'll know what fear truly is."

"Contact left!" I hear as the tires squeal in protest. Hans is jerking us through a turn so tight my eyes hurt.

It is the first spirit I've ever seen in person. Pictures and drawings do them no justice. They are glaring, raw spots of energy, like staring into the arc of a welder. This arc, however, wants to devour us, as Anna said.

We, of course, are here to devour it first.

Ryan is up and moving before Miranda can get clear of the cramped front seat. He is standing on the side rail of the truck, his footing as sure as if it were a flat piece of floor. In his hand is a collection plate, and he has it primed. With a snap of the wrist, he throws it at the spirit. There is an inrush of sound and a feeling of pressure. My ears pop as I see the spirit fold in on itself like a rag dropped to the floor. It vanishes into the plate with a sound akin to a distant shriek.

It all seems to have been so easy. I look around as if to ask what all the fuss is about. That's when I see Anna, arms outstretched to the right side of the truck. Power streams from her hands, and it actually bends the light to produce ripples in the air. I can see a partial sphere of energy formed in the surrounding sky and an eye-searing spike of light as a spirit tries to burrow through her shield.

"Mine!" Miranda shouts as she snaps a collection plate into place just past the shield. It sparks and fizzles before going dark. The catcher is cursing as she grabs for a backup plate. Ryan is still facing the other way. Her claim that it is her target has given him free rein to prepare for anything else that might come up.

Kat's cannon roars, and a single aether-tipped round big as a finger slashes through the spirit, scattering it into glowing motes. It slowly begins to re-form, sliding together with a liquid beauty that ends abruptly as Miranda's second plate opens. With a gasp of released energy, the plate bathes the spirit in emerald fire and absorbs it.

There is a moment of near-silence, broken by the hissing of the truck's steam boiler. Everybody is looking around. I don't know what they're looking for, but I'm looking too.

"Recover," Hans says. The word isn't even fully off his lips before Ryan has leaped from the truck. The red-haired catcher turns a graceful flip in the air and is running when his feet touch the ground. Each hand holds a pistol of some kind, and I notice that his arms don't sway to counterbalance his body as he sprints. The guns are rock solid in his grasp. Seconds later, he is holstering one and snatching up the plate. He pivots on a heel and is running back to us while I'm still trying to analyze his movements.

Miranda has gone to hers as well, though she has empty hands and simply runs without flourish. She is no less graceful but seems to restrain herself.

Five minutes in London. Team 17 has already packaged two spirits.

It's a busy morning. By the time we stop to rest, there are more than a dozen full plates. I've seen enough spirits to know what kind of speed and ferocity they have, and my camera bag grows full with my own type of plates. Hans pulls us into an old fire station to allow the crew to restock from the lockbox in the truck bed. Slade fires a lantern, filling the room with brilliant light, and hangs the lamp on the truck frame.

"You doing all right?" Hans asks. It's the first chance I've had to speak with him. He's drinking from a canteen and extends it to me. I notice my hands are quivering when I reach for it.

"I can't remember my mouth ever being this dry," I say before sucking in a mouthful of the cool water. It feels better in my mouth than I thought possible.

"Goofer dust," he explains. I arch an eyebrow, and he gives me a sad smile from within his beard. "Burned corpses."

I gag, and the water spills from my mouth in a deluge of gray sludge. I've been breathing in the dust of millions of incinerated dead since the moment we arrived. When I vomit, no one chastises or laughs.

"Aether bombs ain't kind," Hans says. He leaves the canteen with me and goes to bum a cigarette from Slade.

"Try a taste of this," Kat offers, holding out a flask made of hammered steel. I feel my nostrils burn as the vapors reach me, and I thank her. The drink is like a foul-tasting mouthful of flame, and I choke again.

Her brother slaps me on the back with a chuckle. "She brews it in the engine room," he says.

I don't doubt it. I look at the unlikely pair, wondering what would bring them to Team 17. I pose the question as Kat takes a long pull off the flask filled with what I now believe must be paint thinner.

"I owed money to a loan shark, and we had to hide," she says in that thick accent they both share. Lars leans in with a shake of his head.

"She tells a story," he says. "We contracted for the job to have a real life. After the war, our military scaled back. People who were strictly gunners were no longer necessary. Here, we have jobs."

"Until we die," she adds with a throaty laugh.

"You'll go before me," Ryan calls from his position in the truck bed. He has finished refilling his bag with plates and is eating something.

It seems a curious moment of normalcy in the middle of a place and situation that could flare into violence without a second of warning. I have to think to remember that we're actually in London. We could as easily be at a dinner party in Vermont. Everyone is spending a few moments just relaxing. It occurs suddenly that the members of Team 17 are simply taking the opportunity to live. Minutes ago, they could have been killed, and minutes from now, they very well might be. For the moment, they are alive, and they are enjoying it.

Miranda has taken the opportunity to lean back in the front seat. She has a rag laying across her eyes, blocking out the light provided by the lantern. Her chest moves rhythmically as she catches what sleep she can. Anna is perched on the open tailgate of the truck, smiling as she watches the interplay of the others. Her helmet is off, and her bald scalp gleams in the sharp light. An unlit thin cigar is clamped in the corner of her mouth.

Not every team has a mage assigned, which makes Anna unique. Sniffers like Hans are frequent, and many make a fine living back home, but those that can truly wield magic are few. And they are prized. I had asked her about her position back on the *Grantville*. Her answer was truly descriptive and involved a play on the word "position." I take a step toward her, intent on asking more about how she discovered her power, but I'm interrupted as Hans shouts out, "Incoming!"

The effect is incredible. Everyone on the team knows exactly what they're doing, and they take up defensive positions in a flash. Guns point everywhere. Hans is holding some kind of shotgun-thing with a muzzle that gapes like a bucket. Miranda has a long-bladed cutlass, the edge glowing with embedded aether. Even Slade has a pistol. The entire crew is taking the few steps necessary to return to the truck.

I've noticed that they never stray far from the vehicle. It is truly their lifeline. With it they can go anywhere, do anything. Even now, the boiler is stoked and the pressure chamber full. Gauges are lined out, and with a press of his foot,

Hans will have us rocketing forth to escape whatever is approaching.

"Step lively, new guy," Slade calls.

New guy. That would be me. Standing slack-jawed as the veterans mount the ride with ease, even with all their collection gear. I'm "that guy"—the one everybody is looking at. They're all in place, ready to defend against anything, and here's this idiot still looking for directions. Ryan holds out a hand from his position in the bed of the truck. I shake off the feeling of being frozen and grip his hand. His eyes bug out and I hear three separate shouts from the others on the team.

It feels cold at first, like I've submerged my leg in an icy bath. My brain spins and loops in a desperate attempt to figure out what's going on when suddenly the cold becomes a roaring, searing agony, like acid and flame racing through my nerves. The leg collapses beneath me, and I'm tumbling toward the floor. Behind and above me, the air boils with raw magic and the projectiles of aether guns. Shrieks as collection plates do their jobs. Screams of panic and a sudden concussion as Lars and Kat open up with their cannons, rapid fire.

I'm also seeing something different but not with my eyes. Flashes of memories that are not my own overtake me . . .

There were hundreds of airships silhouetted in a perfect blue sky. Air raid sirens and panicked voices rang in the air. What looked like flecks of pepper drifted down from the German aircraft. By the time we recognized the flecks for what they were, it was too late, and seconds later, the first explosions began. Weaponized aether bathed the city in that sickly jade-green glow, and the waves of it came closer with every crash of sound. There was nowhere left to run.

I'm lifting from the ground now, and the visions vanish. I recognize Slade as he hoists me up into the air and literally throws me into the bed of the truck. He dives in behind me, and our surroundings blur as Hans opens the boiler to full, spitting a column of steam which quickly fades behind us.

". . . shock!" I hear Slade shouting. He stabs me with a long needle, and I feel a rush of energy that leaves my fingers tingling. I don't know what he has done, but—

The world snaps into perfect focus. I can feel everything except my leg. The air passing across my skin. The combined pressure waves with every shot of the big aether guns that the Torkelsenn twins are using to cover our escape. The sharp, ozone-scented eruption of raw power from the fingers of Anna Purevoy.

"On the two!" Miranda shouts, and the truck shudders into a left-hand turn.

I see it as we pass: an immense group of spirits, easily a hundred thick with dozens more joining by the second. Ryan throws a random collection plate at the group. It may take in as many as three, but all it can do after absorbing them is whine impotently.

Flares shoot skyward from Miranda's position, one after another, signaling our distress. I can smell the propellant from them, hear the muffled *crump* of each shot as she cycles through half a dozen.

"Hold on, news boy," Slade says. He has some kind of jar in his hand, and when I look down, he is pouring it across what looks like a withered piece of red meat. My leg. I should probably scream, but I don't see a reason. What was in that needle?

"Reinforcements in ten!" shouts Miranda. Her gaze is cast skyward, and I look up to see two of the *Grantville's* titanic walking machines dropping down to us on triple parachutes. Their arms blaze green with sustained fire from the rotating cannon mounts, and I can imagine them ravaging the spirits that had emerged to block our path.

The truck shudders to a stop, and I see a constant stream of collection plates being thrown behind us as everyone but Lars and Kat—and Slade, who is still occupied with trying to save my leg—sail the vessels out in a line, our own little wall of aetheric defense. It is at that moment that I realize I'm not wearing my goggles, and I can still see the approaching wave of spirit energy. It looks different without the aether providing a filter. I can see individual faces, bodies, clothes. These were people once—before the German bombs erased them. Somewhere in that crowd of spirits, if he has not already been collected, is the man whose memories I shared, the spirit that attacked me. I look at Anna, and she looks back, a knowing smile on her face. Then her hands come up and a twisting, spiraling flare of energy blows a jagged hole into the approaching spirit ranks. The plates are absorbing energy in mass quantity, but we'll soon be overrun.

The walkers land with earth-shaking force, and enormous collectors spring to life in their legs and torsos. Emerald light bathes everything around us. The amount of spirit energy we're collecting from the dead is enough to power most of the planet for weeks.

The battle stretches for another twenty seconds. The entire area is thick with aetheric waste and the smell of ozone and hot metal. Steam from the walkers, trapped by the humidity of the air, surrounds us in a thin fog. Shell casings are a brass carpet on the pavement. I can no longer make out individual sounds, and the world has become a mixture of discharging guns and screaming spirits.

"Have a little more," Slade says, his mouth inches from my left ear. He drives another spike into my pelvis. I look down to see the ruin of my leg laying on the shreds of my pants. I start to panic for a moment, but then, the drug hits. Again, the leg doesn't matter. Whatever he's giving me is a taste of heaven itself.

Ryan and Miranda are out of the truck now, attending to the plates they deployed. It looks like we used every one Team 17 brought. The massive walkers have closed their collectors as well. The bilious green light has vanished, replaced by the blue-white of the lamps on the huge attack machines.

I reach out a hand toward Anna. She acknowledges me with a nod and a tight smile. She won't compromise her hands by holding mine as she might need them free to unleash her magic again. Around the truck, there is a whirlwind of activity. I see the crew from Team 9 roll up. They call out greetings and take up positions to defend if anything else goes down. The *Grantville* is floating overhead, and I see chain lifts being lowered. One of them, I know, is for Team 17.

We're soon lifted back into the airship for resupply and to deliver the mass quantity of aetheric energy collected below. Slade turns me over to the *Grantville* medical staff. They know what they're doing. I'm not the first victim of spirit attack they've seen.

"You get better soon, news boy," Slade says.

I grin, the drugs still playing through my system and keeping the pain at bay. I lean up closer to him before he can leave, clutching at his sleeve for support.

"We did good," I declare with all the confidence of an outsider. He chuckles.

He tucks a hand-roll into the corner of his mouth and winks at me before speaking.

"Yeah. Not bad for day one."

{§

T. Mike McCurley *lives in a small city in Oklahoma where, indeed, "the wind comes sweeping" and all that. His Firedrake series has now filled three books, with a fourth in the works. He is a founding member of the Pen and Cape Society, an online cabal of authors of superhero prose, and his Emergence setting will soon be featured in Lester Smith's D6xD6 roleplaying game. His supernatural Western series, The Adventures of Jericho Sims, has seen two short releases so far, with a novel in the works. His works can be found linked at www.tmikemccurley.com.*

The Litany of Waking

Scott Fitzgerald Gray

❖❖❖

She awoke to darkness and a grinding headache, her teeth buzzing and her hands tingling with the residual power of the flare that had dropped her. She knew no more than that, thoughts reeling within a storm of shadow. She tried to touch her thumbs to each of her twitching fingers, judging whether any had gone missing. She found she couldn't quite remember how many she'd started with, though.

She ran through the litany of waking, remembering first her name. Sabela. That sounded right. She heard it in her Ma and Da's voices in her mind and was pleased that she knew them as well. She recalled her age, twelve summers. That was important.

She tried to focus on place and action. Where she was, why she was there. And in doing so, she remembered suddenly the imperative of not moving a muscle where she lay sprawled on her back in the darkness. That was more important by far.

It was the familiar information that focused you, her parents had taught her. When power surged as fire and lightning through an open coupling or along a conduit that had looked well grounded at first glance, it could kill you quick enough. Sabela had seen it happen. What was worse, though, was that same power scrambling your mind and memory. So it was that her Ma and Da had taught her the litany of waking, sharpening the instinct to reset the mind and put it through its paces in response to any unexplained darkness. Making sure everything was where it was supposed to be.

She squinted. In the half-light, she could see bundles of cable that thickened and twisted along dark walls, looping around and through each other like the contents of a butcher's offal bucket. She counted them and realized that her numbers had come back finally. She counted her fingers. Nine, just like she remembered.

Why have you come, ghost?

The voice came from everywhere and nowhere at once. Sabela felt her mind settle to an absolute silence, her body doing its best to follow. The only sound was her blood beating steady in her head.

Ghost. I know you hear me.

The voice hung in the air as light as well as sound, like Sabela had seen once at a town-park concert her Ma and Da had taken her to when she was young. That had been great fountains of blue and red and white arcing through the sky, marking the boom and brass of the orchestra. By contrast, the noise-light of the voice was a single shade of pale gold, shimmering through the shadow of her sight like fireflies.

"Go away, voice," Sabela said.

Strong words, ghost, but this is my place you find yourself in. You cannot pass through these halls unnoticed and unseen.

When the voice spoke, its firefly light shifted and drifted through the space around Sabela's eyes. She saw the dark lines of cables and conduits more clearly. She saw condensers set in rows of six by two, hanging limp like sow's teats and dripping dead oil. As she craned her head, feeling the tug of her hair where she'd plaited it to keep it out of her way while she worked, she saw a straight tunnel behind her and a twisting course leading down.

She still didn't know where she was, but she had her choice of escape routes. That was something.

"There's no such things as ghosts." Sabela heard an echo in her words as she recalled how Nicolau had said that exact thing to her. She blinked at the memory as it fell into place, feeling the headache rattle around a bit. She recalled the others as well and was glad of it. Xabier and Cibran, Iago and Rocha and Illiam. Her fellow scrappers. Nicolau was their master, but him and his pig prod, she would have been happy to forget.

"I've got work to do," Sabela said, but the voice and the shadows gave her no response.

✿✿✿

It had been early when Nicolau woke them all, the sky a bruise of blue and gold above the ash fields. Sabela and the rest of the scrappers had been scouring those empty battlefields for the better part of the summer months. Long days spent claiming old iron and bits of mechwork, lost among the smoldering fires that had burned since the end of the war.

It was meant to be a small war, the stories all said. The mechwork had changed that, though.

"The ruins is safe, you slack duff." Beneath the dark dawn, Nicolau had taken on the mocking tone he adopted in response to fear and injury among his scrappers. Sabela remembered him smirking the time he'd cut and sealed the stump of her finger when it was lost. "The experts and the spook squads is gone through it six ways from the end times and claimed it all clear."

"Then ask the experts and the spook squads what's there, and save me the trip."

Something in Sabela's thoughts seized up, so she couldn't remember what Nicolau had said in response. She felt pretty certain the pig prod had been involved, though.

She remembered walking alone toward the ruins, the other seekers working the safer open ash behind her. This was a job for just her, Nicolau had said. He'd heard rumors of something big. Sabela picked her way along pathways of ash, watching for strike-spots of fire and lightning. Ahead was a great field of tangled steel strung with flapping canvas like wind-blown flags. Dangerous for a seeker not at the top of her game.

"There's no such things as ghosts," Nicolau had said. "There's just dead machines for halfwit folk to be afraid of. Not a proven tinker like you. You're not afraid, are you, Sabi?"

Nicolau was the only one who called her Sabi. She hated it.

In the dark now, Sabela found her starling hanging from her belt. In response to her touch, it unfurled its wings and set itself into motion, mesh gears spinning up to a staccato clacking hiss. She set its lamp alight, fingers flicking control studs along its spheroid body, then tossed it to the air.

In the flying scutter's shimmering light, she saw the spark switch whose spasm of white lightning had coursed through her and put her down. The switch was a dead-drop condenser, set up to store all the power shunted into it when its circuit went dark. She should have gone back down the line, looked for a shunt point, and grounded out any stray charge there. It was a novice seeker's mistake, its obviousness burning for a moment in Sabela's heart.

She was no plain seeker, though. She was a tinker, and the best in Nicolau's troupe. She was ready for this.

You are ready for what, ghost?

The words at her ear caught her by surprise. "You can go anytime, voice."

No. You are the one not meant to be here.

"Wrong about that."

The light of the starling showed Sabela where to go as she flexed and flicked an insulated prod from her belt kit into the switch. She had no need anymore to fear the white lightning she'd so effectively grounded out on herself. When that was done, she followed the starling along the spark lines, checking each connection where it split off from the main. She watched the scutter's lamp flash coded signals to mark each point of power detected as it went. She noted which points had worked loose and carefully tightened each in turn, knowing their power would be hungry for her fingers.

The starling was the newest of the scutters that Sabela shaped from mechwork scraps and tatters. The snake she pulled from her jacket pocket was one of her first pieces, simple in design but most effective. It coiled its oiled links around her wrist as its head lit up, giving her a working lamp as she checked and tightened a dozen wire fittings. When she was done, she punched the power from standby to active and held her breath.

With a bang, that power surged. She heard cables crackle, saw slack pipes pulse out with sudden pressure. A humming sounded out as arc glow flared around her, and she shielded her eyes for the moment it took them to adjust.

When she looked out again, she had remembered where she was.

And where is that, ghost?

"*Behemot*," she whispered. "It's mine."

She had tripped across the name by accident, etched into the edge of a shattered wing. Most of the morning had already gone to routine salvage and avoiding the collapse of ash pits filled with rusting iron. Her breather had howled against smoke and ash as she dug deeper to fully realize what she'd found, working her way in through layers of steel and rotting canvas. The remains of the last vessels *Behemot* had destroyed as the legendary airship fell to its doom.

Sabela remembered why she was there. She felt the last pieces of everything fitting into place in her head, locking in tight. "I'm going to make *Behemot* fly again. I'm going to show them all."

She realized she was answering a question no one had asked. She shrugged as she collected her tools, setting the starling to sleep at her belt again.

You should not be here, ghost.

"Got work to do, voice," she said. "Stay out of my way."

✪✪✪

Sabela took the twisting passage leading down, away from the entrance she had carefully opened through a blast port almost as wide as she was. She crawled slowly, checking for stray power coursing where it shouldn't. The interior of the engine core that she had cut her way into was remarkably intact, though. It spoke to the strength with which the great airship had been built, its interior struts and trusses as thick around as Sabela's waist.

Like a sinuous squirrel, she crawled through nests of cables that quivered with the standby power pulsing through them, ready to shunt fire and lightning to the sails and blast ports that had once taken *Behemot* to the air. In the darkest days of the Great War That Was, the airships that unleashed bright death from the sky had coursed like birds across a hundred nameless battlefields. But *Behemot* was the greatest of those airships, whose creation had swung the tide of war and whose fall and destruction had ultimately lost it.

Except *Behemot* wasn't destroyed, and Sabela was the only person in the world who knew that.

What is it you seek, ghost?

"I'm going to make *Behemot* fly. You don't listen very well, voice."

I wasn't asking your orders. I was asking your goal.

"You know."

And how would I know?

"Because I'm imagining you." That realization settled into Sabela's head even as the words were spoken, and she felt the satisfaction that came of having solved that puzzle. "I got the pulse shock in me. Scrambled my thoughts, and you're what's left over."

It was a thing that happened sometimes. All scrappers lived with those risks as they scoured blackened battlefields in search of clean iron and precious brass. Insignias and medallions in gold and silver, sometimes, ready to fetch real coin in the pawnshops in the larger towns of the frontier. And above all else, the precious mechwork that had once turned the ash-grey battlefields red with blood and fire.

How do you know the pulse shock did not kill you? The tone of the voice was flat in her mind, but Sabela thought she felt it mocking her.

"Because if I was dead, I'd remember dying. You remember the things that happen to you."

By your logic, ghost, you were never born.

"I remember my Ma and Da. You lose, voice."

That was half a lie. She remembered her Da mostly, her Ma gone earlier to become just traces of voice and memory now. It was her Ma who had first showed her the tinker's ways, letting Sabela help repair the mechwork that her father collected, and the pieces that came in to their wagon for repairs when they traveled the trade roads.

With those tinker's ways, Sabela turned bits of still-functioning mechwork not large enough to sell to the machinists in town into the scutters that she and the other children used to search and sweep into tangled wreckage and unseen spaces. The dangers of those spaces gave most scutters a short life and highlighted their usefulness in keeping the scrappers from getting hurt, but Sabela was always happy to build new ones.

There were good seekers among Nicolau's troupe. Cibran and Illiam were the best, after her. No one else had Sabela's tinker's touch for the mechwork, though. That wasn't a thing you could teach, her Ma had always said.

The strength and precision with which *Behemot* had been built made the long day's job of restoring the engine core a simpler matter than Sabela would have thought. It was mostly time and rote labor, working her way one by one through power linkages torn free from their conduit lines. She patched and prodded. She repaired bright brass coils melted from the fatal heat of *Behemot's* fall, hunting down free wire from the less important lighting systems to rewrap them. She bypassed and rerouted, listening always to the instinct of her touch and the readings the starling gave her as it flitted through the shadows.

When she was done, she rested a while. She took a drink of water from a skin bulb, tasted the grit of the ash fields that never seemed to wash away.

What are you, ghost? With your tools and your deft touch?

Sabela knew she was talking only to herself, but her pride made her answer. "Tinker. The best thing in Nicolau's troupe." As she shifted along a narrow gantry, she saw a filter pack below that marked the head of an airway. With the power systems patched, the airways would be her first approach to the controls that would test that power.

And what is Nicolau?

Sabela scowled as she remembered the pig prod. "He manages things. Buys and sells what we find for him."

Your captain, then.

"If you like." She pulled the filter pack free to peer into an air shaft beyond, battered but clear.

So when you resurrect Behemot *as you hope to do, it will be on Nicolau's order. He is the one who sent you here, tinker.*

"Won't matter it's his order. I tell them I'm the one who patched *Behemot*, and I'll prove I'm more than just a scrapper. I'll get out from under him. I'll find some place better."

Sabela hadn't really thought the words until she spoke them, but she felt them ring true. She had traveled with Nicolau since her father died because she had nowhere else to go. He kept her down, though. Wouldn't take her to the cities where she could do real work. Always just scrapping because that was what Nicolau knew.

We called you mechs before, the voice said, and Sabela thought she heard a strange wistfulness in its tone. *Tinkers. Working the machines and shaping their power for the captains to control.*

Sabela heard her Ma's voice in her mind suddenly. Not a thing she wanted to think about right now, needing to focus. "Talking to the mechwork isn't something to be taught . . ."

The floor beneath her feet gave way suddenly. A section of support lattice had crumbled to lightning rust, the bars looking iron-solid but turning to black powder with a touch. She was wary but not fast enough, swinging for an out-thrust support with both hands but only slowing herself as she fell.

She tumbled, hitting once. A long space of weightlessness told her the darkness she fell through was larger than she'd seen before. She hit a second time and stopped.

❍❍❍

You should not have come here, ghost.

Sabela felt her heart skip an unexplained beat at the sudden sadness in the voice. She fumbled the snake from her belt and set its glow to full bright, then sent it crawling up high so that light would spread.

Black ash covered the wide expanse of windows above her, thick glass intact but showing fracture lines, rainbow bright. Sabela saw chairs and consoles canted sideways, telling her the angle at which *Behemot* had settled beneath the ash. The confines of the engine core had come with no real sense of up and down, but she was reoriented now as she mapped out the shadowed space of the great airship's flight deck.

Most of the crew who had died were still in their chairs, dry rot stripping their flesh away, eating into canvas straps and dark grey uniform jackets. Their heads were slumped over and down in deference to gravity, but most still had their hats on. Other bodies were tumbled into heaps along the side of the deck, which was below Sabela in the orientation of the crash that had turned left to up, right to down.

Along the walls, she saw the shadows move.

It wasn't a trick of the light. The snake coiled motionless above her. It wasn't a trick of her eyes. She worked the litany of waking again to clear her thoughts, but the words ground down beneath a rising fear as the darkness began to swirl around her. Watching her.

"What are they?" she whispered.

Ghosts, the voice said. *Like you.*

High above her, Sabela saw the deck's power panel, no sign of damage. She frantically sent the starling up, flitting through the air on quick flaps of canvas wing to latch itself onto the panel's key breaker. She read the power spooling there in the codes of the scutter's flashing lamp.

"No such things as ghosts," she whispered, trying to calm herself as the shadows flowed like liquid. She remembered Ma's words as she backed away. "Spirit's in the living body. Spirit's the flow of blood and thought, and the dead have got no use of it."

So the living say. The dead say it differently.

Sabela jumped for the now vertical floor and climbed desperately, the shadow flowing to pursue her. She felt it reaching for her as she scrambled across cable and rough lattice, climbing over and past a body spilled out to hang free when its chair mount had snapped in two. At the height of the cantilevered deck, she slung herself onto the power panel, feeling it pulse beneath her. Ready for her.

There are ghosts in all machines, the voice said. *The special among the mechs can speak to them in their own way. Like you. Even if the ghosts seldom speak back.*

Her hands were a blur as she set the panel switches for startup. The voice was shrill in her head, and with each word, she felt a faint spike in the power she aligned and activated.

These ghosts are screaming now, though, to tell you they are the spirits of this machine of war and they are tired of killing.

"They should have stopped me when I came in, then." Sabela saw the panel lights go green beneath their cracked glass. She grabbed the key breaker with both hands.

We are tired of killing. Please, ghost.

She remembered the stories from when she was a girl, the war not that long done but already more than ready to be turned to dark tales. She felt the fear of those tales now, of mechwork engines that had parted battlefields like steel plows through wet loam. Machines whose skin was cold iron and coursing fire. She knew the tales of the terrible tide of war *Behemot* had unleashed and how the great airship had vanished in the end within a storm of elemental fire like the world had never seen.

She focused to push the visions away. "I don't care whatever war you were in."

We care about the next war, which begins when the monster you wish to resurrect screams its way to the sky once more.

"Folk won't fight again. That's what everyone says. Show them *Behemot* come back, and they'll be too scared to fight."

Other folk have said those same words. And sixteen million died to prove them wrong, ghost.

"I'm not the ghost!" Sabela screamed it, fighting the fear.

You will be, child.

She meant to turn the key breaker. She was ready to feel the power surge that she had spent the long day reshaping. But she pulled the breaker instead, hauling on it with both hands to tear it free of its housing. As the growling hum of *Behemot* ground down to silence, she threw the breaker helplessly at the shadow that swirled around her now.

"There's no such things as ghosts." Sabela's throat hurt.

No, child. "If I was dead, I would remember dying," you said, and the dead do remember. We are the spirits of war, driving death before us. We are what's left when the power of the world is corrupted to destroy that world, leaving ash and madness in its wake.

"Let me go . . ."

Yes, child.

Shadow rose around and past her. Sabela saw it swirling around the starling. She felt something change.

To feel the flow of energy within mechwork is a thing that cannot be taught, the voice said. *Your mother told you true. It is a gift of fate that few share in and fewer still will ever master.*

"Let me go," Sabela said. She felt less afraid now.

Yes, child. We will go.

✿✿✿

A blood-red sunset carried her back toward the camp one slow step at a time. She saw Nicolau watching for her, pushing forward to close the distance as she drew near. Not too close, though. It was dangerous in the ash.

"Got everything I could." Sabela hefted the bag over her shoulder. She had claimed a choice assortment of bulbs and wire, of mechwork bits salvaged from the shattered airships that had buried *Behemot* before she walked away. It would fetch good coin but was common enough that Nicolau would have no reason to go back in search of more.

"Nothing big?" he muttered. "I heard rumors."

"The experts and the spook squads called it clear. Listen to them next time."

Nicolau glared as he swung the pig prod, though with a sense of obligation more than malice.

"No," Sabela said.

She felt the power of the prod pulse to full life, its condenser drained in a heartbeat to arc past its insulated grip. Nicolau's lank hair shot out in a haze of grease and static lightning as he was knocked over backward with a scream.

The other scrappers drew closer. Sabela nodded to them all. She picked up the pig prod where it had fallen, watching as a trace of shadow detached from the snake coiled around her wrist and slipped inside it.

"Must be faulty," she said. "I'll fix it for you."

Nicolau growled as he stood, dusting himself off. "Don't be thinking above your place, Sabi."

"My name's Sabela."

She ran through the litany of waking as the others followed her back to the camp, Nicolau watching confused from the shadows behind them. Her name, her age.

Sabela, the ghost said to her ear. *Twelve summers.*

Place and action. Where she was, why she was there. She'd spend more time thinking about that, now that she had someone to talk to.

{}

Scott Fitzgerald Gray (*9th-level layabout, vindictive neutral*) *is a writer of fantasy and speculative fiction, a fiction editor, a story editor, and an editor and designer of roleplaying games—all of which means he finally has the job he really wanted when he was sixteen. He shares his life in the Canadian hinterland with a schoolteacher, two itinerant daughters, and a large number of animal companions. More info on Scott and his work (some of it even occasionally truthful) can be found by reading between the lines at insaneangel.com.*

Labor Costs

Richard Dansky

✿✿✿

T ell me, Mister Upton, can you see the ghosts?"

Obediently, Peter Upton craned his neck and looked out over the back of his chair to the window. "No," he said. "Should I be able to?"

In fact, what he saw looked moderately pleasant in a workmanlike sort of way. Rows of neat houses crouched down on rolling New England hillsides, shaded by trees just starting to think of shedding their leaves. Here and there, a church steeple heaved itself up a little nearer to heaven than its neighbors while the sluggish waters of the Housatonic flowed past in the distance.

"Not unless you're a prophet. But mark my words, they'll be here soon enough." Asher Perry coughed discreetly into his fist and wheeled himself over to the window to take in the view. The hum of his chair's clockwork harmonized with the steady thrum of the machines on the floor below. When Asher Perry asked to see a man, it meant seeing him where he worked. And he worked in the textile mill that bore his name. "Join me."

Upton stood and walked over to stand next to the older man. Up close, he could see that Perry looked weary, the lines on his face deepened by worry and lack of sleep. "Do you know why I brought you here, Mr. Upton?"

The younger man inclined his head slightly. "I solve problems. You clearly have a problem that needs solving. All that awaits are the details."

"Hmmmph. Don't get too clever." Perry sat for a moment and gestured broadly at the town below. "The thing you have to understand is that this is, for all intents and purposes, my town. I was born here. Grew to manhood here. Mustered into the Union Army with twenty-two of my closest friends on that village green, and came home with the six survivors and no legs two years later. And I built this factory up from nothing—here, when the easy thing to do would have been to pull up stakes and set up shop in Lowell. Do you know how much of this town works in this factory, Mister Upton?"

Upton knew, of course. It was his job to know such things, to know all the pertinent things about any man who summoned him to a meeting and might have use of his particular talents. And he also knew that Asher Perry was blunt, even by the standards of New England mill owners, and had little patience for flatterers and their ilk.

"More than half," he said with quiet pride. "Directly, that is. If you count the shopkeepers who sell to your workers, the riverhands and drovers who move your goods, the men of God who tend to their souls and the ladies of the evening who tend to their other needs in a lovely house on Benefit Street, then nearly all."

Perry grunted in approval. "I love this town. It's my mill that feeds it and pumps the blood through its veins. I put the food on the table in every house you see, and I send the doctor when any of 'em fall ill. It's my coin that buys their cradles and their coffins, and while a better businessman might think my sentiment unnecessary, I find it appropriate. This town made me, now I make it."

Perry turned his chair so that he faced Upton, staring up at him with a curious intensity. "But what happens out there if this place closes? If I'm forced to shut my doors, what happens next?"

Upton closed his eyes for a second and imagined the scene. The great looms stilled, their steamy exhalations done forever. The confused and frightened workers outside of the great doors, chained shut. The flight of those who could afford to go, the creeping poverty and desperation of those who could not. The death of the town by inches, and the disappearance of everything Asher Perry had built.

"I can see it," he said softly. "So that is why you need me?"

Instead of answering, Perry wheeled himself back over to his desk. The chair was a solid contraption of brass, inlaid with cherry wood here and there to make it less utilitarian. "Here's the problem," he said, and he pulled two small bolts of fabric onto the desk. To Upton, they were indistinguishable. "One of these is from my works. High quality, which means I can afford to charge through the nose for it. And the other? From a mill in Burlington. Last year, they were turning out stuff that would rub a horse's backside bald. This year, they're making cloth as good as mine and five times as fast."

"I begin to see your worry."

"Hmm. Do you." Perry steepled his fingers. "I'll be straight with you, Upton. My buyers won't hold the line for long. I either have to adapt or shut down, and I can't shut down."

Upton dropped into a chair across the massive desk. "What exactly are you asking me to do, Mister Perry?"

"Steal." Perry's voice was flat and cold. "Get yourself into the Schnurr Textile Works by whatever means you have to. Find out how they're doing it and who's doing it for them. And then bring that secret back to me, so I can do the same thing here."

"How far do you want me to go to get it? Certain things . . . cost more."

Perry scowled. "Whatever it takes, Mister Upton. You have carte blanche."

He pulled open another drawer, pulling out a small bag stuffed to nearly to bursting. "Here," he said, tossing it on the table. "Airship fare from Bridgeport to Burlington. Half your fee, as agreed. And those other things you asked for, all provided."

Upton swiped the bag with an easy motion, not bothering to open it, and stood. "And from here?"

"One of my men will drive you to the terminal in Bridgeport. He's already picked up your things from the boarding house and is waiting downstairs. And with that, I believe our business is concluded, at least until you bring me what I asked for. Good day, Mister Upton, and godspeed."

"Until I return, then." Pouch in hand, Upton headed for the door.

The sound of the machines got louder once he left Perry's office but not oppressively so. The factory floor spread before him, and of all the ones he'd seen, this was by far the most pleasant. Vast windows let in light while massive fans and bellows kept air circulating throughout the room. Nor could he see children working the looms. It was said Perry had strict rules against it and that he paid his people well.

Upton frowned. Sympathy was a dangerous thing in his line of work. His task was before him. Best that he not think of it in terms of good or evil but merely payment. With that, he strode down the iron staircase toward the front door and Burlington.

✪✪✪

The Burlington airship station was small, crowded, and busy. Blasts of steam and compressed air pushed platforms full of passengers skyward or let them settle toward the ground as gangs of men worked to tether incoming vessels. Everywhere, placards announced new expansions that were coming soon—new services, new platforms, a new world manifesting itself in a million small ways.

As Upton's lift hit ground, he hoisted his bag. The disembarking crowd surged around him, but he held back until the tide had receded and the platform operator stood alone at his console.

"Excuse me, sir. Can you direct me to the Schnurr Textile Works?"

The lift operator, a heavyset man in a too-tight uniform, laughed. "That way," he said, and he gestured with a meaty thumb. "Just listen for the commotion."

"Commotion?" Upton asked.

But the platform operator was already hustling the next batch of passengers onto the platform, securing it for ascent. If he heard Upton, he gave no sign

Upton shrugged and set off. Vehicles whizzed past him: larger steam-driven omnibuses with rumbling boilers and smaller clockwork devices like powered bicycles, zipping in and around the motorcars like flies. Horses were still in evidence here and there, but they were few and far between. A sign of progress, Upton told himself. Clearly, Burlington was going places in a hurry.

And then he rounded a corner and came across a scene of pure chaos. Perhaps a hundred yards away, behind a low brick wall, was a massive building labeled Schnurr in titanic bronze letters. A dozen smokestacks belched filth, spitting black soot and thunderous cacophony skyward. No windows disrupted the grim brick exterior, but that was not what caught Upton's attention.

In front of the factory was a surly mob of hired toughs, hard, unshaven men in grubby clothes and hastily pinned-on badges, all armed with clubs or brickbats or sawed-off lengths of pipe. A fiercely mustachioed fellow gave orders from a platform close to the building by speaking into some sort of metal cone that amplified his voice a hundredfold.

Across from the hooligans was an equally disorganized mob, only they held placards instead of weapons. Many were women, Upton noticed, and they chanted slogans almost loud enough to drown out the mustached man's yelling. Overhead, police ornithopters circled lazily, and a crowd had gathered to watch the incipient confrontation. The air was electric with tension. The more sensitive members of the crowd were already edging away.

Upton edged forward, working his way through the crowd until he was on the edge of the throng of sign-holding laborers. He could hear now what they were saying, though the words made little sense: "Tear them up, let them go! Tear them up, let them go!" The strikebreakers were too close now, their makeshift weapons terribly real across the short gap.

Here and there, workers handed out leaflets. Most were met with hoots of derision and torn up, but the laborers kept at it doggedly. Upton worked his way over to where a painfully thin young woman with a long, angular face was resolutely shoving papers into the hands of anyone nearby. He tapped her on the shoulder and got as far as "Excuse me, miss," before she whirled, paper first, and nearly rammed it down his throat.

"I'm terribly sorry," she said, lowering her hand slightly. Her voice had a slight rasp to it, one Upton instantly recognized as an early symptom of Monday Fever. All the mill girls got it sooner or later. The dust from the looms settled murderously in their lungs. The cure was fresh air and sunshine, far from the textile mills—a cure none of them could afford to take.

"Nothing to be sorry for," he said, lowering his eyes to the paper as he took it. It was the usual labor broadsheet, claiming the workers were united against unfair labor conditions and demanding humane treatment. And at the bottom, an ominous phrase: "Not even death will free us."

When he looked up, the woman was looking back at him. "You read it," she said. "Most don't."

"I try to be informed," he replied. "So is this a slowdown?"

"A strike," she said resolutely. "Schnurr Textiles is a monstrous firm. It must be stopped."

Puzzled, Upton turned his head. "Wait a minute. You said it's a strike. But the factory's still running. And I don't see any replacement workers—"

"Scabs," she interjected

"Scabs going in and out. What's going on in there?"

"That's what I'm trying to tell you," she said. "You see, it's—"

And then all hell broke loose.

A brick came soaring across the line. No one saw who had thrown it: perhaps, one of Schnurr's hired thugs or, perhaps, a bored and restless member of the crowd. It made no difference. The projectile caught one of the workers on the side of the head with a crunching sound, and she dropped to the ground. There was a moment of stunned silence and then screams and bellows of anger broke out as the two sides surged together. Metal and wood slammed against bone, fists slammed into faces. From overhead, the impotent tootling of police whistles served to remind everyone that this would not be settled by law.

Upton found himself face to face with one of the strikebreakers, a squat man with an oft-broken nose and a derby crammed low over his eyes. The man roared, swinging a length of lead pipe. Upton ducked and brought his bag up in a vicious arc that intersected with the man's crotch. He grunted and folded, at which point Upton hammered the back of his neck with an elbow, and the man fell senseless to the ground.

Behind the unconscious man, the woman he'd been talking to stood, staring.

"You should go. You're not one of us."

"That seems to make no difference."

"Please, leave before it's too late!"

But it was, or so it seemed. The line of workers wavered and cracked, and the tide of strikebreakers poured through. They lay about indiscriminately, and the resolute chants turned to panicked screams.

"Come on," the woman said, and she grabbed Upton by the arm. "Let's get you out of here!"

"Get *me* out of here?" he said, even as a billy club whistled past his ear. She turned and threw a fistful of leaflets into the strikebreaker's face. She pulled Upton free from the crowd.

"This way!" she shouted, leading him down an alley to the left.

She led him through a maze of small streets and smaller passages as the clamor of the riot faded in the distance. Eventually, they found themselves in a small courtyard of a crumbling tenement. "In here," she said, leading him through a door and into a cramped kitchen. A pot of soup burbled lifelessly on the stove while clotheslines draped across the room to take advantage of the heat. "You can stay here until it dies down. They never come this far looking for us."

"I appreciate the help, Miss . . ."

"Adelaide. Adelaide Marcus."

"Ah. Miss Marcus, I appreciate the help, but there's no need for you to stick your neck out for me. I've handled myself in worse scraps."

"You've seen nothing worse than Schnurr," she said flatly. "Did you not hear what we were calling for?"

"Tear it up, let them go," he said. "Tear up contracts? Let the workers leave?"

She laughed, a bitter, angry sound that devolved into a rasping cough. "You have no idea. Look, have you ever worked in a factory? Lived in a factory town?"

"I haven't."

"Then you don't know. Don't know they bring you in with a promise of good pay and clean clothes and a nice place to live. They don't tell you they charge for all of that, and they keep charging, and you never ever ever make enough working for them to pay it off because they always find new things to charge you for."

"So run."

"Try it, and you'll get clapped into debtor's prison. There's no way out. Once they get a grip on you, you're theirs."

"For life?"

She turned and stared at him. "Life? What do you think happens when you die and you still owe them?"

Upton ducked under a clothesline, stepped around a child's makeshift toy on the floor. "The debt gets passed along, I assume. That's the usual way of things."

Again, a bark of angry laughter. "Not anymore. They've made things more efficient, you see. Now, when you die—"

And with a crash, the door flew into the room. Shouts of "There she is!" filled the air, matched by a clamor from the front of the building. A dozen burly strikebreakers poured in, clubs in hand. One swung at Upton, who dodged as the man's arm was caught by a clothesline. He sent the man sprawling with an uppercut, just in time to take a belt across the ribs from the next thug. Behind him, he heard a scream and a hiss as Adelaide flung the pot of hot soup at another assailant. There was the thump of another man going down. And a gunshot. And another.

A spray of bright red across the clothes, the clang of a pot against the floor— Adelaide was screaming, and more shots were fired until she went horribly, abruptly silent. Upton tried to go to her, but a sharp blow caught him across the back of the head, and he saw darkness.

Hours later, he awoke. The kitchen was empty, and he was on the floor. His cheek rested in a cold, sticky puddle that smelled like old copper pennies. Blood, he told himself as he sat up. Adelaide's. With the name came the memory and the sure knowledge that she was dead. Her body was gone, he saw, though the rest of the evidence of the battle remained: the dropped pot, the bloodstained clothes. Even his bag was unmolested in the corner.

All they'd wanted, it seemed, was her.

Well, Upton decided, they weren't going to keep her. It was that simple.

❂❂❂

The factory was easy enough to infiltrate. The afternoon's excitement had died down, and the crowds had dissipated. Under cover of darkness, it was easy to get close to the building. Even at night, the factory was still running full blast, and the thunderous clatter of the machinery covered the sound of his steps. Upton tailed an unobservant guard on his rounds and slipped into the building behind him. It was easy enough to disable the man, who went about his rounds like he could not possibly conceive of an intruder. Upton then stashed the guard's unconscious body in a closet, borrowed his keys and gear, and stepped onto the factory floor.

It was vast, bigger than Perry's factory by far, and far more crowded. Looms and hoppers filled every available space, churning endlessly as they devoured raw materials and spat out cloth. Carts ran back and forth between the machines in corridors barely wide enough for a man, running full and empty in turn.

And there were no people.

No workers feeding fiber to the great machines. No one checking product as it came off the loom. No one adjusting feeds or tying knots or doing any of the million and one tasks that Upton knew were part and parcel of this sort of operation.

In the entire juddering building, he was alone. It was just him and the machines.

Each of which, he now saw, had one thing in common from cart to loom to carder. Every single mechanism held a singular canister or light of some sort, a brass bracket holding a bluish glass capsule, with a dated placard underneath. They served no obvious purpose, yet their omnipresence spoke to an underlying necessity. Frowning, he scanned the room checking the posted dates; none were over a year old and one marked the very day. Upton walked over to that one and hoisted himself up to where the canister had been inserted securely into the works. Steadying himself, he reached up and grasped it in hopes of better understanding. His fingers brushed the surface of the glass, and a sudden shock dropped him to his knees.

Not the electric current the device provided, though that was considerable. Instead, it was the shock of recognition, of understanding what was in those blue capsules.

Or rather, who.

And Adelaide, who had died earlier this day and who no doubt owed her employer a great debt, had already been put to work repaying it from beyond the grave.

At least, that was what she had just told him.

When he was able to bring himself to move once again, he removed the cylinder from the machine and listened, gratified, as the loom ground to a halt. He thought about doing that for the others as well, but time was growing short, and he had no way to carry more than one. Instead, he contented himself with a visit to the factory's offices, securing certain papers he found there and burning the rest before slipping away.

✿✿✿

As dawn approached, Upton hammered on Asher Perry's factory door. After a minute, lights came on and voices sounded, and the great door creaked open to show an unkindly giant of a man in a nightshirt with a length of oak in his hand. "Go away," he said, but Upton was already pushing past him into the factory.

"Perry? Perry!" he called. "I've got what you asked for. I've got everything you asked for, by God, and I'll not keep it a minute longer than necessary! Asher Perry, come out and take what's yours!"

A thick hand slammed onto his shoulder and spun him around. "That's enough out of you, I think," said the giant as he pushed him toward the door. "You want to see Mister Perry? You come back in the morning like a gentleman, you do."

"No, no, Hammond. It's fine. I've been expecting him." Perry's voice floated down from the top of the stairs.

"Go on," Hammond growled, and he neatly reversed the direction he'd been pushing Upton. "But make it quick. Mr. Perry needs his rest."

"I have no intention of staying," Upton replied and climbed the long iron stairwell, his footfalls echoing over the long rows of silent machines.

"Not here. In my office," Perry said when the younger man reached the top of the stairs. Dutifully, Upton followed him. "Shut the door," Perry said, and Upton did. "Hammond's no idea that there's any trouble, and I'd like to keep him innocent of such things if I can. Now, what do you have for me?"

"Everything you asked for," Upton replied and reached into his satchel. Out came the battery, blue glass and brass, a thoroughly utilitarian design made for maximum use, not aesthetics. He placed it on the desk, though the sound of it hitting the wood was oddly muffled. Instead of a thud, it came out as almost a gasp.

Perry leaned forward and peered at the container. Deep within, a hazy form could be seen, swirling endlessly. "What is it?"

"The answer to how your competitors were able to up their production. Take a closer look."

The older man stared for a minute, fascinated, before the blood abruptly drained from his face. "Good God," he said. "is it . . ."

Upton nodded. "It is. Every single one of their machines is powered by one of those. Every. Single. One."

Perry wheeled himself back from the desk, putting some distance between himself and the battery. His eyes stayed fixed on it. "That . . . that's demonic!"

"It is. And it keeps their looms running twenty-four hours a day. You wanted their secret, Mister Perry. Here it is." Upton tapped the pile of papers next to the battery. "Everything's in here. Schematics. Notes. Timetables and cost estimates. And if you're smart, you'll take it all and throw it in the fire."

"Indeed." Perry sounded distracted. Slowly, he wheeled himself back toward the desk.

"You weren't in there, Mister Perry. You didn't see the things I saw. Dead girls, Perry, dead girls with their souls wrung into glass bottles like cheap liquor, so they could keep working forever. You want no part of that, I tell you."

Perry didn't answer. Instead, he reached out tentatively with one finger, tapping it on the glass of the battery. A faint blue spark leapt from the container to the tip of his finger. A soft keening was barely audible . "Good God," Perry whispered, and he reached out to cup it in both hands.

"Mister Perry, you must understand—"

"I understand perfectly, Mister Upton." He looked up from the battery, his face haggard. "The remainder of your money is downstairs with Hammond. There's a bonus as well. Take it with my thanks for a job well done, and never darken my door again."

Upton didn't move. "You can't do this. It's hell you'd be building to save your little heaven. Even if it does keep the factory open, how long before they find out how you saved them? How long before they turn on you?"

Perry said nothing, turning the battery over and over in his hands as the ghost danced within. A frenzy of sparks flared through his fingers, but he resolutely ignored them, ignored the hammering of the hazy figure inside the blue glass on its walls.

Upton waited for him to speak but finally turned to go.

When Upton reached the door, Perry looked up and called to him. His voice was low, and his eyes strayed to the window and the town beyond.

"I buy their cradles," he said. "I buy their coffins. What else would you have me do?"

⁅⁆

Writer, game designer, and cad, **Richard Dansky** *has contributed to over 40 videogames. The author of 6 novels, including the Wellman Award-nominated Vaporware, he has also worked on over 130 tabletop RPG titles and published numerous pieces of short fiction. He lives in North Carolina with his wife, their library, and an indeterminate number of bottles of single malt whisky: http://rdansky.tumblr.com.*

The Twentieth-Century Man

Nick Mamatas

❁❁❁

The dinner was as cold as the room. Steam-pipe cold, as when the coal runs out. Jessop, Arkright, and Taylor shivered as they ate, though it wasn't from the temperature but rather due to the firearms pointed at the back of their heads.

"Not hungry, Dodgson?" the leader of the quartet asked me.

I wasn't shivering either. After taking a pistol-whipping from my interlocutor, I'd been placed in Carnacki's favorite chair where he'd once snugged up after far superior dinners and told us of his encounters with the abnatural and perverse.

"I am not," I said. "I have trouble digesting food when nauseated."

"What is this all about?" Arkright snapped. Gravy dribbled down his chin, already congealing due to the frigid air. Our captors were outfitted as though for an Arctic expedition save for the fact that they wore gloves only over their left hands, all the better for the pistols in their right hands.

"Carnacki, of course," Taylor said.

Jessop simply nodded and tucked back in to his roast.

"Carnacki," the head man said. "Carnacki, the ghost-finder."

"Eh? Carnacki the ghost, more like! Innit?" said the man behind Taylor, his accent and gruff tone suggesting a social origin far below that of his co-conspirator.

"This is entirely infra dig, men!" Arkright said. He rose from his chair, and Taylor nearly joined him. I thought to leap upon the head man, but my throbbing head injury kept me planted in my chair. Arkright got pummeled for his troubles and slumped back into his chair.

"Infra dig. Abnatural. There are so many notional spaces we create through nothing more than civilized discourse—there is a thing called dignity, there is another known as nature—and by bringing these spaces into existence with our minds, we bring into existence their shadows. The spaces that they are not."

Our captor was a philosophical sort. It was nearly as though he was simply musing aloud to himself, as if our presence was a matter of accident rather than design. It was universally assumed that Carnacki had passed when he failed to return from a summons up to the Borders. We, his friends, were contacted via post by a man we had presumed to be Carnacki's solicitor and asked that we attend one final dinner where the estate of the great detective and my great friend would be settled. Instead, we were greeted by a quartet of armed men and supper that had been left out too long.

Taylor said, "This was Carnacki's home, and now, it is not." Everyone turned to peer at him. Taylor rarely spoke during our intimate gatherings with Carnacki, and his observation was a peculiar one.

"For your sake, sir, hope this is not the case. We are here because this is Carnacki's home. We need it to be his home, vibrationally."

"You sound like Carnacki," I told him. "Our poor friend Carnacki would not keep us waiting so or treat us so cruelly. And the meat would have been kept over a warmer."

"I am not your poor friend Carnacki," the man said, an edge in his voice. He loomed over me. "But I will take his place. And all of you will be of assistance in doing so."

Taylor snapped, "We'll do no such thing!"

Arkright was still in a daze, and Jessop, his usual practical self, ate his cold vegetables.

"We know nothing of Carnacki's art," I said, trying to rise to my feet, if only to save Taylor a drubbing. "Our fellowship with him was rather non-commutative. He was the detective, the adventurer, the occultist. He shared his stories with us but not his expertise. So we can be of no help to you, sir, which is rather a shame given the number of supernatural menaces that continue to plague our country."

"On the contrary, you'll be of great assistance to me," the man said. He took a seat on the corner of the table in the manner of a movie-house rake and tapped the surface with the barrel of his pistol. "Why do you think," he said with his philosophical tone returning, "Carnacki would summon you and give tell of his exploits?

"You were crucial, do you see? He made acquaintanceship with each of you and cultivated a seeming of friendship in order to harness certain... potentials. Your quaint ghost-story club charged the aetheric battery of the Electric Pentacle itself."

Much like Carnacki, our captor did not feel the need to cease speaking when his narrative was not yet done. When Carnacki was alive, I and the other members of our fellowship would never have thought to interrupt our friend— his tales were at once that chilling, that gripping. A pleasing terror kept us silent in our chairs. Our current situation was similar but as seen through a dark glass: the terror wasn't pleasing, the chill was in the air, and the grips were made of solid flesh and sinew as our captor's confederates clamped their hands upon our shoulders. If that were not enough to convince us to grant our captor an audience, there were the pistols to consider.

"Four men and Carnacki. Five, like the five points of the pentacle. It is no coincidence that Carnacki brought you all here to hear of his exploits. It is the nature of the occult to be hidden, but it is also the nature of the occult to tantalize, to 'hide in plain sight' as the newspapers might say of a wanted fugitive who is found in his favorite chair down at his local. The abnatural is not the other end of the world from the natural. It is rather the void that gives it shape. Do you see, Dodgson?"

Indeed, I did. Our captor would not kill us, I knew that much. That is why he and his henchmen had used their guns only as saps, and hadn't simply executed us the moment we pushed in through the door. He had ambushed us for some plan.

Arkright, who had prepared an impromptu poultice for himself by dipping a napkin into his water glass and applying the damp end to his temple, spoke up. "Not all of Carnacki's cases had to do with occult traffic. Plenty of times, he was made a bit of a fool, such as when some criminals had taken advantage of local tales to secure a hideout for their coterie. They laughed at his Electric Pentacle."

"But I am not laughing, Mr. Arkright. I am deadly serious. The Electric Pentacle works, and it works due to the vibrational sympathies of you four and the relationship you had with Carnacki. I mean to recreate the Electric Pentacle.

"I mean to mass produce it!"

Jessop snorted at that. "Why?" he asked.

"As your friend said," our captor began, gesturing at me with his pistol, and I regret to report that I cringed, "there are still many supernatural menaces about."

"Not so many," Jessop said. "There's no market for it, man, do you understand?"

"And truth be told," Taylor said, "if you are familiar with Carnacki's cases as you claim to be, the abnatural is rather gormless in its way. Carnacki put himself in danger by contending with the forces. On their own, left unmolested, what do ghosts and haunts and vibrational entities even do that's so dreadful? Slam doors, tear bed-clothes from mattresses, clomp about hallways on phantom hooves. Honestly, much of this abnaturalism is an issue of real estate or heirlooms. Half the time, Carnacki defeated manifestations by putting the haunted rooms or vibrational objects to the torch! The greater fraction of the remainder, there was no ab at all but just some trickery by the cleverer segment of the criminal element."

"If I'm honest, I'll tell you that I attended our club suppers primarily for the suppers and only secondarily because of an interest in Carnacki's adventures, which I presumed to be largely a matter of confabulation," Jessop said.

I gritted my teeth at that.

"And you, Arkright?" our captor asked.

"I fail to see even a single whit of sense in this endeavor," Arkright said plainly. "Carnacki was a great man. Were he here . . ." Arkright could not finish his statement, and he lowered his gaze, bereft.

"Were he here," the head man said, "I would enjoy a supper with him rather more than I would with you lot, his supposed boon companions. I had hoped that there would be some curiosity regarding the supernatural here and that we could have a nice chat, just like the old days—"

"With you in place of Carnacki, no doubt," I interrupted. "Of course, we'll not cooperate. You can shoot us all dead, our faces falling flat into the pudding if you like." I glanced at my friends, whose expressions did not betray the same stalwart hunger for sacrifice that I hoped my own face carried.

"In Carnacki's place? A clever supposition, but no. Carnacki's interdisciplinary skills were a marvel, but he lacked my . . . vision. If I'm immodest, so be it. I am a twentieth-century man. Don't you see? It doesn't matter if the abnatural is limited to midnight cantrips, now. It's the implications that are the meat of the matter. If magic is so, then science as we know it is fatally flawed. How would we integrate the notion of vibrational essence into Mr. Planck's quantum hypothesis? It resists logic, denies it. These supernatural manifestations are like termites chewing away at the load-bearing beams of the cosmos . . ."

"And now that Carnacki's dead, the termites can feast . . ." Arkright began.

"Perhaps, even *his* efforts were in vain. Imagine a man trying to rid his library of an infestation of firebrats or other vermin with a pair of tweezers and a looking-glass instead of fumigation!" Taylor exclaimed.

"Ah, thus mass production," Jessop said. "I must say that it would be rather difficult to earn a profit selling spectral security. You can't convince a man to repair the commons out of his own pocketbook, even if the commons is the terra firma, and astra firmament, he is used to being rather more solid than you contend it is."

"Are you entertaining this madman's suppositions?" I demanded. "He has us held captive! Show some courage, men. What *would* Carnacki do in such a circumstance? Think it through rationally, and then, only at the limits of the rational, appeal to the supernatural. The world has done very well so far and isn't about to fall into ruin if we fail to acquiesce to a gunman and his troupe of ruffians."

Our head captor grunted to demand the return of our undivided attention. "Ah, that is the subject I had hoped to discuss, Dodgson," he said to my friend. Then he turned to meet all our eyes. "What would Carnacki do? He would think through the situation rationally, and then, only at the limits of the rational, appeal to the supernatural. I would do the same, and indeed, I have. Which is why I summoned you here to Chelsea and have told you my concerns. I have reformed the supper club and will use its vibrational power to deal with the supernatural, just as Carnacki did but with finality. The five shall eliminate the supernatural from the universe. The five!"

"Aha, so you do plan to take Carnacki's place," I said, incredulous and aghast at the pluck of this man. "You're no Carnacki, sir."

"Not yet," the captor said, and he did something so horrific and so brave that it chills me to this day to detail it. He lifted his pistol, and I cringed. Arkright gasped and made to leap from his chair, but the ruffians held him down. I swore to myself that I would keep my eyes open and take the bullet like a man even as my nervous system impelled my eyelids to squeeze shut.

Thunder filled my ears, and burning powder singed the hairs of my mustache. My breath froze in my throat, then burned. I opened my eyes, steadying myself for the bloom of blood I was convinced I would see upon my jacket, but the blood was on the floor, a halo of red around his head and a coin-sized hole in his temple. His crew sprang into action, leaving their stations behind Arkright, Taylor, and Jessop to attend to the body. They withdrew unusual instruments from the pockets of their heavy coats. They tore at the gunman's jacket and shirt and opened his mouth to insert a sort of spoon attached to a coil that in turn led to a small crank-battery. Though the ruffians worked with the mien and precision of a team of Army medics, the apparatus used was more reminiscent of radio equipment. The man with the harsh accent muttered to himself as he worked the crank, as the others treated their leader's fatal wound.

I exchanged glances with my cohort. Though no longer directly threatened by the ruffians, we were paralyzed by the scene and could only watch them work on the corpse on Carnacki's floor. One ruffian stormed atop the table, a length of copper wire in his gloved fist, and punched up at the light fixture, shattering the bulb and plunging the room into a momentary darkness as he shoved the wire into the light socket. A great spark traveled down the wire like a snake and excited the body into a spasmodic twitching. The air smelled alive, and a low buzzing filled the room. The hair on my arms stood on end, and as the drone subsided, footsteps clomped about in the dark. A door swung open and shut.

"Arkright . . ." I started to say as the door opened again, and the light orange glow of candles spilled forth. Our captor, so recently dead of suicide, held them in both hands as he stood in the jamb leading to Carnacki's kitchen.

"Hello, friends," our captor said. His voice was unchanged, but his cadence was different. No longer limned with braggadocio and hinting at violence, it was warm and chipper. "Clever man, coming to the place I love best rather than to the place I died to offer up this vessel to me."

Taylor said it first, "Carnacki."

"In some flesh, if not quite my own," the man said. "I . . . oh, I have it! Flint! That was the name of our criminal and, indeed, our savior." He turned to his gang and nodded toward a door that I had never seen opened in all my visits to this Chelsea bachelor flat. "What you are looking for is in there, men. The key is behind the clock on the mantle."

The man—Carnacki—placed the candles on the table, pushing them into the bread and puddings for lack of proper sticks, and looked expectantly at me. I rose from Carnacki's old chair and took up my usual spot while Carnacki settled into his.

"The Borders is a marvelous place. I don't regret having met my doom there. There was an old Roman settlement whose original inhabitants had decided to continue to fight for Hadrian long after their tours of duty ended. I'm afraid my pistol didn't stand up to their spectral spears and shields, and I could not complete the Eight Signs of Saaamaaa before they were upon me. Pistols do seem to be rather insufficient to the job of putting the dead into the graves and keeping them there, if I do say so myself.

"I am sure you are curious as to the physical—or should I say metaphysical—and moral layout of the Other World. I'm afraid there isn't much to report. It was the Greeks who have come closest. Hades isn't a realm so much as it is a state of being. As the body decomposes in its grave, the soul decomposes in Hades, disintegrating and joining the Abyss. It's not a painful experience per se, but it is singularly unpleasant. The abnatural as we experience it here on the material plane is the result of this slow dissolution. Some personalities are so fierce, so powerful, that they can leave a vibrational mark here on Earth even as they dissolve into the Eternal. It's wondrous to contemplate, but no wonder at all that there are hardly ever any pleasant abnatural manifestations.

"I would have found a way back at some time in the future without the assistance of our man Flint, who so bravely sacrificed himself for the world to come, but by then, it would have been too late. He is where I was, his spirit flaking to pieces, like a waterlogged corpse being dragged through the silt by a strong current. I propose that we have saved him and, indeed, saved all the world's dead via a positive charge powerful enough to match the immense negative charge of Hades, freeing the dead from their fates and releasing them into the Light.

"Sounds downright Christian, doesn't it? You could find similar conceptions of the Other World in virtually all religions. We know *something* as a species, after all. It's our birthright to fear death, and for good reason. I do not recommend death, even as a fortnight's holiday. Flint's own expertise was theoretical while my experiences were practical. He believed that the Electric Pentacle, mass produced and installed along various ley lines all across the world—Egypt, Rhodesia, Peking, Mexico—would be sufficient to free the world from the dark aether in which it floats. What he lacked was the perspective only death can bring.

"The Michelson–Morley experiment of which you learned men surely are familiar with disproved the existence of 'luminiferous aether' via simple use of the clock. If the aether wind existed, surely the speed of light on Earth would vary based on the planet's relative position vis-à-vis the aether. Light traveling parallel to the aether would be slower than light traveling perpendicular to it. But the speed of light is a constant! No aether, after all, and much of nineteenth century physics was left out for rubbish.

"But those American scientists misunderstood not only the aether but also time. Time is not an arrow so much as it is a table. Everything upon the table of time has, is, and will be occurring. This is also why precognition and postcognition are occasionally efficacious. Time is a vibrational state, a constant, and sensitives do not so much predict the future as they simply perceive it, just as you can see the meal before you and the remnants of Jessop's meal at the far end of the table in one 'look.' The aether is real. It is time that is false.

"This, indeed, may also be why some religious sects believe in praying for the dead. Eternity does not respond to prayer and save a soul from Hades. If a lucky fellow finds himself in Paradise, it is because his relations prayed for him after his death, and this influenced his behavior during his life *before the prayers were said*. The Electric Pentacle can send a similar aetheric message across, throughout, and within time.

"Flint was ambitious, but his understanding was still limited by linear time. He sought to eliminate the supernatural from the world at present, but his plan would, in fact, actually eliminate the supernatural forever, including the past. So this is what I put to you, gentlemen.

"We can set up the Electric Pentacle, and with your help, I can tune it in such a way that it will exist at the dawn of time—at the far end of the table. It will annihilate the aether in which the souls of men are trapped, not just now but always, in the past as well as the future. There will be no aether. There never will have been aether.

"With a flick of a switch, things will be very different indeed. Are you prepared to walk outside into a different world, one where the abnatural has been collapsed into the natural? You may find life to be quite different."

I was surprised to hear Jessop speak first and almost immediately. "Are you speaking of a Utopia, Carnacki? That Greek pun of the *good place* that is in fact *no place*. At the risk of being vulgar, I must ask: what's in it for me?"

Carnacki worked the mouth of the man he inhabited into something reminiscent of his usual mirthful expression. "Flint was right. The supernatural vibrations I made a career of fighting are only to increase. By mid-century, I'd imagine that even the atom would be torn in two, like a hungry man tearing apart a piece of bread. The energies unleashed would be magnificent. And that is of minor concern. With the laws of physics in abeyance, some hungry man could take two minuscule grains of flour, one on the tip of each forefinger, and bring them together with such speed and power that a loaf of bread would spontaneously generate in his hands. If that sounds appetizing to you Jessop, let me remind you that all analogies are limited. We're not speaking of bread but of the cosmic forces that keep the 'uncuttable atom' in its current state. Rather than a loaf of bread between those two fingers, imagine the Sun."

"Incredible," Taylor said. "But . . . what proof do you have? Are you Carnacki or are you our captor, playing pantomime with the help of spirit gum and stagecraft to mimic a grievous wound?"

"I have no proof, but I ask you to allow me to set up the Electric Pentacle in your presence. All five of us must be present. It is why I sought you out and formed our club, after all, though I wasn't aware of my motivations when I first invited you all to supper back when Edward was on the throne. Only now do I understand why I found you, why I made you all my confidants. I have no proof, but if I am a liar, there are no stakes. We set up the pentacle, I flip the switch, the lights flicker, and you walk out the door into the same world you knew this afternoon. If I were here to simply rob you or murder you, I could have done so without this charade. If I am mad, then I am mad alone," Carnacki said.

I glanced over at Arkright. "And you?"

"Aye, let's humor this man. If nothing comes of it, I'll be back here with constables and my own gun."

Carnacki smiled at me, and I smiled at him. I could not tell you then why I agreed to participate in the construction and activation of the Electric Pentacle except that I had heard so much of it but had never seen it until Flint's men retrieved it from the other room. We cooperated with them to move Carnacki's furniture to the corners of the room as Carnacki prepared five bowls of water, taken from the dinner glasses, and chalked a pentacle on the floor. The Electric Pentacle was simple: a pentagonal black battery with five sets of wires coming from each side. Carnacki stretched out the wires and connected vacuum tubes to each, then flipped a switch. The room glowed, not unpleasantly, though it was odd to sit in a place where the light was on the floor and my long shadow on the ceiling with colors shifting from red to indigo and beyond.

After a few moments, it was over. Carnacki stood, wiped his hands, and reached for his pipe on the mantle.

"Out you go!" said Carnacki, genially, using the recognized formula.

And we went out on to the Embankment and presently through the darkness to our various homes. If there was a difference in the world, I did not sense it, and as I speak these words into my voco-stylus, I can see the sun rising in the west as it always does, and I feel safe in the airship bearing me to America as I do every week when I make my trip to consult with the Difference Engineers of Imperial Tabulations, Limited. Carnacki's supper club disbanded, and truth be told, I cannot recall why I ever felt that tales of disembodied hands and phantom boars contained even a trace of verisimilitude.

Perhaps there's something about London that drives men mad. I am considering moving to the colonies, to Chicago, as extensive air travel makes me brood more deeply. Is this all there is?

§

Nick Mamatas *is the author of several novels, including* Love is the Law, The Last Weekend, *and* I Am Providence. *His short fiction has appeared in* Best American Mystery Stories, Tor.com, *Asimov's Science Fiction, and many others. Originally from New York, Nick now lives in California, where he works in publishing. His latest anthology is the SF/fantasy crime story collection,* Hanzai Japan *(co-edited with Masumi Washington).*

Clockwork of Sorrow

Spencer Ellsworth

❖❖❖

Observe a simple scene: a bachelor preparing chicken cutlets and potatoes. His hands smell of kerosene, his clothes of oxide. He gives a carefree whistle, for his purse is fat, and such a thing is a rarity. He little notices the dark and the cold.

Do you see? Between his bedroom and the small kitchen, a light grows. Not a light often seen in sooty London anymore; it has the precise quality of the full moon, soaring from a soft cloud on a clear night in the countryside. The kind of light that makes the old wish for young love and the young lovers pine over those they cannot have.

It grows. It assumes a shape. A girl, thin and worn. Her ragged dress and her bony arms made of the silvery moonlight. Her hair, the hollows of her cheeks and collarbone, and her deep dark eyes made of the sky that frames such a moon.

Our bachelor turns to see her and utters a cheery, "Bridget, darling."

The ghost hangs silent in the doorframe.

"How did you do today?" he asks. He dabs his eyes with a worn handkerchief that, like his hands, smells of kerosene and, like his hands, has been tattered by time.

"I went among the city," she says, and her voice is the soft whistle of wind catching the leaves of a willow. "I watched. I saw a boy selling to the rag-and-bone man, and a woman buying a brush, and a doctor discourse on the health of the pores."

"Wonderful! Mister Rensworth, who runs the toy-shop, often attends lectures on health. He tells me to leave my windows open, to let the pores breathe, no matter the cold." Perhaps you detect an overly affected cheeriness on the part of our bachelor? If so, your senses are keen. "I was paid from that merchant-man I told you of. There is a puppet show in Bethnal Green next week. We could attend . . . you did love puppet shows."

"Puppet shows?"

The bachelor's hand clenches, and there is a practiced air to the next words, like a catechism. "Bridget, do you remember the oak tree on the hill above the church? Do you remember that wonderful day when we climbed and would not come down, and there was sap in your hair, and Mother . . ."

The specter's night-sky eyes are deep and empty.

"Do you remember the children's workhouse? Leashby? I have never seen a man so drunk at ten o'clock in the morning. He called every child by the same names. Do you remember that? Jon and Mary, scrub the floor! Jon and Mary, why is this floor wet?"

No response from the specter.

"Bridget, do you remember when you were so ill, and you couldn't speak for the phossy jaw, and I held you, and I sang . . ." Words go unsaid by the bachelor— the words *please, you are the only one who hasn't left me.* "You remember my name, yes?"

In the consequent eternity, the oven completes its work, and the smell of chicken and buttered potatoes welcome in the cold. But any cheer is long gone. At last, she says, a voice indistinguishable from the night wind, "I am so weary."

The bachelor fixes his face as he attends to his meal. It would not help things for the ghost to see him weep.

✿✿✿

Charles Oakley had a tragic history, as you may have guessed. But at the time of this tale, Charles Oakley believed himself a happy man.

He ran a toy-repair shop where his heart delighted in the tick of tiny clocks, the bursts of jacks-in-boxes, all things with springs and sprockets. He gave three shillings even for bent and twisted hair springs, and at any time, he could be found winding a mainspring, fitting bronze gears into each other. For his heart delighted, even more than gears, in the reward of a child's smile.

His conversation with his sister's specter had unsettled him, on the day our tale truly started. Bridget had lived with him for many years, both before and after her sickness and death. Ever she faded, but she always brightened at his attention. Upon prompting, she always began to remember. Until last night . . .

Charles Oakley had just gotten up to close the door of his shop when a boy snuck past. "Mister Oakley, toy and tackle! Full watch, guv!"

The boy held out a watch and chain, so close that Charles stumbled back. "Eustace! What has you so lit up?"

Eustace, who was a boy not given to restraint, waved the watch in Charles's eyes as if he were our Lord trying to heal a blind man. Charles snatched up the piece and examined it through his glasses. Oxidized green, ash-stained, but fine workmanship. The watch was marked with a stylized R, and below it, the legend "Ridley." Charles knew no Ridley watchmaker.

He reached for his purse. "I'd say you've earned some keep for today, Eustace."

"Eh, guv, leave off the reader for a moment." The boy kicked his feet over the floor. "I been good to you, aye, guv?" When Charles nodded, smiling, Eustace went on, "My sister, sister, skin and blister. She en't never held a proper toy. I hope to bring her down here Saturday, guv, and have a look 'round. Wondering if I might built up a bit of the old 'oof?"

Charles's own heart rattled, its mainspring over-flexed at the mention of a sister, but he hid it well when he leaned over and said, "Bring her in, and I just might find something that could suit her."

While Eustace took in the toys on the shelves, Charles gently began disassembling the watch, scraping away oxidization, removing the pinpoint screws, and prying the housing apart. Its insides were clogged with mud and ash. He pried the alien material from the escapement until he could just turn a gear.

And then—the world slowed. Eustace seemed caught in molasses as he reached toward a toy, fingers creeping through the air. Charles stood and walked to him, asking, "Are you well?"

Eustace might have heard him—Charles couldn't tell by the way the boy turned his head in infinitesimal increments.

Then he observed through his door, the carriages and passers-by and flocks of sheep in the street all moving at a similarly slow pace. The entire world had slowed.

Charles returned to the desk to find that the watch had further come apart—the entire apparatus was completely dismantled. Then, most shockingly, the mainspring itself uncoiled, raised an end as if it were a head, and hissed at Charles Oakley.

He shoved the watch away from him. When it struck the floor, the mainspring, and the hairspring as well, slithered away. The world righted itself, Eustace suddenly moving at the speed of a man again.

The boy took down a felt bear, heedless of Charles Oakley's merry face now gone white. "Oh, this'll be worth that toy and tackle, right."

Charles had a great struggle with his own tongue in order to find the words. "Ridley. Where?"

Eustace said, his attention still on the felt bear, "Found on West India docks, guv. Warehouses. Foreign workmanship, that is."

Rather than going home that evening, Charles closed up and walked to the docks.

Any who saw him that night would have thought it a peculiar sight, such a bumbling gentleman going from one tough to another, asking questions. Amidst the chaos of rail-carts and ships in port, the small, chubby form of Charles Oakley went from stevedore to stevedore, heedless of their spitting and laughing. Charles only had ears for his quarry. Some averted their eyes at the name of Ridley. None would own up to knowledge of that name. It was dark soon enough, the kind of close dark aided by the soot of London. Charles wandered from warehouse to warehouse among the clanging roar of the docks. The blackened air brought water from his eyes and nose until his face burned. He never considered the idea of home. He would find this Ridley, this maker of magicks, if he had to stay all night and day at the docks. He would discover what other marvels there were in this world than his own and perhaps help Bridget in the process.

Deep into the witching hour—cold, wet, and shaking—he stumbled past a small warehouse door only to see the same stylized *R* that had been on the watch.

Charles gently knocked. The door creaked open, but there was no indication of a hand. He found himself quite frightened, but despite the shaking of his hands and his teeth, the thought of his sister's peace pushed him forward.

He stepped into warm darkness.

His eyes resolved with another throb on a small room: a poor dim oil-lamp, a desk, on which was perched a pair of boots, tall and turned-down, shining with new leather. Next to the boots, a small watch, the more resplendent twin of the damaged one Charles had seen.

"Have you seen one before?"

Charles looked up at the source of the urbane voice.

The businessman stood two heads above Charles and, oddly enough, wore no hat. He seemed to suck up what little light there was into his vibrant red hair, streaked with grey, and his vibrant green eyes. The businessman's eyes seemed inconsequential at first glance, but—you must know, you must have guessed—with the wonders and horrors they had seen, they burned like coals.

"Come, come, give fodder to my ego, if you will."

"Ah." Charles was surprised how his words came. "Quite funny, quite funny. Ah, you see, I do a little repair work, and a watch crossed my path." He pulled the remnants of Eustace's watch from his waistcoat pocket and handed it to the man, who examined it closely. "So sorry. Very sorry." Charles was afflicted with apologies when he was nervous.

The businessman was not often surprised, but tonight, he was. He hid it well as he realized that Charles Oakley had managed—and easily—to open the watch, despite a protection that should have made such a thing impossible. "Is this what led you to seek me out, sir?"

"Ah, well . . . I opened the watch, and it behaved most strangely, sorry to say, sir."

"Malcolm, please. Malcolm Ridley. There's no need to apologize."

"Almost as if, I thought, some sort of magic had been done upon it." Charles bit off the words before another *sorry* could escape.

"Are you a man who believes in such things?" his opposite number responded as casually as if he were asking Charles Oakley to pass the butter. Charles could not find the words to respond, but he could tell that this Ridley almost looked pleased. "Wind the watch backward, my good man, and you will find the world slows. For the busy man, a means to make deadlines. For the man who cannot find time for leisure, a few spare hours. No use now, without the spring. Tell me, then. This is not your first time with a marvelous invention."

"I . . ." Charles spoke. "I have a sister."

And so was told the tragic history of Charles Oakley and how he came to live alone with but his sister's specter. His people, save Bridget, fell devastated by scarlet fever in Charles's eighth year—parents, siblings, grandparents, godparents, neighbors. You might well have fired all the cannons in England at his parish and wreaked less devastation. He and Bridget came to a children's workhouse with all the hardships a thing entails: hunger, cold, work, cruel and neglectful masters. He told of his own hard work, for Charles Oakley, even as a child, could not be crushed in spirit. He had been apprentice to a toymaker and saved enough money to lodge himself and his sister comfortably, but she had taken work as a match-girl, and like so many others, the poison of the phosphorus matches rotted her jaw and then her entire body.

Charles could not bear to let her go. So she continued to appear, held in place by his love night after night, year after year.

"And until last night, her smiles were the same as they were in life, sir." Charles stared into those green eyes and thought of how, at home, this very darkness held what was left of his sister. "I am a happy man, Mister Ridley. It is but a little problem, and I must believe that it has a solution—"

At this point, the businessman said. "Sir, I may know the makings of certain peculiar things, but I am sorry to say that death's door is not one of them."

He affected great sympathy, Charles thought. "I understand,"

"I cannot refer you to any who might help you either."

Charles stood and offered his hand. Malcolm also stood, and under his gaze, Charles could not look away. "But in the area of specters and their ills, my good man," Malcolm Ridley said, "there, I have some knowledge."

✿✿✿

Observe now as Charles departs and the businessman withdraws. Observe, if you will, that Malcolm Ridley seems to grow more vibrant, his eyes and hair swallowing all light. Observe that he takes a small sip of something too dark and pungent to be any liquor.

Now, observe a marvel as great or greater than those you have already seen. Malcolm Ridley steps from his warehouse, his boots sinking into mud, and he stalks along the poor footing of the docks and turns and weaves between small warehouses. And now—now, your eyes do not lie. For his body changes, slender legs to thick haunches, refined hands to rough paws, strong chin to angled muzzle, and threads of red hair appear all over his body in place of clothes.

You've heard legends of this, but there is no moon peeking through the London fog—and you, if you be clever, may have already ascertained Malcolm Ridley will not be prisoner of any condition. For if there is one thing such a man craves, it is control.

His nose takes in all the smells of the docks—soot over all, and subtler shades of kerosene, urine, steel, lard. Above them all a peculiar scent, one that sticks in his nose, raises his hackles. Hope.

✿✿✿

For the next few nights, Bridget was a thin, wan, vanishing presence. She would appear and look at Charles, and he would ask about her sights in her travels through London, but she would not answer.

Charles maintained hope. He had a meeting set with Mister Ridley and was assured of treatment for his case if, and only if, he could bring Bridget with him. A solution for the little problem.

So one night, Charles fetched his hat and waited at table for Bridget.

She was even more faded, the moon in her light hidden by the clouds. Charles smiled his long-practiced smile. "Hello, dear. Remember the meeting I told you of?"

Do we dare look into Bridget's mind? She has some sense that she was once human, but Charles's words—oak tree? puppet show?—these are words less familiar. Ash, bone, darkness, shadow—those are real, and Charles's world is a distant echo.

"Bridget, I have found a specialist. A doctor, of sorts." Charles said. "He can help you with your feeling of wear. Remember when I said I would find you a doctor, even at death's door, even beyond? I kept my word."

See how inside Bridget's mind, for the first time, stirs something like a memory—her brother, holding her hand as her body fails, pleading with her to stay. The warmth of his arms, the gentle touch of his cheek. It is but an echo, reverberating through darkness, but it stirs her.

Since past, present, and future are one in her darkness, she will go, she does go, she did go.

The wind lashed the buildings with rain that night, mixed with chips of ice, turning the roads even soupier than usual. The whole world seemed faded, shuttered behind a curtain of wet and cold. Charles looked just behind him and was pleased to see Bridget's form, her white light catching the rapid dotted lines of raindrops. He found the address for the meeting, went to the side of the building as he had been instructed. "Here . . . ah, we are." Charles began to wonder if Malcolm Ridley were playing an especially cruel trick. There was nothing in front of him but two brick walls and the sea of icy mud between them. An alley?

And then a thing peculiar, prelude to the most peculiar part of this tale. Though it was cold, a heart of wintry cold, the air shimmered as if in a heat haze. Charles thought he saw a keyhole, a single black shape against the air. No, he did see it. And following it, a curve of darkness like the crescent moon, what his mother had called the dead man's moon.

A door.

Like the door that had opened into the Ridley warehouse, this one, though made of the air itself, opened into stifling darkness.

Charles's heart rattled like a strained balance lever, but forward he went, looking behind him to see if Bridget followed. And slowly, slowly, she emerged into the darkness with him, her pale form lighting his way.

That journey was a haze. Darkness and then great wheels of flame overhead in place of stars. Whispered words, some in growls like the language of bears and some in a high clear song-speech that made his heart weep.

Always, he saw the thread of a road ahead, pale cobblestones glowing faintly. Always, there was Bridget just behind him, a thin finger of light. Always, there was the tick-tock of blood pulsing in his temples.

And always, he came to realize, there was the soft, ragged breathing, close at hand, of some huge animal.

The path ended among a new sight—rising towers, scaffolds, metal structures ringing in a high wind. The light of the fiery stars in this strange place reflected off steel. Charles Oakley watched as the dark shape that had accompanied them—a dog? a wolf, he decided, by its loping gait—slipped inside one of the buildings through a gaping door like a maw.

And then Malcolm Ridley's voice. "Come in, and see what I spoke to you of."

Once inside, it took Charles a moment to adjust his eyes to the low, pale light. Almost all the light in this place came from a great central orb, elevated on a lamppost, and it all bore the quality of light that Bridget represented—a pale moon caught behind the clouds.

Springs and gears, like the pieces of enormous pocket watches, littered the floor. Scrap metal was piled in the corners. In the center of the room stood Malcolm Ridley next to a new shape. It was taller than Ridley, taller than any man, and made entirely of joined metal: orbs welded to shafts, resting on tightly coiled springs and gears, with two blank eyes like unlit lamps. Hands made of thin wire fingers. In the center of the chest, that stylized *R* for its manufacturer.

Charles could not help, even in the midst of the strangeness, a smile as child-like as those he counted precious. "A mechanical man?"

Ridley said, "Come closer."

Charles ran his hands along the remarkable machine. The joint-welding was perfect: the round globes of metal that made up shoulder, elbow joint, and hand seemed as smooth as skin. The head was merely a round metal ball set with those lamp-light eyes, peering down at him. "Bridget!" he called to his sister's specter. "You must come see this!" The chest-panel was open. Charles saw gears and springs to put any mere pocket watch to shame. "Does it wind up, Mister Ridley?"

"I'm afraid things do not work in such a way in this world," Malcolm Ridley said. His own gaze played between Charles and the floating, thin specter of his sister. "They only move when given an inhabitant."

"An inhabitant?"

"Yes, as I spoke of." Malcolm Ridley watched Bridget float, slow as a wisp of rain on the air, toward her brother. "Help for the specter."

Bridget watched her own face, reflected in the metal of Ridley's man. Her wide, dark eyes, the moon-bright bulge of her cheekbones, and the thin movements of her lips as she said, "Charles, what is this?"

"We've come to solve your little problem, my darling," Charles said. "Look! Physical form. Of a kind. Mister Ridley says that in return, I only need to come to his factory twice a week and aid him in the construction of these mechanical men."

"Him?" For the first time, she shifted her attention, with great effort, from Charles and from the mechanical man onto the businessman. His tall, guarded form, his green coal eyes.

See now as the specter does. There is the twisted-together tick-tock-tick of past, present, and future, the echo of good cheer, the faint threads of hope, the calling emptiness of shadows, all the specter's world.

And then there are the things that frighten even the shadows. Malcolm Ridley is one of them.

Bridget understood, though Charles did not. "He wants me, but he does not like the way you smell."

"What?" Charles turned to their host with a bashful smile. "Sorry, very sorry, sir, very sorry. Perhaps I'd have done better to take my time with her."

"No need to apologize," Ridley said, but his nose twitched as though something indeed had gone rank. "Perhaps, we could only convince her to try it on."

Bridget, though, flitted away like the wind across the room. And Malcolm Ridley continued to advance.

"So very sorry," Charles said. "Bridget, do come back! Try, for me, won't you dear?" He looked upon Malcolm Ridley and could only mutter endless apologies. "So very, terribly, terribly sorry, I . . . let me speak with her and bring her back upon another day."

"I will have a specter," Malcolm Ridley said in a soft growl. "And I so despise the smell of hope."

Charles witnessed what his sister knew by instinct. Malcolm Ridley's transformation, even as we have observed it in the shadows, is a heart-clutching thing, but in front of a man's eyes, a man old and beaten by time as Charles Oakley was, it is the face of all devilry. Rivers of red hair ran along Ridley's skin, and his hands twisted into claws, and a great hump rose in his back, sprouting that smoky red fur, but those awful eyes never left Charles Oakley—even when a gaping mouth of teeth savaged Charles's arm and he stumbled backward, begging for help, crying out against the blood that flowed from his neck and chest. Even then, those twin green orbs of fury transfixed him, two suns of fire, two hells sucking him in, until—

The eyes tore away. Charles sagged into his own bloodstained clothing in relief. His ears filled with howling and roaring, a crack like bone against metal, the limping growls of a wounded animal and then a curious sound. The sound of metal teeth engaging each other, the flex and push of a mainspring. A sound that gave him, as all gears did, great joy.

He found himself looking into lamp-lit eyes, soft as the moon coming from behind a cloud. Two arms—steel and rivets and beams—enfolded and lifted him. "Bridget," he whispered through the blood in his mouth. "You took the body?"

Bridget, if she could be called that, cradled his bloody form to a metal chest. Ridley, beaten and bloody, slunk away. She could no longer speak, but her thoughts to her brother spoke of holding on, of courage as they made their long trip back.

✪✪✪

Observe now as ash and bone are forgotten in the engagement of escape wheel and pinion, in the steady heartbeat of the impulse pin, and in the tightly coiled life of the mainspring. Observe as gears strain and steam roars, as a gleaming figure runs through a dark place to find safety.

Ridley sought to wind the spring on fear and to grease gears with threats, but now, it tenses and releases, tenses and releases, because once Charles held her, and begged her not to leave, and now she holds him, and she will not let him go until she knows he will remain with her.

Spencer Ellsworth *wrote his first novel at seven years old and never recovered. Since then, he's worked in wilderness survival, special education, publishing, and now teaches and administrates at a small college. His work has appeared or is forthcoming in the* Magazine of Fantasy & Science Fiction, *Michael Moorcock's* New Worlds, *and* Tor.com. *He lives in Bellingham, Washington, with his wife and three children. You can find him at spencerellsworth.com.*

The Lady in the Ghastlight

Liane Merciel

✿✿✿

The lady in the glass transfixed him.

She whirled around the lantern's glowing wick, hair a comet of blue flame, tiny limbs of light perfect in every detail. Abernathy could make out fingers stretched in the joy of her dance. Fingers! Each one slender as an eyelash, graceful as laughter. They beckoned to him. He was sure of it.

He stepped away, wiping the astonishment from his face. Uneasily, he looked around, but none of the roughnecks in the audience had seen him gawking. They were too caught up in their own amazement.

Abernathy couldn't fault them. He'd been as astounded as any of them.

This was a carnival, not even a proper exhibition. There wasn't a scientific innovation or legitimate man of learning among them. It was just a bunch of dusty tents filled with freaks and frauds who gulled farmhands with crooked games and tawdry peepshows until their marks had enough and drove them away like a flock of patch-winged crows. Abernathy had only come because he'd heard that Li Chan, a celebrated inventor from the East, would be displaying her creations at the carnival. It was said that Madame Li hoped showing the wonders of modern science to the uneducated might open their minds to the possibilities in steam and might even persuade some of them to pursue the technologic arts themselves or allow their children to indulge in such fancies.

Personally, Abernathy believed that to be foolishness—these rustics would never be able to distinguish Madame Li's masterpieces from mere carnival trickery—but he'd been willing to subdue his distaste for the chance to see her achievements in person. Tales of her inventions had galvanized his circle for months. At the last World's Fair, Madame Li had exhibited a peacock whose tail feathers were organ pipes, each one blowing a plume of colored steam tuned to a different note so that the bird produced a symphony of rainbow and song. She'd shown a steam-powered monkey so cleverly articulated that it could leap from branch to branch just like the real animal. Most intriguing of all, she'd discovered a new chemical compound that vaporized at a lower temperature and into greater volume than water. The implications for steam-powered mechanics were potentially incredible. When Abernathy had heard about *that*, he'd been determined to brave any number of carnival crowds to see it.

Yet upon arrival, he'd been told that Madame Li had left the carnival three weeks ago, accepting an invitation to lecture on the university circuit instead. Her tent had been given over to another exhibition, and it was there that Abernathy now stood.

He'd expected disappointment, of course. No carnival show could possibly compare to Madame Li's whistling peacock or capering monkey, and nothing about the garish paintings outside this tent promised that its entertainments would be any less crude than the rest. "See the lady in the ghastlight," they'd blared. "A spirit of fairy fire!"

He'd thought that might be a trick of electricity. Perhaps, at most, a tube filled with that odd red gas the British chemists had distilled from air some years back.

What he found, instead, was magic.

He knew no other word for it. No painting or projection could create that fiery nymph spinning in her cage. No pyrotechnic chemical could draw those shapely limbs from air, nor drape them in veils of fluid flame.

He had to know how it was done.

Outside, Abernathy seized the ticket-taker's sleeve. "Who owns that lamp?"

"Why, sir, I do." The ticket-taker smiled. He was a small man, ill-favored with the aspect of a toad squatting atop a mushroom stool. His clothes crumpled into him, shapeless and dirty.

"How does it work? Electrical wires? Gas discharge?"

The man shook his head. "Couldn't tell you. She is as she was when I found her."

Abernathy pressed down his frustration. It was unreasonable to expect that a carnival barker would know. How could he? Doubtlessly, the man was ignorant of basic scientific principles. But if *he* could study the lantern, could unravel its secrets . . . the advancement! The acclaim! "How much do you want for it? And don't say it's not for sale."

"Oh, she's for sale." An odd look crossed the ticket-taker's face. Fear, or maybe hope. Or hunger. "For a particular coin."

"What coin?"

Silently, the barker held out a dirt-creased palm. Upon it gleamed a heavy silver round: a Finisterra nickel, one of the solid globe-and-Liberty pieces that had been minted a decade back to commemorate the charting of the last frontiers on the globe. The Earth was known, its wonders measured and mapped, and the achievement had been stamped into a collector's coin.

But this one was different. Its Lady Liberty face had been etched into a skull with a raw, bleeding stump for a neck. Darkness pulsed in the metal's grooves. The sway of shadows across its face lent it an awful semblance of movement—a sense, surreal yet powerful, that something malign lurked and laughed and looked through the empty eyes of that coin.

"She only wants one," the ticket man said. "If it's the right one. Then she'll go to you as she came to me. No other way to buy that lady's favor."

Abernathy tore his gaze away with difficulty, swallowing. He'd seen such coin carvings before, although never one so grisly. A gentleman of his acquaintance was an amateur folklore enthusiast and collected them. Perhaps he could be persuaded to part with one. The Finisterra itself was only a nickel. How much could the etchings be worth? A dollar? Five?

He pulled on his gloves. "A deal."

✿✿✿

His acquaintance, the architect Marshall Brown, wasn't available to help. Brown had embarked upon an educational tour of Italy, return date uncertain.

At first, Abernathy thought his friend's absence a minor inconvenience. He wanted to discover the lady's secret for himself. He'd seen the final effect, and he had a fine scientific mind; therefore it should have been no great difficulty to puzzle out how it was done. All the world's workings followed rational rules.

Yet the mystery of the fiery dancer in the lantern-glass proved impenetrable. No clever configuration of steam valves began to approach what he'd seen in that carnival tent. No sequence of firecracker tricks could trace the faintest shadow of her shape.

Abernathy couldn't crack it. The problem rose before him like a glass mountain, refusing to grant the smallest toehold. It repelled his understanding entirely.

Day after night after day, he threw himself against it. Weeks vanished into sleepless fever. Abernathy broke appointments, neglected friends, let unanswered letters pile up before his door in a paper bulwark against unwanted intrusions. The pressurized locks he'd built to guard his room hissed and groaned in displeasure at his neglect, their pipes and kettles rattling in dismay.

Abernathy scarcely noticed. He had no time for lesser concerns. His hair grew gray and wild. His cheeks sunk into sallow pits. On the rare occasions that he emerged from his study to renew his supplies of colorants and cocaine, the good people of the city drew their children away.

And at the end of it, he was no closer than he'd been the first time he'd looked into a bubbling pot and wondered what magic turned water to air.

He *dreamed* of her. The lady in the ghastlight danced through his slumbers, tiny ballerina feet sketching curlicues of fire across his drowsing mind. He saw her smile as a curved dimple in the flames, heard her laughter like the trill of some faraway bird. Abernathy always woke shivering after such dreams, feeling that he'd stood at the precipice of some discovery greater than any inventor before him had envisioned.

But none of his experiments brought her any closer to his waking grasp. He could see no way to catch her magic in his flues.

Finally, in desperation, he went looking for a carnival coin.

He didn't really know where to find one. His friend, the architect, had purchased his etched nickels from the people who made them, but he'd never named a specific artisan. Perhaps there was none. The point of folk art, after all, was that it reflected a people, not one person. And as Brown remained in Italy, Abernathy couldn't ask him.

But he had a general sense of who had carved Brown's coins, and they weren't his kind of people. A gentleman of learning, Abernathy had always avoided the vagrants and roustabouts who drifted like flotsam around the city's eddies. He knew they followed rail lines, though, and that their camps sprouted like mushrooms in the shelter of briars and thickets.

Choosing a direction at random—almost at random—Abernathy headed west, following the trains' path of iron and gravel. He carried a stout walking stick and a hidden pistol against the risk that some desperate might think to rob him. Within an hour, he had an ugly collection of blisters, and his legs protested bitterly against the unaccustomed exertion, but he ignored the pain. Discovery demanded much from those who would be worthy.

Although Abernathy had gone west to prolong the light—he had no wish to stumble upon any desperados after dark—it was well into twilight before he glimpsed the first red flicker of their campfires between the trees. The day was a fading gasp of blue in black by the time he actually reached them.

Five gaunt men in scarecrow rags sat around that fire. A dented tin pan rested on a rock in its center. Something brown bubbled inside. It didn't quite smell like meat. The men raised their heads as he neared, watching him hungrily and without smiles.

Abernathy patted his pistol pocket for comfort. "Gentlemen."

No one answered.

Clearing his throat, Abernathy tried again. He took his hand from his pocket. "I'd like to make a purchase."

"Of what?" asked one. A gray beard, filthy as a saloon doormat, hung down to the derelict's chest. His mouth was a pocket of darkness in its gnarled mess.

"A coin."

The men around the fire exchanged a look. Abernathy had the sudden, uncomfortable sense that they had known his purpose before he'd appeared and that his answer conveyed not information but willingness.

Willingness for what? Apprehension twisted low in his gut.

The gray-bearded man stirred the bubbling mass in the pan. "What kind of coin?"

"A nickel. A carved nickel." Abernathy held his thumb and forefinger apart, absurdly, as if they might not recognize the coin without a show of its size. "The Finisterra. With a skull on it, I suppose. I don't really know."

Another glance around the fire. A current of fear, this time. Abernathy felt it amplify through each of them. It hit him last and hardest.

The graybeard shook his head, staring fixedly into the pan. "Can't help you."

Abernathy's tongue was dry as a gravestone. "Surely one of you must carve—"

"Not the kind you want." The vagrant looked up at him, finally, and there was such a bleakness in his rheumy yellow eyes that Abernathy stumbled back, reaching for his hidden pistol. He tried hard to believe the gun's promise that *he* could control whatever peril might be here.

The graybeard didn't react. He poked at the pan, ignoring the weapon trembling at him from fifteen feet away. "What you want, you buy with your own coin. Ain't none of us going to pay that toll for you. Not here, not at any camp around here. Go on and ask if you want. You'll get the same answer. That cross is yours to carry."

"I don't have any idea what you're talking about."

"Good for you." The vagrant shrugged, bony shoulders rustling against his shabby jacket. "Stay lucky, you never will."

✪✪✪

Abernathy bought his own Finisterra nickel. He bought twenty. He bought engraving tools, too, and he set about learning them with the same intensity he'd devoted to mastering the skills of medicine and machinery.

Engraving was close kin to his other arts, and it didn't take long to develop a basic proficiency with the tools. Soon he was able to mechanize the process of grinding Lady Liberty's features into facelessness. Having delegated that task to a coal-bellied machine, Abernathy could focus on the finer details of the work. By the fifth nickel, he'd mastered the lines and hollows that transformed the Lady's face into a skull's fleshless grin. By the tenth, his carvings were grislier and more detailed than the one the ticket-taker had shown him.

They had nothing of its menace, though. He could sculpt the face of fear, but he couldn't grip its clammy essence. Abernathy's carvings remained inert, with none of the awful, pulsing life he'd felt flickering under the thin metal skin of the carnival coin. Somehow, he knew in the deep coil of his bowels that he'd never win the lady without that.

To learn how to find it, he turned to those who had mastered the science and art of fear.

For science, he found a muttering phrenologist who purchased the heads of the criminally insane and boiled them down to skulls in his mold-streaked basement. Abernathy took notes on the deformed dimensions of the craniums that lined the phrenologist's shelves and tried to replicate them in his carvings. The skulls of madmen, he thought, would surely serve him best. Their very bones had swollen with the extremities of agitation. Ideal.

For art, he sought out a writer of penny dreadfuls, who told him lurid tales in exchange for liquor and laudanum. Every night, after the writer passed out, Abernathy went back to his workshop and tried to scratch the man's delirious visions into metal. Sometimes, he almost succeeded, especially when he could use shadow to create the space for suggestion that existed between the writer's words, but the coins never quite came alive in his hands. The metallic tang of their dust never transformed into the cold sweat of real fright.

That was the key. It tickled at his fingertips, just beyond his grasp. Abernathy needed *life*. That was what he'd felt thrumming in the carnival coin. That was the secret of the lady's dance.

He didn't have the power to create it, not by any art or science. No one but the Lord above could draw life from the simple earth.

But maybe he didn't have to create it. Maybe he just had to catch it.

Ain't none of us going to pay that toll for you, the vagrant had said.

How wrong he'd been.

❀❀❀

He'd planned to begin with animals. Pigeons, maybe, or rats. They could be cheaply purchased, and the bodies were easy to hide. He'd expected to need a few weeks to experiment before he'd be ready to try trapping a human soul in a coin.

Fate had other plans.

A carriage running at reckless speed. A man who didn't look before crossing. A scream and a squeal and the wet crush of bone. Teeth scattered over the cobblestones like hail. The driver cursing, the horse shrieking. Nothing from the victim save the grotesque soggy labor of breath, the difficulty of it overmastering him.

Abernathy ran forward. Scarcely able to believe his luck, he stooped on the red-slick street, mouthing inane noises of concern. The driver had control enough of the horse to keep its hooves from his head, but its flailing deterred other passersby from coming too near. *Perfect*.

Abernathy cradled the deflating ball of the victim's skull in one hand and pressed a fat silver nickel to the sticky pulp of his mouth with the other.

Time faded to nothing behind the hammering beats of his heart.

If no one noticed, if no one stopped him . . .

The victim's breath blew scarlet bubbles between his fingers. Smaller and smaller they came until the last lacked the strength to break its bloody film. It stuck to the nickel and was still.

Abernathy stepped back, frowning gravely. He picked his fallen hat up from the cobbles and replaced it with a solemn air. "Gone, I'm afraid," he told the onlookers. "Nothing anyone could have done for the poor fellow."

Then, victorious, he walked away.

There was a change in the Finisterra nickel, a thrill and thrum in the metal that he'd never sensed before, but Abernathy felt an unexpected tremor of superstition when he thought of looking at it on the walk home.

No. Patience would be rewarded. He'd wait until he got back to his workshop.

When he did, sweaty and breathless from nerves and the eager speed of his walk, he opened his shaking fingers to find a red-smeared skull grinning up from his palm.

It was better than any he'd carved. It was better than them, and it *was* them, all of them at once: the early ones with the gross, unintentional deformities etched by a clumsy hand, and the late works that rivaled Durer and Dore for their sophisticated depictions of suffering. Every affliction that plagued the phrenologist's subjects was stamped into that skull, even the ones that could never coexist. The cranium simultaneously dimpled and bulged; the nostrils were both wide and narrow, straight and crooked.

And the horrors . . . the horrors of the penny dreadfuls were all there, lovingly assembled, each and every one tattooed into the nickel's face.

No mortal hand could have made such a thing. He didn't like to think what could. Trembling, Abernathy put the coin aside and swept a sheaf of letters over it, burying the image in paper and dust.

He could still feel it, though. He could still *see* it, staring at him with horrible empty eyes, grinning at him with horrible metal teeth.

Shuddering, Abernathy fled his workshop.

That night he lay in a little tent of blankets on his bed, a lamp burning on the side table as it had when he was a boy, and did not sleep.

A week later, the carnival was back.

It wasn't the same one. This caravan had two strongmen, not one. In place of a dancing bear it had the Astounding Fish Boy, whose hands were fins and whose skin was scales. The peepshow girls were dark rather than fair, billing themselves as the Sultan's Daughters instead of the Czar's White Swans. The barker at the gate wasn't a dwarf on stilts but a pair of conjoined twins who juggled spinning batons in a double-eight between their four hands.

But it was loud and gaudy and full of bald-faced frauds, and it had a tent billing the Lady in the Ghastlight, the Fairy in the Flames.

Abernathy jostled to the front of the line.

The ticket-taker was the same man he remembered. Older, squatter, more jaundiced, but indisputably the same. "You're back."

"I am."

"You have the coin?"

Abernathy held out a nickel. Not *the* nickel but an ordinary coin. "Let me see her first."

The toadlike man made it disappear. "Go on in."

She was there. Others were, too, but Abernathy paid no mind to their crushing crudeness or the sour smell of the press. The gawkers in the audience counted for nothing. Only *she* mattered.

The lady danced within her lantern, enchanting and eternal, so pure in her beauty that Abernathy's eyes filled with tears. The blue flame of her hair whipped across her curved cage, leaving a trail of dazzlement across his sight. He longed to touch her, possess her, lift away that protective glass and feel her fire on his skin.

He stayed until the final show and then, shaken, stumbled out. Around him the carnival's lights were blinking out, row by row, their steampipes creaking as they cooled. Stale ozone and hot grease suffused the air. Between the tents, the marks and spectators drained away, returning to their workaday world.

The ticket-taker was waiting. "You still want to buy?"

"Yes." The word came out ugly, guttural, the need in it too raw. Abernathy couldn't help himself. His fingers curled into his pocket, seeking the solidity of the coin he'd made. He offered it with a shaking hand. "I have your price."

The ticket-taker wasn't as quick to seize this one. He looked at it for a while, and then he looked up at Abernathy. Something like pity flickered across his face. "Not many come back with that. Lots ask, but not many come back. Five, in all the years I've been here."

"You've sold her before?"

The man's smile was impossibly wide. It showed no teeth, only wet emptiness between his gums. "What makes you think I'm the one does the selling? It's the lady makes that choice. Tells me where to take her, when to go. Five times before she's done it. Now you're the sixth."

"How—"

"She didn't stay with any of the ones who came before." The ticket-taker nodded at the graven skull. "That's the beginning, not the end. A fire don't just need a spark. It needs *fuel.* You might think you understand that, and maybe you do, but none of the fellows who came before you did. They couldn't hold her."

"But you can?"

The man shook his jowly head. "She don't belong to me. I just carry her around. Show her to rubes and gawping gulls. Every so often, to someone like you." He pinched the coin from Abernathy's hand. "You've paid your price. A wiser fellow might change his mind right about now, but then, I reckon a wise one wouldn't have come back in the first place."

Abernathy nodded, only half listening. She was his. That was the important part. The lady in the lantern belonged to *him.*

He waited for an eternity of seconds until the ticket-taker returned. When the man finally came back, Abernathy exclaimed in dismay. The fairy was gone. Only the wick—a slim, straight core of bone—glowed weakly within her lantern. "What trick is this?"

"She'll come back when you call her. She likes to be admired."

Scowling, Abernathy took the lantern. He clutched it protectively to his chest as he returned through the dark streets and gaslit avenues to the familiar bricks of his workshop.

There, hastily but reverently, he cleared a space for her amid his gravers and diagrams. The need for those tools was past. The lantern was his.

He cupped the warm glass between his hands, willing the wick to ignite. *Come to me.* He wasn't sure if he said the words aloud, and he wasn't sure if that mattered. What did a fairy hear? *Dance for me. I need you.*

In a flurry of fire, she answered. The bone wick ignited into splendor, and around its white pillar, the lady spun her dervish spell. She whirled, and she laughed, and she kicked her tiny feet high, and the flurry of her veils whipped his senses away. Her song was a high, sweet piping to shatter an angel's heart, and her smile was a secret like none he'd ever known. Every pirouette was an epiphany, every fouetté a revelation.

And then she was gone, and nothing he did could call her back. He pressed his fingers to the glass, but it gave him nothing. Even the memory of warmth within its curves quickly faded.

She likes to be admired.

He tried, feeling more foolish with each attempt. But his words of praise met with deaf silence, and flowers heaped outside the lantern just wilted and went to black. Offerings of ribbons, fragrance, and bright paste jewels failed to move her. The lady of the lantern shared none of her mortal sisters' tastes.

There was only one coin Abernathy knew she'd take. One way to fuel that fire.

Neither oil nor gas burned in her lantern. It contained nothing but a wick of bone, and now that Abernathy had it to study, he saw that ivory needle was charred to ash at the end of her dance.

Carefully he prized the lantern open and, using medical tweezers, extracted the wick. It had been sanded down considerably, as if whittled on a lathe, but he could identify the familiar knobs and crevices of finger joints. Human, of course.

The lady, he now felt certain, was nothing so innocent as a fairy. She was a hungrier sort of spirit, and her appetites were bloody. That was why she required a dead man's coin. The admiration she wanted was that which the gods of old had demanded: sacrifice. And that was her test of faith.

The tweezers clattered against his desk. Abernathy sank back in his work chair, frightened and disheartened. He had hoped to comprehend what he'd seen, and he thought he'd begun to . . . but the answer was one he couldn't accept.

Death alone didn't deter him. Medical advances required a willingness to experiment—and to accept certain costs in the course of those experiments—that swiftly weeded out the weak-livered. The technologies of steam and steel could be lethal, too, scalding or crushing those who failed to treat them with due respect. Abernathy had made his peace with that years ago.

But this wasn't science. There was no rationale to dead men's coins or fingerbone wicks. Every step had led him deeper into an ancient and murky way of thinking, a realm where unreason reigned and superstitions held power. The *only* power. The lady had lured him with glimpses of understanding, but it was a nonsense understanding, filled with the illogic of dreams.

She had showed him magic, and rationality held no sway where magic ruled.

Death was not a price too high. But reason was.

Surprising himself with the sudden violence of the gesture, Abernathy knocked his engraving tools and carved coins into the feeder basket of the grinder he'd used to do his early roughwork. The sharp blades nicked his arm, tattooing crooked red beads across his shirtsleeve, but he welcomed the pain as penance. He hit the switch, feeding coal and air into the machine, and water gurgled in its kettle as the grinder woke. The basket tipped up, spilling into its maw, and the discordant clangor of the tools being pulverized into powder broke a burden from his soul.

Let the stamped reality of Finisterra nickels be their only reality. Abernathy didn't want to scratch through their metal faces in search of mystery, not anymore, and he certainly didn't want to find it. Once, he'd been a man of science, and he'd believed the world was ruled by natural law. He wanted that assurance again.

Squeezing his eyes shut, Abernathy laid a handkerchief over the cold lantern, feeling like he was draping a flag over a coffin. In a way, perhaps, he was. A white flag, a dream's shroud. A farewell to a magic he had barely known.

To the lady in the ghastlight, whose dance could not be of his world.

Liane Merciel *is the author of novels including* The River Kings' Road, Dragon Age: Last Flight, *and the Pathfinder Tales books* Nightglass *and* Nightblade, *as well as the forthcoming* Hellknight *(April 2016). She lives in Philadelphia, where she practices law, plays with dogs, and tries to grow fruit trees on the roof. Sometimes it works.*

Cuckoo

Richard Pett

○○○

Her sound is with me always. Her heartbeat is behind my heartbeat, the song of below. A steady susurrus of wheezing is my second bride, and hers is the song I hear most even from so far away. One day, she will see me to my grave and still her song will go on. No one will ever see her to hers. Her lot is to toil, not to rest.

It is night, the cloying darkness of below where the work doesn't stop. Sweat cannot escape and hangs in the stale air, drowning in human toil. I cannot sleep, and the more I wonder about why I cannot sleep despite my weariness, the more awake I become, waiting for tomorrow's shift. Or is it tonight's? Darkness strips away rationale and nurtures primal feelings and fears. Where concentration should be easy is the easiest place to become confused.

I abandon my attempts to slumber, so I rise, bleary-eyed. Outside in the bedroom, my daughter cries. I hear her mother whispering. I flounder for cigarettes, a blind man feeling for comfort. The sulphur burn is blinding as I strike a match, the fire's echo dancing in my vision. Sucking on the teat, I fumble to stand and light the pyrebeetle lamp. Her victims crackle and spit, crawling from each other as the flame engulfs them and their immolation turns them into light.

The room gropes into uneasy view as though ashamed at being disturbed. Simple function lurks in all the corners: a stove, a tawdry washstand with the broken shard of a grimy mirror hanging above, the old wooden larder lurking by the leaded window that somehow clutches at the odd shard of daylight lost down here.

"You have a window," they tell us. "You are lucky."

We do not tell them that we have two, that both have long surrendered to opacity beneath the grimy spit that encrusts their exteriors, places untouched by humans since they were first fitted.

The horsehair couch creaks as I rise and begin to function as a person in the new day. I light the stove to make tea, awaken slowly, and prepare myself for work. All about me is the distant ceaseless toiling song of the fleshgines. Some call it their hymn. To me it is more a song of distress.

I comb my greasy, angry hair and shave my protesting skin. The blunt razor pulls rather than cuts. I bear the smell of cheap waxy soap that has gorged on too many chymicals, perhaps it is my feral scent, my spoor tattoo. It is the smell of me, of scrubbing and dirt and the mask of sweat. The mirror has cracked twice before and now bears only a sullen vague face in its depths. I stare, perhaps hoping it will change, pulling skin back to remove years. Movement from the other room draws back a creased smile in my echo. I tell my darling I'm going to work, tell her to remain in bed until they are both better. Tell her not to worry.

The machine is waiting.

I join the dance to industry. Segs on metal echo through the shaft, countless shuffling feet descending into the bowels of the city through winding iron spiral stairs. The work clock clicks out four, and outside, the salt rain begins to fall through the slumbering night into the soul of the city. High above, on the cauldron streets of Brine, the tidal storm will be drowning the city streets. Twice a day, the tides rush beyond the levee and scream into the city below, driving her countless waterwheels of industry. The dampness follows me down into the bilges of the city. Drip, drip, drip. As I descend, my watery pursuer echoes my descent and threatens to drown me in her embrace. Perhaps, water is my third bride. I try to remember the last time I felt truly dry and fail.

In the sweaty air below, the machine waits for me to tend her.

I smell the machine long before I see her. Her dry sweat of labor pervades high beyond her reach, telling me she still works, telling me she has not halted in that awful stillness that comes if a machine ceases. They do not die, but sometimes, they fracture or halt and are discarded. I try not to think of the stories I have heard. What would she give to escape? Does the thought ever occur to her? I enter the chamber. Somewhere nearby, her two sisters toil away as endlessly as she does. I've never seen her companions, nor their attendees, but sometimes they call to each other, these machines of gristle and bone. I imagine they are talking, but about what, I never guess. Sometimes, I could swear they are singing. Just once, it seemed that the song was taken up by them all, the countless engines calling to each other across the bilges of the city. Some said it was the end of the world approaching.

As I arrive, my fellow takes his leave. I try not to meet his stare, not after the beating I gave him for the one he gave her—an anger that nearly cost me all.

"Beasts are to be beaten," the overseer had said afterwards. "We do not beat men anymore."

Not their flesh, anyway, I thought afterwards.

I enter the sough, slithering into the fold. Above me and about me, her thin limbs stretch and arch upward, arms pumping and dislocating. Within, like a behemoth crippled spider, is the fleshgine's body. From inside that fleshy cathedral, her eye stares at me: perhaps recognizing me, perhaps just hungering. I move toward her, soothing, and reach out to stroke her calloused flesh. Why do I bother? Does she feel it? I carefully check the copper pipes that enter her spine, her suckling mouth for feeding the elixir—the lowest grade of elixir—that keeps her moving. Endlessly moving.

Every hour, on the hour, she must be fed the elixir. We You know the consequences if you fail. I fill the empty trough before her with water, and from her wide mouth, a tongue lolls out, lapping. Why did they give her a mouth? The water splashes across the floor, joining other pools of moisture to create the echo chamber I occupy. Her lapping disturbs the image, fractures it. I am the only one who gives her drink. It does not need it, they have told me, the elixir gives it everything it needs. I do not care what they tell me; I know only that she likes it.

She laps at the water greedily as my watch begins. Her rhythm goes on, taking the water from the mines far below and back up to the levee, gulping air into the windpipe of the city.

Why do I call it *her*?

Because I make her suffer.

I prepare the elixir away from her. I try not to let her see it, even though there seems no logic to my secrecy with the machine. When I feed her, she suffers, her body tormented by the very thing that keeps her alive. Burning within her, the stuff of life jolts her into continuation. I inject her as quickly as I can to get it over with, using soft words as I do.

Her body shudders as the elixir boils within her, feeding her, driving her on. The whole chamber shakes with her misery, her movements slowing as it seethes into her veins and arteries and muscles and nourishes them, feeds them, drives them.

Soon, but not soon enough, the first of twelve doses is within her, and her work and mine goes on.

Much later, I leave my ward as the other man returns. Eyes not meeting, we pass like strangers. He only watches.

"She is a machine," he says, "a machine of flesh and blood made to toil. She feels nothing. She only serves. You are sentimental."

It is soon night again. I lie awake smoking and wondering. Beyond, all is silent save for the distant wheezing of the flesh machines. No one stirs.

Something moves in the dark: cockroach or manyleg, perhaps. I wait for it to halt, its scratching noise taunting me. I rise. I know the stories about insects and babies. I determine to resolve the battle in my favor. I heroically grip my shoe and fumble for my matches, phosphorous flaring as my eyes stare into the corner where I heard the noise.

I see nothing. I wait, alert, eyes fixed on the floor.

A noise echoes from the wall by the washstand. I stand clumsily, look around. There is nothing.

The noise echoes again right behind me. I turn and face myself in the mirror shard, momentarily confused. The noise is from behind the mirror.

No, not behind.

Within.

Then I see it. A thing behind me. I turn and there is nothing. The room behind me is empty.

Yet it was there in the mirror.

Not enough sleep?

I saw it.

The long face.

It was there, behind me in the glass.

But just within the mirror.

I know the stories.

I tell my beloved that everything will be alright. Soon, they will both be better.

When I leave, the mirror is in my pocket.

I wrap my clothes about me and slumber to work through oily corridors and decay and meaningless graffiti. I am Gideon Weal. I am Gideon Weal, and I tend the machine. In the streets above, I wonder if the sun has groped through the smog or if it is dark. When did I last feel the wind on my face? When did I last see the sun? I imagine it imperfectly as I wander on, holding the mirror tight.

As I reach the long spiral stair, I grip the mirror in my hand. Momentarily, I am of two minds, but within seconds, the glass is shattered on the metal walkway, shards fracturing into slivers beneath my feet.

I've heard the stories.

I tell the machine about the thing in the mirror. "The thing in the mirror is gone," I tell her, "its threshold shattered and lost."

She says nothing. Her arms arc and grip and wrench and toil in the clammy chamber we share for half of my life.

She has an odd face: too much flesh trying to stay in too little skin. She is blemished.

She is my friend, my wife, my lover.

Bolete.

I tell her about the mirror. She asks me what I saw.

"A face—a long face. A face without humanity," I tell her.

She puts her arm around me and tells me she understands why I broke the mirror. The baby comes first. The baby grins up at me, and I hug them both tightly.

One day things will be different.

That night, I sleep like a log.

She is there again in the morning, lurking in her mist of sweat. The Machine. The instrument, the fleshgine: thing of gristle and muscle and bone. Always moving, always toiling, her limbs dislocating back and forth, pumping air into the mines beyond our homes.

I wonder if they are kin, the machines?

Do they think?

I pause, wiping the sweat from my brow. The heat clings to me, her smell enveloping me. I ready the elixir for her, sensing her despair. Her muscles tense; her movements become more nervous, erratic. I move as quickly as I can. I clamber up the iron rungs and over her body. Her flanks heave below me as I reach for the copper pipes to feed her through. The elixir hangs at my belt. Momentarily, I see something move across the puddle of water below me. A thing too swift to be mundane. I wait, staring at the slippery floor. It moves again at the edges of the slick oily tar beneath me.

Long face.

This time, the face is hungry, envious. It leers up at me from the liquid. Is it smiling? It drags its crooked fleshy form up toward me. I'm lost in its familiarity, its brotherhood, yet appalled by just how different it is.

The figure staggers to the edge of the reflection. With one swift movement, its hand reaches up, overly long digits groping at the edges of the oily water, violating the chamber with its presence as it tries to drags itself from the reflection and into the mundane world.

I look about me, seeking a weapon.

"Daydreaming again?"

The voice of the overseer below. She stares up at me and immediately senses my fear, which she takes to be fear of her. She wraps herself in it and scowls up at me, her uniform starched like her soul.

Below her, my echo fades into a confused blur of ripples as she walks across the moist floor, lacerating the image. The fingers slip into the oily liquid and are lost. I breathe a sigh of relief.

She is angry. The fleshgine is sluggish. It may need replacing, but for now, the elixir must be stronger, she says. The dose will be doubled, and the production had better double with it.

I agree with the overseer: we have been slack. She is right.

She tells me she has seen Sedge, my partner. The word seems wrong when she pronounces it, laced with hidden meaning. He brokers no nonsense from the machine. His methods are stricter and more productive. She hopes I'll take a lesson from his ways.

I tell her I shall.

But when she is gone, I hate her and him.

I stare at the machine as she continues to toil. How would they dispose of her, I wonder. She cannot die. How would they end her? Would they do so?

I stare back at the rippling waters below and look for my mop, determined that, for once, the floor will be dry.

That evening, the stairs take an eternity to climb; a mountain ridge of industry and time rises beyond the clock. I am exhausted from my labors, but for now, the echo has gone, lost in a panicked cleaning of the floor. I stagger upward, warily eyeing every dancing rusty smear for a pool.

I see none, but by the time I reach home, I'm almost sleeping on my feet.

Bolete leads me to bed and closes the door behind me. Beyond, I hear her whispering to our child. I try not to sleep, but exhaustion soon claims me.

✪✪✪

It is dark when I awaken, but I am not alone. There is a steady breathing beside me. She stirs as I stir and then is still once more.

My mind begins to wander back to the machine and to the thing in the mirror—the echo vision. I idly wonder if the overseer has a softer side and decide she probably hasn't. What will happen if the machine fails? Will we be punished, will we be dismissed? I try not to worry. I try to focus upon happy things.

She stirs again beside me, shuffling in the darkness in our bed.

Then I hear my wife singing a lullaby to our daughter in the room outside.

I pause, frozen, wondering at the weight beside me as it turns in the bed. Our bed. I'm caught between outrage and terror: a need to see and to shout and a wish not to know.

What is lying beside me?

I gather my thoughts as I withdraw into myself, arching and pulling back my limbs as though trying to absorb them, my anger and violation breeding and boiling as I cringe further into myself.

I've heard the stories about Between.

I reach for my jacket and matches: breath paused, eyes fixed in the darkness to my side. I strike the match and move back from the bed.

In the room beyond, my wife stirs, an unspoken bond teasing her into alertness.

It has a human shape, but I take a further step back as I realize it is long for a person—too long. I drop the burning match into the lantern. Her passengers begin to hiss and blister as light blossoms. My claustrophobic surroundings take on an oily slowness: the bedstead, the crib, the trunk all grow from the shadows. Our tiny second window glowers from behind inadequate curtains lurking beside a trio of paintings of stern kin long dead. The leering wardrobe cowers in the corner, and I spy the walking cane on top—images of Bolete injured after a fall, a hobbled bride. I see the cane's brass head and stout shaft and make for it.

The bedclothes move as something starts to slithers away, exposing wan skin. It is waxy, fluid, a concoction of me but stripped bare. Stripped beyond flesh, I sense my moods and inadequacies and fears hanging upon its flesh like clothes as it slithers across the room, its reflections tethered to the glaring echoes of the lantern in the polished surfaces of the room's poisoned black window and glassy portraits.

I reach the cane and strike out at the fluid thing and its reflection. I thrash out again and again, fury burning at the impotence of my efforts as I smash at the flowing form of the long-faced man. And as I strike, he becomes even more like me, a mocking echo.

From somewhere outside, I hear a baby crying and a woman screaming.

My anger grows, my feeling of violation seething.

I move forward, trying to hem my foe into a corner, trying to force it out of the window. It lurches back toward the space, its revoltingly distended form brushing the curtains aside as it is caught in the lantern's light reflecting in the window's glass. It is trapped in the reflection. I give out a long scream and drive the cane forward through it and out into the raging rain outside. I hear and feel something slither away from me and fall.

I drop to the floor as the rain pounds in. Is it gone? I stare around frantically for the echo, smashing the remaining glass in the portraits and window until there is nothing but ground glass fragments. No escape or entry for it.

Then I realize I am not alone. The door behind me lies open, and Bolete stares, clutching our child deep into her chest.

Her look is of terror.

Don't worry, I tell her. It is gone. The beast is gone.

Long face is dead.

She says she understands.

I try to console her, to touch her and keep them safe. "It is dead," I tell her. "We are safe."

As I try to touch her, she backs away. Perhaps, the baby needs to be taken away, just until everything is safe, until we know everything is safe for her.

I agree, saying everything will be all right.

Everything will be all right.

✿✿✿

The overseer tells me she has heard my wife has left me. She is sorry, she says, but it cannot affect the work, or everyone will suffer. She cannot let that happen. If one fails, all fail. She is sure I understand.

I tell her I do. It is the first time I have heard her say that she is sorry about anything.

The machine must work harder, she says as she hands me more elixir, stronger elixir. This will make the machine better, faster, she says.

I ask her if the elixir will make the machine suffer more.

"The machine is just a beast of burden," she tells me. "It has no feelings. It is born to work, nothing more." I am to stop referring to it as living.

I say I shall, even though I mouth the words only to please her, use them without meaning.

I think of the word *born*.

✿✿✿

Night. I know my eyes are open.

There is a noise.

A subtle noise.

A sound behind the walls.

"Who's there?" I call out, fumbling for a matchbox. I find it, sulphur and balsa and damp, and strike the match. It blossoms.

I know who is there.

The wall judders as though a fist drives against it from outside. Yet outside is outside, and there is nothing there.

I stare around the shadowy room. All is normal: the window, the larder, the sofa, the washstand. They are as they always have been, but they are different now. I have removed the echoes, blackened the windows, grimed the sheen—there are no reflections here. No way in.

The walls pound again. I lean against them, sobbing. "What do you want?" I ask it. "What do you want?"

I hear a whisper from the other side of the wall and press my ear against it to hear closer.

From somewhere beyond, I hear a figure do the same, sense as something presses against the other side and listens.

It is something weeping. "I only want what you have," it says in my own voice.

What you have.

I tell the voice it cannot have what it wants.

As I lean there in vigil, I vow to put this to an end, to face my enemy from the mirror—to draw him out and snare him.

❁❁❁

The day after, I speak to the man that procures things and ask him to find me a mirror. He seems surprised. Mirrors are bad luck, he says and begins to tell me the stories.

"I know the stories," I tell him. "I'm in one."

He demands a high price.

A day later, I clutch the package tightly, careful not to expose the glass that will draw my enemy out of his hiding place and into my clutches. Soon, the mirror hangs as the old one did, but this time, I am ready for my echo, the would-be cuckoo in my nest.

❁❁❁

I fumble like a blind man in the stairwell. The clock glowers above me, but her angles are changed.

Maybe, I am only dreaming that I'm returning from work. The day has been long. The journey up the stairs is interminable. The reach and stretch above and before me are like a nightmare, their form fluid somehow. I must stop working so hard.

I reach the little door in the bleached and bare corridor and walk in, my movements automatic. There is no one home.

I wander into the functional living room, the horsehair couch and the larder and the washstand are waiting for me. Above the washstand is the mirror.

I walk up to it and peer through.

Outside, in the other place, I see the three figures I always see, living warm and safe in the mundane world I once shared with them.

I wander the space of Between now, sometimes shouting, sometimes weeping, sometimes delirious. The chambers so like my own yet nightmarish, crooked. I share my world with no one else. Even the machine lies still and silent: not dead, simply ceased. When I cannot stop myself, I go to the mirror shard and gaze through. As often as I try to leave it alone, I am drawn back, madness embracing me perhaps.

The scene is always the same, through a glass darkly: unreachable.

Bolete, happy to see me, smiles. I smile back, and we leave the room: my cuckoo and my wife and child. Sometimes, he stares back at me as he leaves the room, this duplicate—stares back and smiles.

Inside the mirror, I am trapped forever.

{{

Richard Pett *got the idea for "Cuckoo" from watching* Eraserhead *too many times while sitting alone in a cellar at his remote Derbyshire farmhouse and drinking strong cider. He thinks the machine is very sad and hopes you agree. A veteran of the gaming industry with over 100 titles to his credit, he's appeared before for Broken Eye Books, who published his novel* Crooked—*also set in the sweaty, tar-drowned, fleshgine-city of Brine. Amongst several gaming books, including the mammoth half-million word* The Blight, *he's working on a collection of unpleasant short stories set in Brine and its crooked sister Between, which he happily describes as* Alice's Adventures in Wonderland *meets* Frankenstein.

The Shadow and the Eye

James Lowder

✿✿✿

Professor Thaxton ignored all the warnings he received about the Eye of Kafiristan, and there were many of them. Once word got out that he had acquired the infamous gem, the London dailies all published editorials proclaiming its dangers. So, too, the major scientific journals, with rhetoric a little more learned but no less steeped in panic. The House of Lords debated the military and economic implications of Thaxton's plans to exploit the Eye—or what they could piece together of those plans from speculation and secondhand report, since he refused all direct inquiries on the matter. The archbishop herself called upon the professor's home in Kew. She hoped to implore him to abandon all uses of the Eye and carried with her letters to the same effect penned by the mahdi, the pope, and several other eminent religious leaders. She returned to Canterbury frustrated, her good counsel undelivered. Thaxton wouldn't even open his front door for Her Grace, though in deference to her great age he kept the clockwork mastiffs penned until she had retreated most of the way to the main gate.

A pair of those clanking, hissing beasts still prowled the estate's front lawn when I arrived later that same day for my appointment with Olivia Thaxton, the professor's wife. At first blush, I took her for a rather plain woman of middle age, self-assured, dressed neatly and for comfort rather than show. When she welcomed me, she did so with genuine good humor. "The hounds won't bother you," she said as she shepherded me briskly along the walkway to the house. She looked back over her shoulder at me and smiled. "Truth be told, they're more sound and fury than actual threat."

If it had been even a few days later, I would have taken her at her word, no matter how absurd the claim might seem. I came to trust that remarkable woman implicitly in almost everything. At that moment, though, my host's apparent desire to be clear of the watchdogs as quickly as possible, coupled with the hounds' bear-trap jaws and generously taloned paws, made too strong a counterargument. I clutched my small suitcase in front of me like a shield and hurried to stay hard on her heels.

Mrs. Thaxton led me through the foyer and past a wide central staircase to the den. It was the perfect place for a sitting, cozy and book-lined, with several large windows for natural light and more than one nice spot for seating my subject. As I admired the room, I realized that the house was not at all what I had expected. No automatons rolled through the halls, busy with domestic tasks. No crazy contraptions buzzed and sparked from the alcoves. The tables held vases of peonies, not unruly stacks of lab notes or newspaper clippings, fragmentary clues to some larger mystery begging to be solved. The shelves were free of strange artifacts. Nothing at all commemorated the professor's adventures and misadventures—his 1897 expedition to locate the Wandering City of Patagonia, his descent into the erupting Mount Rainier a few years earlier. There wasn't even a trophy to celebrate his victorious race across the Gobi on the aether-powered mechanical elephant he'd designed. Nothing.

I was, I must admit, a little disappointed.

Then Thaxton himself arrived.

His abrupt appearance startled me. One moment the doorway was empty, the next he filled it. He stood with arms akimbo and feet planted shoulder width apart, barrel chest puffed out and bald head bowed just a little, as if bracing for impact. Charles Augustus Thaxton wasn't the immovable object, daring anyone in the room to try to push past; he was the irresistible force readying for a charge. Everything he did or said came across that way—a promise of relentless action and tireless progress. As I looked at him, I found myself backing up a step. Before I'd even understood that there was a game on, I'd ceded him the field.

Mrs. Thaxton was suddenly at my side. Her gentle hand on my shoulder stopped my retreat. "This is Bhagesh Chatterjee," she told her husband. "He's here to paint my portrait."

"Oh. The artist," the professor said through the speaking box clutching his throat. It was a gorgeous, insectile thing wrought of glossy black metal, beautiful in the way some mechanical devices can be. It clicked and whirred as it worked and gave his voice an inhuman edge. Without it, he could only grunt like a beast. "Those imbeciles milling at the front gate didn't cause you any grief, did they?"

"Not a bit," I replied. "No one even asked why I was here."

My invitation from the Thaxtons had been quite clear: I wasn't to speak to anyone at the gate about my visit, just arrive on time and wait for Mrs. Thaxton to grant me entrance. The crowd there had been comprised mostly of reporters, with a scattering of policemen and political functionaries. You could tell the latter by their bowlers and Savile Row suits, and by the way they segregated themselves into little knots, presumably based on party affiliation, given how the groups glowered resentfully at each other.

"Those cowards would like to rush in here and demand to know what I'm doing," Thaxton said. "They can't. Fear rules the lot of them. All they can do is huddle in the street, mooing like beeves in the slaughteryard."

"It's a wise bovine that knows when to be alarmed," Mrs. Thaxton countered.

The professor uttered a surprisingly foul obscenity, but his wife continued unfazed. "People have read that the Eye destroyed fifty square miles of the Hindu Kush, Charles. The press accounts may have gotten it all wrong on what triggered the devastation. Their descriptions of the aftermath, on the other hand, were quite accurate."

Like everyone who had read a newspaper in the past twenty years, I was familiar with Professor Thaxton's temper. He'd been at the heart of brawls at scientific conferences on six of the seven continents; only Australia has, so far, been spared. Typically, the skirmishes were sparked by a colleague or close friend challenging one of his offhand remarks, like Mrs. Thaxton had just done with his characterization of the crowd outside the gate. So I expected the worst, and Thaxton seemed ready to deliver just that. His face was florid, his fists clenched, as he rumbled, "This is what frightens them—" Angrily he plunged a hand into the pocket of his black-brown tweed jacket. It emerged clutching a gem that filled his palm. "This. A flattened oval of corundum. Cut and polished mineral crystal."

Mrs. Thaxton neither backed down nor softened her tone. "That oval of corundum could be used to create a blast that would encompass much of

London," she said. "The doomsayers can be excused their premature panic, if only until their knowledge of the Eye is made more complete."

The professor cursed again and tossed the Eye across the den. Astounded, I could merely watch as it tumbled through the air. My artist's eye noted the change in color as the gem left the professor's grasp, the way it glowed as it moved through the sunlight-infused room, but no other reflexes goaded me to more constructive action. Fortunately, Mrs. Thaxton was prepared, whether from long experience with her husband's volatility or by her natural disposition, I cannot say. But she caught the Eye as if it were nothing more startling than a tennis ball flipped to her on a practice court.

Noting my astonishment, Mrs. Thaxton held out the Eye and said simply, "No worries, Mr. Chatterjee. The gem itself is inert."

"So is our artist friend, from the way he reacted just now—or, rather, failed to react," the professor said.

I am not, on the whole, quick witted. I'm no dullard, mind you. I just need time to mull over new ideas and situations. So it was only in retrospect, in the months since my stay in Kew, that I hit upon no fewer than a dozen brilliant replies I might have uttered that afternoon to turn aside Thaxton's scorn. As the professor glowered at me, though, all I could do was shift my feet uncomfortably and stammer something incomprehensible, even to me.

It was the intruder that saved me from further embarrassment.

Cold presaged its arrival. Thin ropes of bitter air exploded out from a point near the center of the den. They made no sound, but wherever they came in contact with flesh, they left a slash of reddening frostbite welts. Then the room—I was going to say dimmed, but that's wrong. The afternoon sun still filled the den with light. What happened was the colors lost their vibrancy. They bled from the peonies and the curtains and the people, leaving us and everything around us looking like the subjects in a badly faded tintype. Only then did the figure appear.

None of us knew what it was that first time, and even now, some of us who lived through the events of that troubling time in 1902 can only guess at its true nature. Darkness comprised its entirety, a shifting murk that coalesced into something vaguely shaped like a man. It lacked features, so whatever meaning we assigned to its presence was derived from its gestures and the noise it made. That awful wailing left the most lasting impression on me. It was not a human cry but something more savage, more chilling. I couldn't accurately describe it until only recently, after I attended a party at which a friend was showing off his new and outrageously expensive American Graphophone. As he arranged the device for demonstration, he carelessly shifted the cylinder backward beneath the stylus. The burst of noise from the horn was horrible—and the closest thing I ever hope to hear to the intruder's voice. The sound it made was not a scream, but rather a scream reversed. The mournful wail flowed into it rather than from it.

The Thaxtons reacted to the intruder swiftly and calmly, as if they'd had much practice with these sorts of strange visitations. The professor snatched up a statue of Ourania from a nearby end table. The muse of astronomy stood upon a heavy base, so when Thaxton upended the bronze and gripped it like a club, he had a formidable weapon. Thus armed, he took a threatening step forward. Eyes fixed on the shape, he bellowed out an order to an unseen ally elsewhere in the house: "Hayes! Activate the damping field! Full power!"

Mrs. Thaxton was on the move, as well. She slipped the Eye of Khafiristan into a pocket even as she interposed herself between me and the thing. Unlike her husband, she had no need for a makeshift weapon. She reached down, brushed aside the hem of her long skirt, and produced a derringer from a holster attached to one of her high, lace-up boots. Her hand was steady as she trained the pistol on the intruder.

The figure stretched one shadowy limb out to Thaxton and then to the professor's wife. The air in the den had quieted, but the hand shifted like smoke in the wind, making it difficult to read its intent, whether accusatory or beseeching. Then, with one final, terrible howl, the thing vanished and the room returned to normal.

Footfalls echoing from the central staircase and hall announced the imminent arrival of the professor's assistant. Technically, Darcy Hayes was a reporter for the radical paper *Uncommon Sense*, but I saw her operate only as Thaxton's aide. She hurried into the den juggling a trio of devices. Their blinking lights reflected in the dark circles of her goggles. "The damping field is up. I brought whatever meters were close at hand."

"Someone tried to force open a gate but couldn't stabilize it," Thaxton said, as if there could be no other explanation for the incident. "Assassins after one of us or thieves after the Eye." He replaced the statue of the muse and turned to his wife.

"The glass men again?" she said as she holstered her pistol.

Thaxton scowled and shook his head. "The Patagonians don't need a gate to sneak in here. They have their invisibility formula."

Miss Hayes looked up from the meters. "No help here. Normal readings across the board."

"The Deuxième Bureau, perhaps?" Mrs. Thaxton offered. "They're partial to showy entrances. The way their agents arrived at Angkor Thom last year was nothing if not dramatic."

"No. The more I think on it—" the professor's hand strayed unconsciously to his speaking box and the wicked scar that ran along his throat, almost from ear to ear "—the more this has the stink of the Russian about it."

Though he was the subject of many discussions during those two weeks, "the Russian" was the only way I ever heard Thaxton refer to his nemesis, the scientist-spy Pyotr Davidovitch Korolev. No two words have ever held more venom. There was poison enough there to end the man, the tsar who employed him, and a host of their countrymen besides.

As the professor paced around the den, he expounded upon the Russian's perfidy. He rattled off the names of a dozen different countries where they'd clashed, but offered only tantalizing fragments of the adventures that had occurred in those faraway places—allusions to mechanized dream thieves and massive sonic cannons, flesh-hungry yeti and flying machines forged from starlight. The daily papers and popular journals had carried reports of a few of these wonders, but most were new to me. Their full stories remain untold, to the general public at least. Thaxton only referenced them that day for his own benefit. He was simply thinking aloud. In the end, he concluded that the failed gate was a feint, an empty show intended to distract everyone from the Russian's real scheme to steal the Eye.

No sooner had that proposition snapped and susurrated from the professor's speaking box than he turned his piercing eyes on me. "You're fortunate I place so much trust in Miss Hayes. She thoroughly investigated your background. Otherwise, I might wonder why someone who was paralyzed with fear at the sight of the Eye could show so little reaction to the event we just witnessed." With that, he turned abruptly and stalked from the room.

I appealed immediately to Mrs. Thaxton. "It was as you said: I only knew enough about the Eye to fear it. The apparition wasn't frightening. It was bizarre, surely, but it struck me as more mournful than threatening."

She held up a restraining hand. "No worries. That was my husband's way of letting you know you still had our trust. But I'm afraid that this afternoon's events prevent me from sitting for you today. I have to see to some precautions about the house and grounds." She turned to Miss Hayes. "You and Mr. Chatterjee should stay here and get acquainted, Darcy. Charles is going to want an hour or two by himself to mull things over. In the meantime, you can answer any questions our guest might have. If you get bored, perhaps you two can uncrate the canvas and paints the courier delivered this morning."

On her way from the den, Mrs. Thaxton paused at a shelf that appeared to house a carefully arranged row of leather-bound books. At a touch from her hand, a section of false spines opened to expose a meter. She adjusted one of its knobs and flicked a switch before closing the façade and moving on to another shelf, which held a similar hidden device. A final stop at the door revealed a cleverly concealed speaking tube, which Mrs. Thaxton used to communicate with her husband in his laboratory before she headed off to another part of the house.

"The rooms on this floor hide a stunning amount of technology," Miss Hayes said after Mrs. Thaxton had gone. "Groundbreaking, but practical. She designed all of it, either based on her own research or adapted from some of the professor's more theoretical discoveries. That's the long way of telling you to be careful what you pick up or poke."

Now that the reporter was standing close to me, I could see more clearly the harsh, lingering reminders of what must have been a prodigious aether addiction. I've never tried the stuff, but I've known quite a few artists over the years who have. They dabbled, hoping it would open up their senses and allow them to experience life in new ways. Most found it more distracting than enlightening, and they gave it up long before the drug's effects required them to wear goggles in order to see the world the rest of us see. The weaker ones couldn't live without the distilled aether and consumed more and more of it, until their minds shattered and their bodies withered. The only place I had ever seen scars like the ones blighting Darcy Hayes's face and hands—the blackened tip of her nose, the transparent fingernails—were on men and women caught up in the drug's death spiral. The only difference was, her scars were no longer fresh. She must have possessed a remarkable will to get that far down the path to an addict's oblivion and then turn back.

We chatted for a time about our respective professions and the mutual acquaintances we had in the art world. Her research on me had been, as the professor suggested, quite thorough. She even knew about the gallery opening at which I managed to offend, among others, John Singer Sargent and James McNeill Whistler.

As the afternoon wore on, I grew bold enough to ask about the professor's plans for the Eye. The answer Hayes gave was both more and less than I had asked for. She told me a little of the ruby's history, how two soldiers-of-fortune had stumbled across it in 1889 while trying to establish themselves as kings of Khafiristan. The unlucky pair used the gem in a rite that triggered its ability to channel and focus aetheric energy. After the blast, the surviving soldier smuggled the Eye out of the Kush in the severed head of his former partner, then vanished into India. Thaxton learned about the Eye from the Intelligence Bureau and had been questing for it ever since, sometimes coordinating his efforts with Her Majesty's agents, sometimes competing with them. He intended to utilize the ruby as a power conduit, though in a much more controlled fashion than its previous owners.

When I pressed for more details, Miss Hayes circled back to that embarrassing gallery party and asked about the gossip that had me offending not just Whistler and Sargent that night, but Enrico Caruso, as well. The topic of the Eye had been closed.

As dusk approached, a dozen globes in the tin ceiling rotated to reveal electric lights, and arms descended and shifted until the bulbs were positioned perfectly to illuminate the room. The mechanism had been camouflaged to blend with the patterned tin. I came to recognize many such marvels scattered around the den over the next two weeks. Mrs. Thaxton and I spent whatever hours we could cobble together there each day. My subject demonstrated incredible patience. It took me far longer than usual to capture her in my sketches, even excusing the time lost to the mystery of the intruder. Mrs. Thaxton proved unflappable, though. Not even the weird trespasser could dampen her spirits.

We all had different names for it. "Intruder" seemed most apt to me—even after our discoveries about the thing's nature on the final day it showed itself. The professor would refer to it only as "the distraction," in keeping with his theory of its purpose. It appeared at least once a day, sometimes as often as six times in the course of twenty-four hours. A blast of cold would tear through a room, followed by the disappearance of all color. Then the shadowy intruder would manifest. The incidents favored no specific location or hour. Sometimes the thing lingered in a single room. Other times it wandered between rooms or even floors. It passed right through objects and people in its way. The unstable nature of its form continued to mask its purpose, but it never made any gesture I would class as threatening. If anything, it reached out imploringly to whomever it encountered, while making that alarming, inhuman sound.

Professor Thaxton set up a few pieces of equipment around the house the first evening. It was left to Miss Hayes to check the stationary monitors and deploy the portable ones as needed. The reporter revealed her findings to Mrs. Thaxton during one of our sittings. I understood very little of what they said about power fluctuations and field distortions. The conclusion was clear enough, though: apart from quantifying some disturbances in the aether, the data provided no positive insights. They could only say with certainty that the phantasmal visitations were unlike anything they had ever seen before. For the professor, this made the phenomenon a little more interesting, but ultimately confirmed his belief that it was mere light show, intended to distract. He refused to allow himself to be pulled into that sort of dubious mystery. Better that the rest of us pursued it as we wished, while he continued his work with the Eye.

A feeling of unease soon settled over the household. Strange noises in a distant room demanded immediate investigation, no matter how often you told yourself that, this time, you would stay focused on whatever task you had at hand. A sudden cool breeze could paralyze with anticipation of the intruder's imminent arrival. Every room and hallway twitched with odd and oddly moving shadows that vanished if you tried to focus on them. Sleep became difficult, and the lack of rest further soured everyone's mood. By the fifth day, my sleep-deprived brain concluded that the intruder was always there, unseen, biding its time between appearances. Mrs. Thaxton made comments to the same effect, only she felt that the invisible presence was watching her. By the end of the first week, the cook had resigned and fled the house. Had the gardener not been an automaton, he surely would have deserted the place, too.

Miss Hayes had it especially hard. She divided her time between the professor's laboratory on the lower floor, where their investigation of the Eye continued at a furious pace, and the rest of the house, where she did her best to gather whatever data could be wrung out of each incident. She seemed always to be scrambling from one place to another, no matter how much aid Mrs. Thaxton and I offered. Headaches plagued her intermittently. The reason for that, at least, was no mystery. Her addiction had left her particularly sensitive to disturbances in the aether.

The attack Miss Hayes suffered the morning after the cook left was typical. I had just asked her about a piece she had written on the Zulu king's spectacular airship embassy to England when she grimaced and brought her fingertips up to her temples. "It's returning," she said. "Close by."

The intruder manifested in the hallway, just outside the kitchen, with the now-predictable burst of bitter air and extinguishment of all the nearby color. As we got close, the figure cried out in that terrible voice and moved off down the hall. It glided along slowly on shifting, shadowy legs, feet never touching the floorboards. We trailed it at a respectful distance. Miss Hayes scribbled details about the visitation into a little notebook. I found myself captivated by the absolute blackness of its core. The darkness there was so complete that it pained me to stare at it, yet I could not tear my eyes away.

We followed the intruder down the central stairs. It stopped in the open doorway to Professor Thaxton's laboratory, hovering on the threshold. The whir of machinery and the sharp crack of energy arcing between leads came from within the workroom, but we could not see past the shape. The thing had lost its vaguely human form and swelled to fill the doorframe like a black curtain, hiding everything beyond. A loud cry rang out from the murk. Then the darkness dissipated, revealing Professor Thaxton's laboratory.

This was my first sight of the place. I'd been curious about it, certainly, but no errand had brought me there before that morning. It was everything the den was not. In that cavernous space resided the artifacts the professor had recovered during his travels and the trophies commemorating his victories, right down to the working scale model of his racing mechaniphant, which trundled self-importantly back and forth along one wall. If fantastic objects such as these were not enough to dazzle the mind, an overwhelming display of inventions surrounded them on every side—toiling automatons wrought of various metals and weird machinery beyond the dreams of Tesla or Babbage.

At the center of it all, a complicated network of grasping arms held the Eye of Khafiristan. A beam projected from an aether-burning device bathed the ruby in an eerie blue-white radiance. Thaxton's face looked cadaverous in the strange light as he stood close by, adjusting the beam and jotting down readings from the half-dozen or so meters arrayed around him. "If you're done dallying with the distraction, Miss Hayes, come assist me," he said without looking up at us. "You, artist, may go away."

I was more than happy to comply. There was something about the laboratory that made it inhospitable to mere humankind. Such mundane, fleshly expressions of nature were unworthy of inclusion alongside the invented wonders and rescued marvels. Hayes surely seemed out of place as she crossed the room to join the professor. Her scars were vivid reminders of her fragility, a stark contrast to the machines' shining metallic perfection. Even Thaxton looked the trespasser, until you noted his mechanical speaking box. That marked him as something more than human and, therefore, worthy of his surroundings. The thought depressed me utterly.

Wrapped in a cloak of overwhelming gloom, I made my way to the den. I had scheduled a sitting for Mrs. Thaxton that morning, but neither she nor I could rally our spirits enough to make the effort worthwhile. I frittered away the rest of the afternoon in the library, scarcely aware of the rare volumes through which I was paging so idly: illustrated editions of *Inventio Fortunata* and Homer's *Margites*, *On Sphere-Making* by Archimedes and Livy's *Ab Urbe Condita Libri*. Like the marvels in the professor's laboratory, I regarded these treasures through weary, careless eyes.

I retreated to my room after dinner, eager for sleep and the temporary respite it might grant me from my dark thoughts. Yet sleep would not come. I tossed and turned for a time, as twilight dwindled and died, and night fell on Kew.

The hollow, metallic growl of clockwork mastiffs in the garden below my window finally drew me from my bed. A pair of the intimidating beasts stood on a stone path, the now-familiar figure of the intruder trapped between them. The mastiffs advanced a step or two, closing on their target from opposite directions, then hesitated. One tilted its head from side to side, trying to get a better look at the shape. The other mastiff gave a high-pitched whine and crouched—not to ready for an attack, but to retreat. The two automatons backed slowly away, until the wavering figure stood alone in the doubly pale garden.

It was the pallid hues of that wan, sickly nightscape that reminded me so vividly of a midnight in Jalalabad two decades earlier, and my uncle, and the things he tried to teach me about the way of matter. I never got to explain that moment of inspiration to the Thaxtons or to Miss Hayes. I only shared the results early the next morning, just as soon as everyone had gathered in the dining room.

"Perhaps the intruder isn't an empty distraction or someone trying to open a gate," I said. "Perhaps it's a ghost."

Professor Thaxton laughed. The speaking box translated the derision into a sound very much like the growling of the clockwork mastiffs.

I had already steeled myself against that sort of reaction from the professor, so it did not fluster me. "In Hinduism," I continued, "it's said that the disembodied souls of the unenlightened can become trapped in the world until their new bodies are born. But the world is not just what we see. It's the akasha, too. The aether. They can become trapped there."

"I want to know what that thing is as much as anyone," Mrs. Thaxton said. "But I don't like where this is going."

"Neither do I," Professor Thaxton said. "Religion is the stuff of superstition, so of course it leads us to this ridiculous discussion of ghosts. Next we'll be consulting a psychic detective. Didn't you interview one last year, Hayes—that quack alienist Low?"

"I'm not suggesting it's a true ghost," I explained. "I don't believe in them either. But perhaps we should investigate the intruder as if it were some sort of aetheric creature. If someone could look directly at it . . ."

Mrs. Thaxton scowled. "That's what I thought you were going to suggest. Do you have any idea of the risks that course of action might pose to Darcy?"

Miss Hayes had been standing quietly. She surely knew that there was only one certain way to view an aetheric creature and seemed more saddened by the proposition than frightened. "Taking the goggles off isn't difficult," she said. "Getting them back on is another matter entirely."

"It's your decision to make," the professor said with surprising kindness.

Miss Hayes nodded, and a faint, cynical smile quirked her lips. "And it's already made."

We didn't have long to wait.

The final time the intruder appeared it manifested in the great room, in the maw of a mammoth fireplace that dominated one entire wall. Mrs. Thaxton saw it first and shouted for the rest of us to hurry, in case this visitation proved to be short-lived. Sometimes the intruder lingered, as on the morning we trailed it from the kitchen to the laboratory. Other times it arrived and departed before anyone could raise an alarm. If there was a pattern to its movements, we never uncovered it.

Miss Hayes and I reached the great room together, the professor a few moments later. There was no discussion, no second guessing the plan. The reporter waved at us as if she were departing, which was no idle gesture. I've known countless artist-addicts who have lost themselves in the aether by looking into it once too often. That Hayes understood her peril was revealed in her hands: they shook as she pulled down the goggles until they hung useless around her throat.

No scientist yet has been able to duplicate the addict's eyes, to show what they show of the aetheric world, just as no painting or music or poem has fully conveyed the complexity and the chaos of the addict's visions. I cannot imagine what Miss Hayes saw, but it was clear that she saw something startling. "Oh, no," she gasped. "I—I understand." Arms outstretched, she ran forward to embrace the dark shape. She never reached it. Just as she got close, the intruder vanished with a soft sound like a weary, defeated sigh.

Miss Hayes dropped to her knees in the fireplace ashes. With growing ferocity, she clawed at the air where the shape had been. Professor Thaxton rushed to her. She turned at his touch, gibbering nonsense words and meaningless sounds. The professor yanked her to her feet with one hand and tried to pull the goggles back into place with the other. I glimpsed her face then. The orbs of her eyes were roiling like a thundercloud-choked sky. Tears streamed down her cheeks. They changed colors as they fell, leaving tracks that glowed blood red.

It took all three of us to restrain her so the goggles could be shifted back into place. When she was once again looking out at the world through the thick black lenses, she calmed. After a time, she could speak, though she was still having difficulty focusing her thoughts. "Couldn't communicate with us," she said, her voice a harsh rasp. "It was a warning."

Her words had not been directed at anyone in particular. She'd been looking from face to face as she spoke, struggling to anchor herself in the real world—or in the world she shared with us, at least. Then Miss Hayes turned to the professor and leaned in close.

"Gone." Hayes reached out weakly toward Thaxton's face and faltered. As her hand fell back, it brushed the glossy black metal of his speaking box. "Burned away."

Thaxton and his wife ushered their friend to a chair across the room, where she again spoke to them. This time, they were far enough away that I could not hear what she said. I could, however, judge its weight by the horrified looks on the Thaxtons' faces. Miss Hayes was still talking when the professor staggered back a step before turning and fleeing the room.

The intruder never returned to that peculiar, marvelous house in Kew. But it also never left.

It lingers in my portrait of Mrs. Thaxton. I have never spent more time on a work and probably never will again. There was too much to get right to hurry it. The dark shape presented the biggest challenge. It had to be there, though, lurking in the background, all but invisible to the casual eye. The portrait would not have been complete without that detail, just as it needed hints of those secret meters and hidden weapons to suggest my subject's true strength. Her expression is bold. I like to think that I've captured her as she was in the days after the final visitation. She would not speak directly of the mystery or its resolution, save to quote her friend Marie Curie: "Nothing in life is to be feared, it is only to be understood. Now is the time to understand more, so that we may fear less." The Thaxtons intended the portrait to hang in the professor's laboratory, a permanent lodgment of humanity amidst the cold technological marvels.

Work in the lab involving the Eye was halted. Miss Hayes's revelations about the intruder had so shaken the professor that it was set aside. Set aside, but not cancelled. After a year or so of relative quiet, the gem became a topic of public debate again last year, in the wake of the debacle with the experimental clockwork policeman Thaxton unleashed upon London. The bodies of the victims had not been interred before the papers resurrected their panicked editorials about the Eye. This time I shared their alarm. From my experience with the professor, I knew where the speculation about his likely actions overlapped with the truth. "He cannot stop moving ahead for long" was how Miss Hayes summed it up just a few weeks ago, when I ran into her outside the National Gallery. "It's his nature."

It was a friendly enough visit, though she once again refused to tell me what or, more to the point, who the intruder was. I think she knows that I have figured it out and I'm only asking now to confirm my conclusion. She's seen the portrait. It's all right there, if you know what you're looking for. But her loyalty to the professor prevents her from sharing the details of what she saw when she removed her goggles that day. There might be a measure of kindness in the refusal, too. With uncertainty comes the luxury of self-delusion. Only those who have stumbled across a hard, irrefutable truth understand that luxury's value.

It was impossible to miss the genuine horror on the professor's face that day in the great room. Little wonder. Barring conversion to a faith he disdained, he was being forced to acknowledge the existence of a thing with no future, its eyes turned forever to the past. The intruder could escape from the aether to the physical world for a few moments at a time, but it was too weak, too damaged to communicate. Some catastrophic mistake had ended its life and robbed it of its voice, even its mechanical one. All burned away. The truth of its identity remains, nevertheless, inescapable.

Many men are haunted by their past. Only Professor Thaxton is haunted by his future.

I said that I came to trust Mrs. Thaxton implicitly in almost every matter. The exception, to my despair, was an important one. She was wrong when she claimed that nothing in life is to be feared, only understood. I understand the intruder now, and I am still afraid.

James Lowder *has worked extensively on both sides of the editorial blotter. As a writer his publications include the bestselling, widely translated dark fantasy novels* Prince of Lies *and* Knight of the Black Rose, *short fiction for such anthologies as* Shadows Over Baker Street *and* Extraordinary Renditions, *and comic book scripts for Image, Moonstone, and Desperado. As an editor he's directed novel lines or series for both large and small publishing houses and has helmed more than a dozen critically acclaimed anthologies, including* Madness on the Orient Express, Hobby Games: The 100 Best, *and the Books of Flesh zombie trilogy. His work has received five Origins Awards and an ENnie Award and been a finalist for the International Horror Guild Award and the Stoker Award.*

Golden Wing, Silver Eye

Cat Hellisen

✿✿✿

It is winter in Pal-em-Rasha and all the roosters have been strangled. We are in mourning. The prince was born white and strange, his dead sister clinging to his heel, and since then, three weeks have passed without cock-crow.

People work with their heads bowed and their lips pinched. In the markets—normally ringing with calls and shouts and trades—money falls from palm to palm in muffled offerings. Even the People of the Dogs wrap the hooves of their shaggy red oxen with rags when they come down to the city from their mountain homes. Peasants chase the monkeys away from the orange groves and the tamarind trees, and the leaves hang dry and limp. The little brown doves do not heed the king's order for silence, and they line the buildings, chuckling at each other in low coos, taking turns to steal the fallen rice from between the road stones.

Our city is divided like a lotus, each petal some stronghold of trade or class. My Bee lives in the cogworker's district on Iron Ox road in her father's house. She has no memory of him. Like many men, he has fallen to war. There is only her and her mother, both pretending that this house they run, that they inhabit like snails inside a shell, belongs to them. They eke out his small fortune, watching it dwindle with every passing day.

Her mother climbs the stairs to the loft where Bee has her workshop, and I follow dutifully. I am not permitted to serve food these days. It pains me to see Old Mother struggling to carry the heavy tray up the narrow staircase and know that I am forbidden to help her. She pants as she manoeuvres the tray into the crook of one arm so that she can swing the door open.

Bee waves her mother away as the old woman clears a space on the clutter-strewn desk for the tea tray. "Kavi," Bee says without looking up at me. Her voice is low. Even in our own homes we speak in whispers, scared of offending the dead. Bee is at work on one of her creatures, its innards spread out across her work table: minute shining cogs and coiled wires fine as the tongue of a butterfly. Her eyeglass is strapped in place with leather bands, flattening her dark hair against her skull, and she looks like a drowned monster hunched over an open treasure chest.

I wait respectfully for Old Mother to leave before I answer. "What is it, my little bee?" The fragrant red sweetness of the tea lifts some of the oppressive funk of the dimly lit room. Even with all the shutters open wide, there is not enough light. The skies are weeping too, cold and bitter with dry snow.

The queen is dead, her children monsters or ghouls.

"I'll need new lenses," Bee tells me. "This one, even on its highest setting . . ." she pauses to unbuckle straps and pull the offending thing from her face. "It's not good enough." She takes the tea, sips, sighs. "It's simply not up to the kind of work I want to do."

The city of Pal-em-Rasha is famous from the high mountains to the bay of Utt Dih for its clockwork beasts. The temple mages from the mountains may sneer and call our people toymakers, but it only shows how scared they are of what we could do. The toymakers are the little gods building horses of bone and wood and metal for princes to ride into battle and birds to take messages, beetles to watch from the walls. Not all their creatures are simple cog and gear contraptions, wound to life with a key. The very best toymakers have also graduated from the floating university.

They are artists and metalworkers and magicians, skilled and powerful. My Bee builds creatures from shining metal and breathes life into them. She has made fine work. Not the finest, perhaps, but she did her time in the university, and her skills are much in demand. Just last month, she completed an order for a hair ornament for a prince merchant's wife. A moth made of silver, delicate as a live creature. After she'd breathed her soul into its metal heart, I pinned it to her own hair. We stood together in front of the bronze mirror her father had brought back more than twenty years ago from some borderland skirmish. Her reflection was bronzed as the mirror. The moth stirred its grey wings softly, shimmering against the black coils of her hair. I stood at her shoulder. Already, I was too pale and unhealthy against her brightness. She'd smiled in satisfaction, and I'd carefully caught the moth and boxed and wrapped it.

Now, she is working on something grander. My Bee is done with crawling things, small mechanical lives.

While she leans back in her chair and sips at her tea and nibbles on her mother's little coconut pastries, I pick up a feather from the open drawer in her beast-box. She spent many nights perfecting each one. There are flight feathers of heavy gold and thousands of down feathers no bigger than a baby's pinkie nail, each one made of metal filaments. The one I hold is from the wing, heavier than a real feather, of course, but otherwise almost identical.

My Bee is a master. One day, soon, I think, they will know her name in the palace tower. She will be richer than the merchant princes who buy her art now. She will teach kings the meaning of life.

"You'll need to go down to the Oculary and buy me something better, higher magnification," she says. "I don't have the time now to go myself."

I'm her servant, true, but I am more than that, and I frown at her in wounded annoyance.

She catches my look and runs one hand through her hair. "Sorry, love." Her smile is tired, these long nights eating away at her brightness. "Please," she adds, almost as an afterthought.

It's not always easy: love. Especially when you love someone caught in their own genius, like a child trapped in a never-ending dream. Sometimes, they forget we are out here. Sometimes, they forget everything.

I nod. I will leave Old Mother a note telling her what Bee needs, and she can send one of the delivery boys out to collect it with the household orders. "Magnification?" I ask, carefully writing Bee's words down. I can still do this, at least. The quill-beast responds to my touch, clattering as it reacts to the pressure of my finger, the lightest brush. Bee made this one for me, back when we first fell in love.

We passed our hearts across doorways, secret and nervous. She, the treasured only child, burdened with talent and an expensive education, and I, a women's maid, burdened with hairbrushes and pins and pots of shadows. I had every excuse to touch her, and I took them all. These days she has no time for preening, and I drift through the house, neither one thing nor the other.

❂❂❂

The rooster takes shape, day by day. First the skeleton, in gleaming bronze, its skull polished under the floating gas lamps Bee has gathered in the corners of the pitched roof. Then, as the hours pass and I watch, quiet from my cushion, the muscles and sinews of cogs and wires. At the end of every night, Bee folds her tools back into velvet, sighs and taps the creature, and sets it bobbing and pecking. The eyeless skull bowing to her.

"Why a rooster?" I ask her. I've enjoyed this time without the pre-dawn shrieking of the backyard barons.

She shrugs. "They are handsome, gold and green, crests and wattles like new-spilled blood, dragon eyes and claws. What's not to like?"

Because, I say inside my head, *because then the spell will be broken, and I will have to go.* I'm not the only one to have enjoyed this brief reprieve. We pass on the streets and nod to each other in unspoken acknowledgement. We watch the city hens with their trains of new-hatched chicks and wait for these little suns to grow feathers instead of fluff and brash voices instead of peeps. Some of them will grow spurs and proud tails, will crow the day awake.

And then we will leave.

The rooster's eyes lie on a work cloth darkened with metal dust. They look like beads strung on black wires. Bee has made them silver grey to stand out against the golden feathers. I watch them, and they watch me in return.

"Make something else." At her elbow is a glass bowl of leg scales made of electrum. I stir them with one finger as I talk, not looking at her face. "There are jungle crows in the south that have feathers of gold—you would only have to make a few small changes."

"The queen's standard was a rooster," she snaps.

"You think he will care?"

Bee stands in a huff, throwing a fallen loop of her silk wrap back over her shoulder. "Jealous, Kavi, because you have no art? Or scared that success will ruin what we have?" She dashes one hand across her eyes as though flicking away a lazy fly. "I'm doing this for us—if I can get a royal patronage, we can buy our own home, go anywhere we like. We can pay for the finest doctors and do as we will."

She's bitter because she's tired. She forgets because it's easier that way.

I say nothing. The rooster grins at me with its metal beak.

"Sorry," Bee says. "I don't mean to be so sharp. It's been a long day." She holds her arms open to embrace me. Her apologies always were as quick and raw as her attacks.

I step out of reach and slip past her.

$$\text{✧✧✧}$$

Old Mother is waiting for me on the stairs.

We stop across from each other. Her wrinkled face, cross-hatched with sadness and fear for her daughter, peers up at me. I try to keep my own face a mask to hide my guilt. Guilt? What have I to be guilty for, I ask myself as I wait for Old Mother to speak.

"You should go," she says.

My answer catches in my throat, rust and broken edges.

"The longer you stay, the worse she gets," Bee's mother says, and the tears wash through the tiny valleys that map her cheeks. "You are driving her mad. You are hurting Bijri, and I do not think you want that."

I know, I want to say. But it's not me who chose to kill every rooster in the city. Perhaps, even now, the king sits in his high tower, in the Pistil of Pal-em-Rasha, holding his queen's cold hand and praying for miracles. I nod at her instead. I have heard, I have understood.

I wander into the little room that used to be mine when I was still just a servant. It's unoccupied, and I lie down on the narrow bed. It is colder and harder and meaner than Bee's, but it doesn't feel right to go lie there now.

Through the wooden walls, the voices drift. Old Mother, coaxing Bee to come with her to a friend, to take in some fresh air and clear her head. Bee argues, but eventually, she gives in, and their feet patter away, down hallways and staircases.

Alone in the house, except for the maid and cook who avoid me anyway, I take the opportunity to go into Bee's loft. The gas lamps are dead, but thin winter light still bathes the room enough that I can see. Bee must have been tired—she bowed to her mother's wishes. Far more telling: she left her tools out on the work bench, not rolled up in their velvet and put gently to bed like fragile children. She was working on the eyes again. Near them lies the clockwork heart, a bright ticker waiting for winding.

Childish temper, fear, anger. I don't know what it is that drives me, but I flick those watching eyes from the bench, and they rattle and bounce, lost to the wooden floorboards and the dark corners. I press one finger through the mechanics of the heart, upsetting the delicate balance of cog and wheel.

This will hurt her more, I realise. Not because I've broken a trinket, but because it will only make the leaving harder. I search the floorboards until my skirt and hands are streaked with dust. When I find the eyes, I put them back carefully next to the broken heart. That at least, I know Bee can fix. I leave the destruction and go hide in my old room. It is familiar-strange, a place I only came back to when I hurt, when I didn't want to distract Bee with my pain. It's hard to cry, but I find myself dampening the sun-bleached bedding with my faint tears.

✿✿✿

"Found you," Bee says, her voice bright again, waking me. It seems the walk has done her good. "What are you doing here?" She lies down next to me on the servant's bed, gently shoving so that I will make room for her. We fold each other in our arms. We kiss and sing the song that only those who love know, that sweet low song.

"I was just thinking," I say when I have air again to speak.

"Don't," she commands. "It's made you miserable, whatever it was you were thinking about." She kisses me again, her lips warm, her tongue soft. She has eaten honeyed figs and drunk imported tea from the Ten Thousand Island Heaven Empire. "Never leave me," she says between kisses. "I know I'm a pain, but you make me human," she says between touches. "You are my right eye, my right hand—"

"Shh," I tell her.

"My right ventricle, my right foot, my right big toe—"

I quiet her with my mouth.

✿✿✿

The rooster is almost done. The gas lamps are turned low, and the beast stands regal on the table. The feathers are soft gold, warm and welcoming. The tail curves high, black and green, each filament enamelled. It is a thing on the scalpel-edge of living. I look to the open windows where the darkness is still looped with stars. Outside, the birds have not yet woken, but they stir in their dreams of rice and grain.

"So?" Bee spreads her hands and looks to me. Under the arrogance is her fear. *Am I good enough, or have I wasted my time, my money, have I deluded myself, tell me, tell me, tell me that my work is sweeter than palm sugar, more precious than salt. Please tell me.* "What do you think?"

"It is very beautiful."

She sniffs. "Of course," but she winks after she says it and smiles shy as a child.

"When will you present it to the king?" I lean forward from my seat and touch its beak. It shivers gently.

"Tomorrow," Bee says, and before I breathe deep at my momentary stay, she continues, "but first, I need to make sure it will work."

I tuck my hands back in my lap, and the bangles she gave me as marriage gifts clatter softly.

"Pray for me, Kavi. Pray to your funny little house gods." But she doesn't wait for me to say yes or no, so eager. She's a child showing off, caught up in the joy of her creation. Bee bows her head, her eyes closed. She looks like a temple reverent, her dark lashes spider leg shadows on hollow sockets, her ringlet hair unbrushed for days. Like all students of the floating university, the first thing she ever learned was stillness, to tame her breath, to use it to call up power from the earth and channel it. Her breath is her magic, machinery her art. The air changes as the magic builds, gathering in her belly. Minutes pass as she charges her breaths, pulling energy from the lifewells that track below the skin of the world. Before, I wasn't attuned to these currents of power, but now, I can feel them. I can see ribbons of light. The dark hair on my arms stands up, and a million spiders dance out a strange new song against my skin.

The breath moves from body to body. From warm lips to cold bright beak, and like paper catching fire, the energy crackles along every wire and cog, turns the dead heart into a lightning pulse. The rooster opens one dragon eye on me.

Oh, enemy.

There is still time before dawn, before daybreak, but my lover's art has no care. It throws back its gleaming head, heavy feathers flushed with warmth and magic.

First crow.

The sound is harsh and over-loud in the loft, and it tears the anchor of my heart, uproots me.

"Kavi!" Bee says, cheeks and eyes shining. "Look! Oh, Kavi, our fortunes are made." She turns away from her monster to catch my hands and draw me to my feet, to spin me around in a tight dance. She is hot and breathless, and her kiss tastes like bitter tea and too little sleep and funerary coins. "Oh, love, you're so cold," she says when she draws back from me, brow crinkling in concern. "You've been so patient with me, and I've been ignoring you." She holds me tight, drawing me close to her until I can pretend her heartbeat is mine.

Second crow.

My feet disappear first. Bee cannot see them, hidden under my long skirt of red ochre. My legs and hips fade, and all that is left is painstaking embroidery and rustling linen. I grow light.

"Are we still fighting?" she asks me, her breath damp against my ear, and I will her magic into me. If I were made of cogs and wires, she could make me dance again.

"You forgot," I whisper back, but the rooster has thrown back his sharp head, opened wide his savage beak. He crows again and there is no more time left.

Three crows to call the dead home.

We leave Pal-em-Rasha in a sea of misting grey, thick as dreams. The shades that have spent the weeks since the king's command in a hell of waiting. The pull rushes us, whistling hard in our ears, dragging us willing or no. I force myself to turn my head and look back down at the house where I died alone, retching up blood in a servant's room so that my lover would not see.

Bee dances in her loft, the empty pleated skirt and tunic top held crumpled in her arms. Her tears fall bright as feathers. On the workbench, the golden rooster struts and calls.

{{

Cat Hellisen *is a South African-born writer of fantasy for adults and children. Her work includes the novel* When the Sea is Rising Red *and short stories in* Apex, The Magazine of Fantasy & Science Fiction, Shimmer Magazine, *and Tor.com. Her latest novel is a fairy tale for the loveless,* Beastkeeper.